PENALTIES OF JUNE

McSWEENEY'S

SAN FRANCISCO

McSweeney's and colophon are registered trademarks of McSweeney's,
a nonprofit publisher based in San Francisco.

Cover illustration by Lina Müller

ISBN 978-1-963270-07-5

10 9 8 7 6 5 4 3 2 1

www.mcsweeneys.net

Printed in Canada

PENALTIES OF JUNE

A NOVEL

JOHN BRANDON

McSWEENEY'S

SAN FRANCISCO

THE MOTEL WAS TWO stories, but the entire upper floor was cordoned off with frayed white rope, some of the doors ripped off the hinges and nowhere to be seen. The cab dropped Pratt in the parking lot. He stood there a minute, duffel bag at his feet, nervous for reasons he couldn't identify, among ash-hued cars that appeared to have been struck by lightning. He supposed it was the strangeness of complete freedom. The better part of three years. That's how long he'd been inside. The clouds looked the same out here as from the prison yard, low and billowy, undergirded with dark silver, but somehow they didn't matter as much. Out here, there were other things to worry about than the weather. This place *smelled* worse than prison. Urine. Gasoline. Roadkill. He'd asked to be taken somewhere cheap—what did he expect?

Pratt toted his bag into the cramped check-in. There was barely room to set it down. Empty, scarred coffee maker. Faded wood paneling. Pratt didn't feel like raising his voice. He was searching for a bell when a guy in a purple Kangol hat sauntered out and lowered his weight onto a squeaky stool. Once he'd finished chewing and got his bulk arranged, he looked up at Pratt drearily and told him it was cash in advance and checkout was ten sharp. The man had stained teeth and a solved Rubik's Cube sat on his cluttered parcel of desk.

"No smoking," he said.

"Okay," Pratt answered.

"No needles, neither." The guy picked up the cube and scrambled it, then quickly turned it back to perfection. "You got pills or weed, don't let me see it, don't let me smell it."

"I don't think I do drugs anymore," Pratt said. "I'm pretty sure."

"No parties and no hookers," the guy said, rattling his hand around in a box of keys.

"I won't have any caviar either. And I promise not to block in anyone with my Porsche."

The guy tipped his head at Pratt, looking short on patience, his Kangol clinging fast to his head.

"Oh," said Pratt. "I thought we were just naming shit I can't afford."

The same cracked paneling from the check-in covered the walls of Pratt's room. Dank carpet, like all these places had. Mouse droppings in the corners. When he went to sleep, he knew, the roaches would come out. He wasn't having a party, but the roaches would. Two nights at most, one if he was lucky. The question was: Where would he go instead? He couldn't leave the state—that much the law had made clear—but it was a big state. What he needed was a car, even if it'd cost him. And the *real* question, of course, wasn't where he would go, but would Bonne let him go there? Would Bonne bother to track him down if he left town? Was the old man mad at Pratt? If so, did he want to yell at him, or never see him again? Maybe the last thing Bonne cared to have was a reminder, in the form of his kid's best buddy, that his kid was dead. Jacksonville. It was north. It was a place a guy could get lost in—at least it seemed that way, spread out and mostly medium poor, the one time Pratt had been there. He had his parole check-ins, but he could always day-trip for those.

Before all that, though, there was Kallie. He couldn't just blow town if she was nearby. Her surprisingly deep voice. Her sly smile. Her steady gaze. He imagined them so often in prison—his idea of her was probably way off by now, warped. He didn't want anything from her, which was easy to say because she likely didn't want anything from him either. He wanted only to lay eyes on her. He'd breathe easier if he could only see her and know she was okay. He owed it to Matty to do that much, didn't he? To check on Kallie. He would find her or he wouldn't, then he'd be able to leave knowing he'd at least tried. He'd be able to start fresh.

A car. No matter what, he needed a car.

He pulled the curtain closed, then opened it again. He didn't want to be shut up with no view like he'd been in his cell, but he didn't want the luckless derelicts who resided in this place looking in at him like a fish in a tank. He closed the curtain except for a slit in the middle, so some late-afternoon light could shine in. Cranked up the window-mounted air conditioner and held his hand in front of its tepid output. Went to the bathroom and unwrapped the tiny soap and smelled it. It smelled different from prison soap, but not better. He washed his hands. Washed his face. Sat down on the mattress and pulled the phone book from a drawer in the scratched-up table near the bed. Last year's edition. White pages in the front. Pratt flipped the thing open on the stiff bedspread. N, O, then P. Padilla. Pagan. Palmer. Pantoja. Here it was—Pappas. Two of them. Pratt's eyes scanned fast; neither name was familiar. Alexandra and Brock. Brock? Pratt didn't remember Kallie's father's name, but it sure as hell wasn't Brock. Kallie had no one else. Just her and her dad. She hadn't even been living with her dad before Pratt went away. She'd been with five other girls in a dilapidated plantation-looking place they rented by the room. No way she was still there. He would check, but there was no way.

Pratt closed the phone book and grabbed the *TV Guide*, leaned back against the headboard and leafed through the onion-skin pages. Sitcom reruns. Talk shows in the early morning and talk shows late at night. Dramas about hospitals. Dramas about aliens. They'd had most of this stuff on the inside. In Pratt's block, there'd been a Cuban guy who always watched *The Simpsons* and an aging farm boy with gout who lived for *Walker, Texas Ranger*. Pratt saw the remote on the dresser, unguarded, but he left it where it was. He didn't want to be doing the same thing out as he'd done in—staring at a TV screen. He was tired, but a nap wasn't what he needed either. He could hear someone next door. Water running, a door opening and closing. Soon he heard a man's voice, high but sandpapery, enunciating the same name louder and louder. He was on the phone. He kept repeating the name, first and last, until he was yelling it, and then he slammed the phone down and yelled it even louder, into the void of his room. Something hit the other side of the wall, not far from Pratt's head— maybe a phone book like the one he'd just looked through in vain. He heard a table topple over, then something small and metallic exploding into pieces.

In the morning, Pratt put on a pair of stiff, tan-colored jeans that were big for him now and an old polo shirt that smelled like the airless metal locker where it had been stored. He could hardly remember what his hair used to look like back when he worried about what his hair looked like. With his hand, he pushed the shapeless medium-length mass of dirty blond into an almost-part, then set out for the day, taking a low-riding cab that smelled like popcorn to a used car lot called Budget Plus Auto. The office was a double-wide trailer that sat amid a gravelly lot of maybe seventy-five cars. The wind carried a scent of motor oil and sulfur, the latter from a water-treatment plant a half mile upwind. Pratt walked straight to the pickup he'd seen advertised in the paper, a Tacoma with a six-cylinder engine and a dinged-up tailgate. The tires were almost new. So were the windshield wipers and mud flaps. Whoever had sold it to Budget Plus hadn't planned on doing so.

Pratt turned around, and a dude with a scraggly red mustache and a knit tie was speed-walking toward him. Before he even had Pratt's hand in his own, he said the pickup had already sold. Twenty minutes ago. The buyer couldn't pick it up until later. There were other pickups on the lot, he told Pratt, but they were a bit pricier.

"Why don't you put a sold sign on it?" Pratt said. "I let the taxi go because I thought I'd drive away in this one."

The guy detached a walkie-talkie from his belt and told someone named Vernon to come yellow-tag the '92 Toyota. He explained to Pratt, his tie folding over in a hot gust of wind, that the cars were lined up least expensive to most, with the high end near the palm trees and the low end near the sinkhole. He said they featured a no-haggle pricing model that earned a lot of positive feedback from customers. Said to give a wave if Pratt needed any help.

Pratt watched the man walk off in his cheap dress shoes. He saw a kid who must've been Vernon strolling toward the pickup, a big, bright sticker in his hand. Pratt turned and stepped toward the sink-hole. He wasn't going to pay for another cab to take him to some other lot that probably wouldn't have anything he wanted either. On Pratt's budget, there were only so many roadworthy cars around.

From the edge of the lot, he could see down into the oblong grassy chasm. Trees, some of them ten feet tall, grew out sideways from the walls. At the bottom was a small pond, still as a mirror, that reflected the weak blue of the sky. Pratt measured the distance to the other side of the pit, wondering if he could throw a baseball across it. Too hard to judge, the light hazy and deceptive. He wondered how long it had been since he'd thrown a ball. A long time. He still had most of his muscles, the important ones, and could still move his just-under-six-foot frame when he had to, but he'd avoided the sandlot games in prison like the plague, unable to stomach everything baseball made him think about.

He switched his attention to the inventory. The first offering was a rusted-out Datsun that didn't look like it could make fifty-five without a stiff wind behind it. After that was a prissy white LeBaron convertible. There were three minivans, and after those a Volkswagen Beetle whose peeling layers of paint hinted at its numerous past lives. Pratt approached the cloth-topped Chrysler. It was ridiculous-looking, especially for anyone under retirement age, but it had no rust and the inside looked spotless, down to its tape deck and orange-slice air freshener. The price was right, down here by the sinkhole. Someone had put whitewall tires on the thing—probably the cheapest used set at whatever service station the car had limped into. What the hell, Pratt thought. A to B. He could be done looking. He waved his hand, and after a minute the plexiglass door of the trailer-office pushed open. He wondered if the convertible top actually worked, but truly he didn't care—unless you were trying to sun-fry yourself like an egg, why would you ever put it down? He stepped around the back of the car and saw a single bumper sticker: PEROT '92.

"This one will do," Pratt said.

"The LeBaron?"

"Yeah, the LeBaron. Why, what's wrong with it?"

"Nothing. Nothing at all. The LeBaron is great. It's a solid American-made automobile. A lot of trips left in this baby."

Pratt offered the dealer three hundred less than the price posted on the windshield, and the guy's shoulders slumped. He took the end of his tie in two fingers and kneaded it pathetically.

"I told you about the no-haggle pricing," he said. "That's our thing. That's what sets us apart."

"How about you re-price the car for three hundred less than you did the first time," Pratt said. "From that point, we won't have to haggle."

"You know, people say they don't want to dicker at car lots, but really they do." The guy seemed sad to report this disappointing foible of human nature. "They like it, is the truth. They complain, but in reality, they enjoy it."

Pratt shrugged.

"You at least gonna finance?" the guy said.

"Not me," said Pratt. "Never took out a loan in my life. Not starting now for a Chrysler with a hundred sixty thousand miles on it."

"Well, congratulations," the guy said. "Just congratulations to you, Mr. No-Debt-Loves-to-Haggle."

Once Pratt had confirmed she no longer lived in the plantation house—which had been fixed up and inhabited by what looked like several generations of a wholesome blond family—Pratt thought he might find Kallie at the bakery where she'd worked part-time after high school. It was a shot in the dark because who kept a part-time job that long? Plus, Kallie had been taking classes at the community college for social work. She'd planned to pile up enough credits to transfer to one of the big state schools. If nothing else, Pratt could ask about Kallie at the bakery, maybe get enough of a report to go away satisfied that she was off to greener pastures.

Settled into his creaky LeBaron, he did the limit down the Olde Dade artery, passing its fossil shops and discount shoe stores and occasional hot dog stands manned by teenage girls in Daisy Dukes. Driving felt surreal, but maybe that was because the car was unfamiliar. The steering was full of play, the brakes mushy, and the mirrors kept misaligning in a way that made the road behind him look vague. He followed the traffic, feeling at once anonymous in the flow of daytime commuters and also exposed, out here in the world where anything could happen, where anyone could see him. Suddenly, as if he'd zoned out and missed time, he was in the humble south-county warehouse district, the endless crumbling parking lots encircled by

brown ditches, and this was the turn—he and Matty had picked up
Kallie here dozens of times—and here was the flat, high-windowed
front of the bakery.

Pratt slowly rounded the building, its stucco walls stained rusty
with hard municipal water. There were no windows low enough to see
inside. Or to see out, Pratt reasoned. He cruised around back to where
the employees kept their cars. Before Pratt had gone in, Kallie had
a tiny pickup that was always breaking down—a toy pickup, he and
Matty had called it—with eighty-eight horsepower and just enough
room in the bed to haul two kegs of beer. She'd had it forever, and
the thing had been on its last legs. Pratt didn't spot it in the lot. He
saw a brand new Saab 900 and a bunch of junkers. At least the owner
of the place was doing okay.

Pratt parked on the shoulder of a ditch, close enough to watch the
glass doors at the back of the bakery, with no plan as to how long
he was going to sit there. Some part of him might've been relieved
not to see Kallie. He didn't feel ready to speak to her. She wouldn't
be angry with him, he knew. What he feared was her indifference.
She wouldn't bear a grudge, even though she'd tried to visit him in
prison twice and both times he'd rebuffed her. He couldn't to this
day, to this minute, explain why he'd done that. He was so bitter
then. He'd felt guilty. Cheated. He didn't want her to see him in
there—that was a big part of it. Lots of guys in prison were like
that. They eagerly committed felonies, but didn't want anyone they
cared about to see them as felons. No one else had visited him. Uncle
Jack had been long gone, and Pratt didn't blame him one bit. Bonne
couldn't visit—he understood that. Matty, before he'd overdosed,
likely had orders to stay clear of the prison. The first time Kallie
showed up, Pratt had claimed he was sick. The second time, he
hadn't even made an excuse. He just shook his head at the guard,
who said, "Are you crazy, dude? She's fine." After that, it was two

and a half years of nothing. He'd wanted to be left alone, and, boy, had he been.

The back door of the bakery swung open. A middle-aged woman with a blue pixie cut emerged and sat at the break table and lit a cigarette. As soon as the door settled, it opened again—a much older woman this time, wearing a hairnet and glasses that dangled on a chain around her neck. The old woman held the door for someone else, and the sight of that someone materializing into view froze Pratt's blood. He didn't know whether to duck or sit up straight. It was her. It was Kallie. She didn't know Pratt's new car, he reminded himself. And she wasn't looking in his direction. She held a cordless phone to her ear, nodding—that way she had of showing impatience by slightly widening her eyes. The old woman sat, but Kallie paced. White sneakers and ankle socks—Pratt had always loved how they looked against her cinnamon-tan legs. She was still gorgeous, even in an apron. Her hair tied up off her neck. Pratt could see sweat shining on her forehead. She got off the phone and rolled her eyes, said something that made the others laugh. Pratt didn't move. He felt snuck up on, somehow, even though he'd driven over here expressly to find Kallie. He wasn't going to walk over there and he wasn't going to start the car and draw attention. He watched Kallie put her hands on her waist and crack her back. She looked exhausted when she leaned against the wall. Someone stuck their head out the door and asked her something, and she answered. A moment later, someone else stepped out so Kallie could sign some papers on a clipboard. She was a supervisor. Or, at least, someone the other employees came to with questions. That made sense. That's how she was—everyone trusted her as soon as they met her, and they were right to. There was so much talk about being a good judge of character, but usually it was more a matter of who you were judging. Someone like Kallie—it was obvious she was good to the bone. Anyone could feel it.

* * *

Pratt was rewarded for his lack of action. He decided to wait Kallie out, to sit tight in the LeBaron, and only fifteen minutes after she had gone back inside from her break—if you could call it that—she walked back outside with no apron and shook her hair loose on the way to her car. Pratt heard the engine whine, then saw her drive out of the lot in a beat-up Pontiac Fiero, rolling the windows down as she maneuvered around sad planters that held only dead grass. If she was a supervisor, she wasn't being paid like one. Her car's tint was peeling and the tires were bald.

Pratt let her escape the web of warehouses before starting his engine. He found Kallie out on the main road and stayed two or three lights behind her as she steered them south, into the hinterland between the North Suncoast towns and the outer Tampa suburbs. There was an old cineplex that had been turned into a church. A paintball range. Pratt, just then, was gripped by the memory of the first time he'd met Kallie. When he'd seen her less than an hour ago, his blood had frozen, and now it sped up, his palms slick. It was junior year of high school, Pratt barely sixteen. He'd been lingering in the school parking lot after baseball practice, a new enough driver that the Cherokee Mr. Bonne had given him use of was still a strange and wonderful place to hide out, to kill time. Pratt hadn't been ready yet to go home for dinner and face one of his uncle's lectures. In time his uncle would give up on him, but junior year Jack had still been game to complain about Pratt's grades, about the way he spent his weekend nights, all too happy to explain to Pratt that all the perks and luxuries he got from Bonne weren't free, that a bill would one day come due. Matty had sped off in his mint-green sports car, chirping the tires toward whatever sundown bowl-smoking session he'd caught wind of, leaving Pratt to nurse his Gatorade and watch the flag corps drill for a while—the corps such a lowly athletic endeavor that its practice facility was a strip of empty handicapped spaces. Pratt had watched the girls' soccer team step one by one by one up into an idling yellow bus. The bus waited five minutes, ten, then finally rolled out onto the road, leaving Pratt alone.

He'd sighed and started the engine—if he was *too* late, it would only lengthen his uncle's lecture—and then around the corner squealed a compact Nissan pickup, clipping a curb, screeching to a stop at a wild angle. The driver hopped out immediately and stood on her tiptoes and scanned the lot, pivoting this way and that, white soccer socks bunched around her calves. White soccer shorts. Pratt hadn't seen this girl before, and he would've remembered—even pounding on her hood and spitting on the blacktop, she was adorable. Muscled legs. Hair shining in the late-afternoon sun.

Pratt put the Jeep in gear and pulled around, close but not too close, the girl glaring at the sky, fuming, her hands in hard fists by her sides. Pratt approached her slowly with open, I-come-in-peace palms.

"They left two minutes ago," he said. "Seems like they were waiting for you."

The girl moved her attention from the heavens but placed no large part of it on Pratt, showing no surprise at his presence. He noticed that her eyes were dry. "Thanks," she said. "That's really helpful. It makes a big difference right now to know how much I missed them by."

"Soccer," Pratt said. "That's the one where you use your feet instead of your hands, so that way no one ever scores. I think I've seen it."

The girl ignored Pratt. She leaned against her truck, shaking her head, and Pratt had the odd thought that she was getting her perfect white uniform dirty.

"Fuck," she said. "Just... fuck."

Pratt took a small step toward her. "I guess you should've left sooner," he said, smirking.

Maybe she hadn't seen the smirk. She squared her body to his and peered right into his eyes, her anger perversely causing Pratt's nether regions to stir. "Oh, should I have planned that my drunk-ass dad would fall out of the trailer and dislocate his shoulder? I should've anticipated that's what I was going to find when I got home from school, my dad with throw up on him and his arm out of joint. Should I manage my time better so I could take him to the ER and fill out forms and answer a bunch of questions about the suitability of my home and still have time to catch the game bus? Is that your advice?"

"Shit," Pratt said. "Sorry, I wasn't... I was making a joke. I'm sorry that happened."

"A joke," the girl said. "It was hilarious. So well-timed." She took in a big, slow breath through her nose, her fury seeming to cool a few notches because what was the point.

"Is he okay now?"

"What?"

"Your dad."

"He's okay. He's always okay. I'm not okay. I can't miss this game. It's not fair. I shouldn't have to miss it."

"Where is it?" Pratt asked. "Can you drive?"

"It's down by Busch freaking Gardens. Farthest game of the season. Who are you, by the way? Like, what's your deal? Why are you...?"

"I'm Pratt. I'm just a regular dude. I saw you over here."

"Oh, good," she said. "A regular dude hanging out in the school parking lot." She stood away from her truck and pulled a wad of pink gum out of her mouth and flicked it dejectedly toward a palmetto thicket. "You want some information, Mr. Regular-Dude-with-a-Brand-New-SUV? No, I can't drive to Tampa, because I got enough gas to get me to next Tuesday and not a drop more, and I don't have any money. If you don't know what no money means, it doesn't mean

I don't have cash on me at the moment—it means I don't have *any* money. Not till Tuesday of next week."

Pratt's stomach fluttered in a way it hadn't since middle school. He felt he could listen to this girl forever, even if all she ever did was curse him out. He pulled out his wallet with the caution of a driver revealing a weapon at a traffic stop.

"Listen," he said. "Don't make this weird, but I'm gonna buy you a tank of gas." He showed the two twenties and the ten, then held the twenty out toward her. "There's nothing better this could be used for than getting you to your game. Just take it. Don't think about it—just take it."

A half laugh escaped the girl. "Okay, you're giving me money for no reason and it's not weird. Wrong—it's very weird. I don't even know you. It's weird as hell."

"I told you, I'm Pratt."

She shook her head.

"It's unusual," Pratt said. "I'll give you that."

"I don't think so, man. But thanks."

"Come on—how often can a problem be solved this easy? It's a twenty. It's not like I worked in a salt mine for it." Pratt had almost said, "There's more where that came from," which was true, but he didn't want to be the kind of guy who said there was more money where that came from to a girl he didn't know. He understood that her dad either couldn't or wouldn't buy her a tank of gas, or that she was too mad at him to ask. He understood that her making no mention of a mother in the drunk-dad-to-the-hospital episode was not a happy sign.

"Twenty dollars with no strings attached, he says." The girl's face was full of skepticism. Her truck was still running behind her, chuffing out exhaust.

"All I want in exchange is your name," Pratt said.

She cupped her forehead in her hand and exhaled, like she was starting to see the humor in the whole thing.

"What's the option at this point?" Pratt reasoned. "I'm supposed to keep my stupid money and think all night about you missing your game. The team losing. And me still with my dumb cash."

"They probably will," said the girl, not exactly to Pratt. "They'll probably lose without me."

Pratt further extended the crisp bill and shrugged in a pleading way.

"Kallie," the girl said, reaching for the money. "And I'll pay you back next week."

"No rush," he said. "Whenever."

"Next week. That's when I'll pay you back." Kallie folded the twenty and slipped it down into her loose sock. "Thank you, Pratt. Regular dude Pratt."

It was the next thirty seconds that would haunt him. He'd wanted to tell Kallie how nervous she was making him, tell her she was beautiful, tell her *something*. But he'd been paralyzed by the knowledge in his gut that she wasn't just another girl, hamstrung further by his wariness about taking advantage of the situation, the fact that he had money and she didn't. He'd wanted to grab hold of her hand, but he hadn't—a complete stranger in a parking lot, it was true. He managed to invite her to a party he and Matty were hitting that Friday, and by the time Pratt arrived at that party, the ship had sailed—Matty and Kallie flirting, inseparable the whole night, arms around each other's waists. A couple days later, Matty handed Pratt a twenty, said he'd heard about Pratt helping Kallie out. The two of them—Matty and Kallie—were already an item. Pratt and Kallie became friends and learned everything about each other—the troubles Kallie had because her mother had passed away, the troubles Pratt had because his parents were gone—any affection they harbored funneled into platonic devotion. But the attraction had never really snuffed out, not on Pratt's side. Being off-limits to each other had simultaneously taken the romantic pressure off them and ensured that Pratt would always want Kallie. In a hundred years, he would still want her. But in a thousand years, he'd never betray Matty.

They were headed to Tarpley, Pratt saw. He knew Tarpley. It was a collection of plain ranch houses and small apartment buildings, all relatively safe and—because there was nothing around that rich people sought, no beach or golf or biking trails or malls—Tarpley rents were dependably low. Pratt stayed far back as Kallie pulled onto her street and stopped her car in front of a duplex that looked, from a distance, run-down but not falling apart. Once she'd traversed the yard and let herself in, Pratt crept the LeBaron closer and sidled up to the opposite curb, avoiding a ring of broken glass and a rusty hubcap someone was doing without. The yard of Kallie's duplex was mostly weeds, the myrtles posted at the lot's front corners stunted and bloomless. Kallie had made an effort to gussy up her half of the property with a spoonbill statue and a wooden bench up on the porch, but the other side was a wreck—an old Cougar up on blocks, beer bottles strewn about.

Pratt had made a mistake, he gathered. If he'd wanted to imagine Kallie off to bigger and better things, he should've done just that. Imagined it. Now he *couldn't* imagine it. Now, when he drove off to some other county probably named after some other Spanish explorer, it wouldn't be in ignorant bliss. He closed his eyes hard for a minute. When he opened them, everything was the same. Exactly. The glass in the street shimmered like diamonds. The breeze was soundless and weak.

*   *   *

Pratt had chosen a bare-bones diner on the edge of Bethuna Pond's six-block downtown, a place he was unlikely to see anyone he knew. He didn't feel hungry, but he knew he needed to eat because he was lightheaded, his mind dull and legs heavy. It didn't make sense, his lack of appetite—he should've been ravenous. After getting released, he should've been ordering everything on the menu instead of picking at toast. What he should've been doing, really, was driving. He knew this, and yet here he was. Leaving—it would be so final. Heading toward nothing but a void, toward nothing but more questions. It probably didn't matter how fast he got on the road—if Bonne wanted him, he reasoned, he'd have found him already.

Pratt looked around jealously at the other patrons—a team of housepainters in spattered overalls wolfing down eggs, a line of old men sipping coffee at the counter, their attention on the dusty TV above the register. They belonged here. Nothing was chasing them away. Soon the church crowd would pour in—combed children in shiny shoes, fathers with ironed slacks and pagers clipped to their belts—but Pratt would be gone before then.

The waitress, who'd introduced herself as Tammi—probably forty but looking closer to fifty with her sun-cracked skin and knotted knuckles—was making her way over with another iced tea. She stopped and side-mouthed something that made the old men cackle, then did the same at the painters' table. This was the real skill, brightening the days of bored and weary men; anyone could carry platters and coffee pots around.

When Tammi reached Pratt's booth, she expressed skepticism that an order of toast was enough to found a day on. She raised her eyebrows at all the tiny jam packets he'd opened and scraped clean.

"Too proud to go after them things spoon to mouth, huh?" She picked up Pratt's used cup, only ice now, and set a new one down.

"Pride's not a trouble of mine," he said.

One of the men at the bar called out for more coffee and Tammi told him to pipe down or he'd get it on his lap. She turned back to Pratt, fist on her hip in the classic pose of waitresses.

"I know what you're angling at," she said. "You want to be a regular. That's what everybody wants. You come in tomorrow and say 'the usual' and I'll remember. Even though it ain't a very usual order at all. Not for a healthy young man, anyway."

Up in the corner, a news show came back from commercial. A reporter on Fred Howard Beach was demonstrating the stingray shuffle, speaking about how bad the stingrays were, worse than ever. It was forty-five minutes from where Pratt sat but looked like another world. The Gulf. The sparkling sand.

"Look, kiddo," said Tammi, "you gotta have eggs or bacon or something."

"I'm good," Pratt told her.

"I highly doubt that," she said, shrugging her shoulders and turning on her heel.

Pratt watched her return to the old men at the counter, chiding them good-humoredly. He took another bite of his toast, loaded heavy with sweet goop, and looked out toward the murky, weed-rimmed reservoir that gave the town its name, squinting at the slanting sunlight reflecting off its boggy surface.

He'd been twenty-two when he'd gone in. Now he was twenty-five. It didn't sound like much when you put it that way, but before prison he'd been known as an athlete, a guy whose exploits on the diamond were a big part of his identity. He'd been a guy with enough money in his pocket to do what he liked, a guy who would hit three or four parties—mostly because of Matty, the social part, but still—on a typical weekend night. And now, determined as he was not to return to his old life and old job, even if he did want to stay around here, he'd have to do it without the respect that came with being one of Bonne's men. That flash of fear or envy it inspired. That dark-edged aura that had ushered him into rooms all those years. Now, unemployed and a felon, and without Matty, he imagined most people would simply despise him. He'd rather be hated by complete strangers, people who'd never heard of Arthur Bonne. Around here, he had to avoid everyone. All these people who, no matter what they'd heard, didn't really know what happened the night Pratt and Matty got tailed. They didn't know the real story, but they *did* know—this part they had right—that everyone involved had lost big, and that Pratt, who had nothing now, was the biggest loser of them all.

He finished his tea. He'd eaten all he could of his toast. He gazed in the direction of the LeBaron for a few moments before it dawned on him that it was his. It was his own car he was staring at. A rueful half smile crossed his face. He thought of how different this would all be if Matty was here. Matty would've thrown a bash for his release. Rented out a bar. Weed. Dance floor thumping beneath the high heels of dozens of girls. Pratt would've been forced right back into the social fray, his new freedom celebrated, and would've fallen back unavoidably into his old life. It was the one thing to be grateful for: he could find a new path now, a road he could drive without paying tolls to Bonne. A road that could lead anywhere, but not back to prison. If Matty was still here, he wouldn't even think about leaving. For better or worse, he wouldn't have considered it for a second. After Pratt's parents had died, he and Matty had more or less become family. Pratt didn't live at the Bonne house, but Matty had treated him like blood. That first Christmas, when one of Matty's uncles had mailed him two crisp fifties, Matty handed one over to Pratt the second he saw him. Before that, Halloween—Pratt had gotten a late start trick-or-treating because his uncle had wanted help detailing his car, and at the end of the night, when Pratt took out his fangs and Matty removed his cape, Matty didn't bat an eye at pouring all the candy into one pile so they'd have the same amount. Later, it was more important things. In tenth grade, when a couple football players had cornered Pratt behind the school gym—pissed about their team's awful record and the rumor that one of their girlfriends had been flirting with Pratt in the cafeteria—Matty had happened on the scene and immediately, no questions asked, pulled his switchblade and gone crazy eyes on Pratt's harassers, veins bulging, screaming at them that he'd spend the rest of the school year making their lives hell if they even looked at Pratt again. Now Matty was back in Maryland, in the cemetery where generations of his forefathers were buried. Pratt could never have left Matty. As far as Bonne, though—Pratt had to hope the old man respected that Pratt didn't want to wind up in a cemetery, too.

He was about to raise his hand for Tammi when something on the TV screen stopped him. Speak of the devil. The guy in the suit behind the news desk wasn't two sentences into the story before Pratt knew he was hearing about Roger's and Nairn's work—and so, really, Bonne's work. The short of it was that a Gulf Coast con man had been apprehended and maimed and dropped a block from the county hospital, just outside the view of the cameras that lined the hospital's parking lot. One of the old guys at the counter reached for the remote and turned up the volume, and everybody's head turned toward the screen. Apparently, this guy had been ripping off grandmothers with a lawn-service con. He'd worked his way down to Bradenton and then north again, hitting low-hanging fruit in Pasco and Hernando, walking up clean-cut and buttoned and meek, petting dogs, explaining to lone grannies that he was establishing a good family business based on old-fashioned Christian values and that he was from a long line of proud yardmen and that he saw keeping neighborhoods neat and respectable as God's work; eventually, with his khakis pressed and his hair parted straight as a ruler, he would get around to the cash special he was offering as a promotion—pay in advance and get 25 percent off.

The news guy said the "alleged" con man had limped into the waiting room of the ER with all the fingers of his left hand cut jaggedly off, bleeding like a spigot, his head sloppily shaved, his feet bare. The men at the counter nodded their resigned approval, tapping their coffee cups together in subdued celebration.

"Serves him right," said Tammi, wiping down the table where the painters had been. "Could've been *my* mom. Lord knows she can't afford to get stole from."

This had always been part of Bonne's model. He took care of petty crime in the area, which, by keeping him in the good graces of the citizens, took pressure off the police to crack down on his operation. Pratt wasn't the only one who saw Roger and Nairn all over this story; people were *supposed* to know Bonne was behind these doses of justice, or what was the point? He was the evil Bethuna knew—an evil that ran off other unsavory elements and donated money to the community under the flags of his many retail and wholesale fronts. Stretches of road were marked MAINTAINED BY NATURE COAST CIRCUS OF CITRUS. Little League teams ran around in jerseys stamped EAST HERNANDO LANDSCAPE.

"Mr. B. got another one," Pratt heard one of the old men say.

"You don't know that for sure," said another, causing the rest of them to scoff in chorus.

In prison Pratt had heard, whether he'd wanted to or not, that Bonne was running his territory tighter than ever, bracing for all the development already in progress ahead of the new expressway to Tampa. With opportunity came opportunists, and they'd soon be able to get up here at eighty miles per hour. Bonne never went out in the evenings anymore, it was said, not even to any of his favorite restaurants, where a table was always found for him on the busiest nights and the poor schmucks he forced to wait were thrilled to have been butted in line by the famed Mr. B—something they could tell their coworkers on Monday. Bonne never went and smoked a cigar with the ancient Cubans at the chess park. Never sat in the stands anymore to cheer on his baseball teams. Hardly even ever went home—only to sleep a little, if at all—preferring to haunt the landscape company's warehouse.

Pratt arose and stepped toward the register, getting in line behind a guy about his age who'd come in during the Bonne news without Pratt noticing. The guy was picking up a breakfast sandwich to go and a little carton of milk like what everybody drank back in grade school. Tammi, ringing up the order, looked over the guy's shoulder at Pratt and said, "See, he's a regular. If he can do it, anybody can."

When the guy turned to see who was behind him, Pratt recognized Tony Castillo, and Tony Castillo recognized him. An achingly wide smile spread across Tony's face. It was a genuine smile, Pratt knew.

"Zimmer!" Tony blurted. "Holy shit—it's great to see you, man." He stepped around and gave Pratt a firm hug around his shoulders. A hug. Not something Pratt was used to.

"Good to see you, too," Pratt said placidly, and he sort of meant it. Tony was maybe the nicest guy he'd ever known, a guy you couldn't imagine wishing anyone ill. If Pratt had to run into someone he knew before he dragged himself out of town, Tony wasn't a bad choice.

"You come to this place?" Tony said. "I'm here once a week. Kind of a ritual."

"First time," Pratt said.

"The service sucks," Tony said, loud enough for Tammi to hear him and send a wink his way, "but the egg and chorizo is amazing."

Tony dropped a few bills in the tip jar. "You been back long? What have you been up to?"

JOHN BRANDON

This was Tony. Tactful enough to say "back long" instead of "out long," forthright enough to acknowledge that Pratt had been out of circulation instead of awkwardly avoiding it. It had been years since Pratt and Tony ran in the same circles. They'd been buddies even before Little League, had known each other before they knew what baseball was. Tony was so good-hearted that Pratt could remember wondering if he was *too* nice—a pitcher who never went up and in, never wanted to revel in a strikeout because it might embarrass the batter. Pratt had wondered if he was too kind to make it in the world, but from what Tony was now telling Pratt about his pawn operation, he was making it just fine. He'd done a business degree at the community college, he explained to Pratt, after Pratt had noncommittally revealed that he hadn't been up to much: two years at Pasco-Hernando and the last five fostering brisk trade in the resale market.

"Come over to my place tomorrow night," Tony said. "Let's catch up."

"Thanks," Pratt said, "but I'm sure you have better things to do."

"Some nights that's true," Tony admitted, "but not tomorrow night. I live alone. I get bored. Come on, don't be difficult. Don't be a diva."

Tony turned and grabbed a pen and a takeout menu and wrote down directions to his house. Pratt considered whether he'd be more of a jerk turning Tony down for no apparent reason—or for accepting the invitation even though he'd be in a different area code by tomorrow night.

Tony handed the menu over. "Gotta run to the store. I'll see you tomorrow. Come by around six, or whenever."

Pratt nodded.

"I'll see you then," Tony said. As he strode toward the door, he glanced back at Tammi and said, "Treat my guy here good, okay? Not like you treat me."

"Easy," Tammi called out. "I like him. You, I don't care for."

* * *

Pratt had the LeBaron in gear, about to pull away from the curb and go top off his gas tank, when a raised Ford Bronco pulled up alongside him and blocked him in, braking hard enough to chirp its oversize tires. Pratt immediately knew who it was. He heaved a heavy sigh and shifted back to park and turned the engine off. Here was the music. He'd stalled too long, and now he had to face it. That, or he'd known all along it was going to play. The minute he decided to evacuate, the band would strike up. What kind of song would it be—that was the question. He fixed his face so he wouldn't look flustered, a mouse caught in a trap.

He rolled his window down to match the Bronco's, which loomed above him. Roger, a quiet Black guy who had to be pushing forty, sat in the passenger seat reading a leather-bound book, annotating it with a yellow pencil. Nairn—pure, unadulterated white trash and much younger than his partner—hopped down from the driver's seat and rounded the front of the 4x4, leaving it blocking a lane of traffic. He stood between the two vehicles and settled himself into assholish comfort, his cowboy-booted foot up on Pratt's tire and his ramrod-straight back leaning against the Bronco's quarter panel. He had a dip the size of a Ping-Pong ball lodged in his lower lip and brown stains down the front of his pearl-button Western shirt.

"Whose fuckin' car you driving, boy? You elbowin' into my market?"

This was a reference to the fact that Nairn was known to date lonesome divorcées twice his age. Pratt had heard him boast about how these very experienced ladies couldn't wait to spoil a young piece of ass like himself rotten.

"Howdy, Nairn," Pratt said. "Nice work on that lawn guy."

"Oh, that," said Nairn, his colorless eyes glinting. "That there wasn't work. That's recreation. I'd do that for free, for the love of my craft."

"Hello, Roger," Pratt said, angling in his seat to see the older man's face.

Roger looked away from his book. Tucked his pencil behind his ear. He wore a guayabera shirt and a pale fedora.

"Boss wants to see you," he said.

"I ain't got a boss," Pratt told him.

"Whatever you call him, he wants to see you."

Pratt sighed. "When? Today?"

Now it was Roger's turn to smile. "What, you got big plans? You gotta check with your secretary?" Roger always had his nose in a book, always seemed to exist at a remove, but Pratt had personally witnessed him knock a biker cold with a single right cross and then catch the guy by the vest so he didn't bust his head and make a mess.

"Ain't got a boss, my ass," Nairn said. "Hell, I'm your boss now. Things gonna be different, now you ain't Bonne's precious darlin'."

"How do you know I'm not his darling?"

"After losin' him all them pesos?"

"Anybody needs me, they'll have to use the telephone," Pratt said.

Roger chuckled. "I don't think that's how it's gonna play out."

"Get yourself thrown in the hoosegow and then his boy winds up blue in a box." Nairn spit a wad of dip juice toward the LeBaron's tire, probably staining the whitewall. "That's why you was around. Think it was your professional expertise? It was to keep Matty out of trouble. That one thing, and you fucked it sideways as it could be fucked. There's alive and there's dead. Two ain't nothin' alike."

Pratt didn't want to let Nairn get to him, didn't want to give him the satisfaction—at least not this easily. He could feel the muscles in his neck coiling. Nairn had never liked Pratt, and he hadn't liked Matty either. Special treatment, as he saw it. Nepotism.

"Oh, Pratty's feelings are hurt now. He's turnin' red. Poor little Pratty. His mommy and daddy got killed a hundred years ago. Everybody feel sorry for Pratty."

"Have I ever asked anyone for pity?" Pratt said.

"You're just pitiful," Nairn said. "You ain't gotta ask." He pulled off his beat-up trucker hat and yanked it back on tighter. Pratt looked over into the diner and saw Tammi standing behind the counter, a rag over her shoulder, holding court with the old guys.

"I got plans elsewhere," Pratt said.

"I think those are canceled," Roger piped in. "Don't know for sure, just reading the tea leaves."

"Your folks died drunk on a boat," Nairn said. "Know how my daddy died?"

"Blew himself up with a crack pipe?" Pratt ventured.

"I'll tell you how," said Nairn. "Way that old cuss ended is from me endin' him. Cause of death for that sumbitch was you're lookin' at it."

"I'm sorry for your loss," Pratt told him. He'd actually heard all this before. Had heard it right from Nairn himself. He had no idea if it was true, but it may as well have been.

"Fourteen years old," Nairn continued. "Did that particular exercise with a tire iron. But you keep jokin', Pratt. You keep tellin' your punch lines nobody thinks is funny and see where it gets you."

"We done here?" Pratt said. Staying calm, or faking it at any rate, had worked. Now Nairn was the one turning red. "Because apparently I have an appointment. Apparently there's a request for my company."

Nairn, with an air of forbearance, stood up off the Bronco and stretched. He scraped his boot toe on the pavement. Took a minute to look around, his wolfish smile returning. He leaned down and filled up Pratt's window with his acne-scarred face. "You wanna be done?" he said. "I guess we can be done for now. We'll have us another date, though. Real soon."

"Long distance," said Pratt.

"Shit," Nairn drawled. "You ain't goin' nowhere."

Pratt didn't answer. He let Nairn stare through him, if that's what Nairn needed to do. He sat still and quiet, gazing out toward the line of dilapidated three-story houses on the other side of the pond, until Nairn finally straightened up again and tapped the soft roof of the LeBaron. He strode around the front of the 4x4 and climbed up and gunned its big engine, Roger reabsorbed already in his enormous tome, so engrossed he seemed to have forgotten Pratt was there.

It wasn't until Pratt was five minutes up the road, driving the eerily familiar route to the landscape supply, that Nairn's reek—rotten corn and stale beer and wet moss—was fully blown free of the LeBaron. A couple new outfits had popped up on County Road 40—a diabetes center, a vitamin shop—but the smokers' emporium and the Chinese buffet and the Bible superstore were right where they belonged. Pratt might have appeared cool during his chat with Nairn, but now sweat ran down his back and his eyes ached in the sunlight. He didn't want to accept what was as obvious as a thundercloud: if Bonne wanted him here, this is where he'd be. Pratt possessed just enough optimism to entertain the thought that Bonne only wanted to see him—something like the way he himself had wanted to see Kallie—that Bonne would thank him for doing the time and grant his official release. Since he was fantasizing, he might as well imagine Bonne telling him that Matty's death wasn't Pratt's fault, that he absolved him of everything and that he could depart with Bonne's blessing. Yeah, right. It was like Roger said—as vague as Pratt's plans had been, they were erased now.

He passed the little amusement park with manatees and mermaids. The brown sign reading BEAR HABITAT, even though Pratt had never once seen a bear in the area. Four or five run-down churches—one-story buildings with dingy day cares attached to them. Here was the one Pratt used to go to, with that inexplicable blue line still painted around its exterior walls like a belt, those two tall pines in the side yard they'd used as an end zone for their little football games. Pratt's parents hadn't been religious, but the day care was safe and clean enough. Still in business, so it couldn't be that bad. Pratt's mom used to drop him off with extra snacks so he could share with the poor kids—not that his own parents had been rolling in dough. He remembered how vast the play area had seemed. It was only about the size of two infields, he saw now. He remembered doing Bible-themed word searches with entries none of the kids knew—*Leviticus*, *rapture, covenant*. This was before he'd ever met Matty, but he'd already known Tony Castillo. Tony had gone to that same day care. He'd been there from the beginning, or as far back as Pratt could recall, already collecting old toys way back then, repairing cap guns and Teddy Ruxpins, hoarding broken crayons.

Pratt followed the road as it curved southeasterly, the sun glaring harsh through the windshield. He reached to his collar for his sunglasses and didn't find them there. Weren't in the console, either. He'd left them at the diner. He pulled the visors down. One of them was loose on its plastic hinge. In the full sun, he could see that the fake leather upholstery on the passenger seat was speckled with tiny cracks he hadn't noticed before. That's exactly why you had to talk car dealers down—because of all the shit they weren't telling you.

In the old days, working for Bonne, Pratt had driven a brand new Jeep Cherokee with four-wheel drive. Genuine cowhide. The Jeep had seemed a part of things, like working for Bonne in the first place had seemed a part of things. Pratt had never *decided* to work for him. It was a matter of course for Matty, being the only son, and so it was for Pratt, too. Bonne. The old man. Pratt tried not to think about what he would be like now. He'd never been gregarious, never nice—in fact, the way you knew he was pleased with you was he gave you something else to do, something more important—but now Pratt was prepared for a hardened shell of even that man. He had no idea what to expect from this meeting he was closing in on at two over the speed limit. It was worse than the day he got sentenced. That day he'd known what he was in for, at least—just not how long he was in for it.

He twisted a little wand on the steering column, trying to set the cruise control, but the car instantly lost momentum. He got back up to speed and tried it again. Still nothing. Okay, no cruise control. The one in the Jeep, he remembered, would give you extra gas going up hills and apply the brake going down. The Cherokee had of course disappeared during his stay in prison. Bonne had liquidated it, no doubt—someone was probably driving it around in Mexico. Wincing, Pratt thought of his uncle. Thought of him telling Pratt that no kid his age should have a car that expensive, saying it was nicer than any car he himself had ever owned, him, a person who'd actually done something in his life to deserve a vehicle like that. He'd called his uncle jealous, and his uncle had stared at him with the most disappointed face Pratt had ever seen on anyone. Mortifying to think of it now. Pratt had grown wiser in lockup. He'd been dead set against it, against learning any lessons, but it had happened anyway; he could look back on his younger self—merely a few years younger—and see a stupid punk. An idiot. He hadn't talked to Uncle Jack since the day he was sentenced, and now he understood how wrongly he'd treated the guy, a single man in robust middle age who'd been thrust into parental duty by a freak accident in the Gulf. A guy who never wanted to be in Florida. Never wanted to be responsible for a kid. A guy who'd told Pratt over and over to get out of Bonne's business, and whom Pratt over and over ignored. Pratt had heard from a social worker that his uncle had moved out West, maybe to New Mexico,

and the fact that he hadn't told Pratt himself where he was headed
spoke volumes.

Pratt turned off the road just beyond the unassuming wooden sign
and guided the car past several hulking red hills of mulch—the
highest hills in the state, Pratt would guess—and past a couple guys
shoveling grit into a drum, their shirts tied around their necks like
scarves. Farther back on the grounds, a forklift milled about like
a depressed zoo animal. And here, across the clay parking lot from
the warehouse, were the towering metallic chutes that emptied into
the chippers—dormant now, but Pratt had heard of Bonne dangling
guys inside them when he needed information.

Pratt pushed open the car door but didn't stand up right away,
letting his heart slow down. He didn't know what to be afraid of
yet, but he knew he didn't want to be here. The building was gray
and still as an old warship. No windows on this side of the structure.
Nothing but closed bay doors and sun-warped circuit boxes.

He slowly lifted himself out of the car, stood straight to crack his
back, then strode over and pulled open the plain, heavy door. Not
locked, but Bonne always knew when it opened because a buzzer went
off in his office. Pratt stepped inside and let his eyes adjust, the door
easing shut behind him with a click. Vacuum-sealed quiet. Not a person
in sight. Fluorescent lights in the rafters, so many burned out that the
cavernous space was as dim as a dead mall. Pratt advanced across the
hard floor, listening to the squeak of his sneakers, breathing the stale
air—no fans turning and no air conditioner humming, but somehow
it wasn't as hot as it ought to be, a little kingdom that operated by its
own rules and its own climate. He made his way through the belly of
the place, past shoulder-high pallets of fertilizer and industrial canisters
of herbicide, toward the only room in the entire facility with a door

on it. He raised his fist and thought about knocking, then pushed the door open instead, revealing the well-ordered room and its blank walls. His back to Pratt, standing at a window and gazing toward a bare, bleached-looking tree, was the man who'd summoned him here. The window wasn't broad, and still Bonne's gaunt frame barely interrupted the view through it. The tree was a relic, white, dry as chalk, but beneath it, azaleas bloomed wildly in livid fuchsia.

Bonne turned slowly. He didn't seem to register Pratt right away, his mind elsewhere, his brow dagger-lined in thought. It was June, but he wore a thin sweater. It hung askew on his bony shoulders. However much Pratt had aged, Bonne had aged more, his neck sinewed and jerky-like. He put his watery eyes on Pratt and shuffled over and leaned close, closer—for a second, Pratt had no idea what was happening, then Bonne was hugging him, something he'd never done before. It was a long, awkward hug, an embrace that let Pratt know the man was still somehow strong, and Pratt did his best to return it, Bonne's cologne-and-coffee scent filling his nose.

Finally, Bonne released him and took a step back, looking chilled despite his sweater, or maybe because of the sweater.

"I gotta send for you?" he said. His voice was the same—vaguely ribbing, vaguely Northern, so assured it was almost a parody of confidence.

"I know how you don't like unexpected guests," Pratt said.

Bonne looked at him, that look that said if this was what he had to work with, he'd work with it. "You're skinnier than me," he told Pratt.

"I eat when I'm hungry," Pratt said. "The rest is out of my hands."

Bonne went over to a tiny fridge in the corner and retrieved a bottle of seltzer. He looked over to Pratt to offer him one, but Pratt shook his head.

"How's Mrs. Bonne?" Pratt asked. He was being polite, but he did want to know. The woman had never been anything but kind to Pratt.

Bonne twisted open his seltzer and took a dainty sip. "Thanks for asking, but she ain't good at all. Something called Lewy body dementia. That's why she was acting so screwy, but she's worse now. Worse every week."

"What's, umm…"

"Lewy body dementia?"

"Yeah, what is that?"

"I got no idea, really. Something about protein deposits. I can't follow it. I come home, she says the lady came around selling blankets. I gotta remember to pay the lady for the blankets. Thinking of when she was young in Baltimore, maybe."

Bonne sidled behind the desk and sat down, signaling Pratt to the chair across from him, an out-of-place yellow-upholstered kitchen thing that forced Pratt to sit up straight like a kid at a piano lesson. Once settled, Bonne faced a quarter turn off center, looking into a corner of the office at an oaken coatrack hung with a half dozen cheap brown ponchos. There was absolutely nothing on Bonne's desk. The walls were also bare, though Pratt could see the darkened rectangles where frames had been.

"Know how much three hundred dollars is if you gamble it?" Bonne said.

"Usually nothing," Pratt answered.

Bonne nodded. "Know how much it is if you save it?"

"I guess… three hundred dollars."

"Know how much it is if you drip sweat on it?"

Pratt shrugged.

"Yeah, I'm not sure either," Bonne said. "I lost track. Three bills is what I started with. Graduated high school and Old Lady Mancini gave me one, two, three Bennys. I worked at her car wash three years. Said it was a bonus, a hundred a year." Bonne held his seltzer bottle up and examined the label for what felt like a long time, his face pinched, then set it back down in its ring of moisture. "IRS took her down a couple years before she could retire—this is before I had the wherewithal to help with something like that. Gave all us kids jobs, bought us cakes on our birthdays. Worked her ass off for four decades and the government we all pay for decided to nail her to the wall because her deadbeat husband filed their taxes left-handed once or twice."

Pratt had not heard this story before and didn't know why he was hearing it now. Bonne had never been a storyteller, never a dweller on the past. It had to do with getting old, Pratt guessed—things left undone, now haunting Bonne—but like every change in the man, it was mostly because of all he'd lost. The guys from the early days—there weren't many of them left. Bonne's wife was as good as gone, or so it seemed. Most of all, and most of all by far, Matty. Pratt could tell Matty wouldn't be mentioned at this meeting. Matty's absence was in the air they were breathing, but Bonne wouldn't utter his dead son's name. The hug had been acknowledgment of Matty, and it had been all the grief Bonne was willing to share.

"I got a lot more than three hundred bucks now, but it ain't so much that losing two hundred and sixty grand don't sting."

"Two-fifty."

"Closer to two-sixty, and I always estimate conservative."

Bonne opened a drawer of his desk and looked down in it, Pratt had no idea at what, then gave a little nod and shut it again. He was wearing a ring on his left hand, Pratt noticed, that had belonged to his own father, Matty's grandfather. Matty had always worn it on his thick ring finger, but Bonne had it on his middle finger and it still hung loose on the knuckle.

Looking back now, Matty's overdose was bleakly predictable. Without Pratt around, of course the drugs and the girls had both gotten worse. Even before Pratt went in, Matty had been doing anything his father couldn't smell on him—ecstasy, meth, cocaine. No telling what he'd gotten into on his own, and how much of it. Eleven weeks. That's how long it had taken him to turn up dead. Pratt's sentence had actually been light, considering Pratt had priors for shoplifting and assault and considering that the DA had tacked on fleeing and resisting and had interpreted Pratt shrugging a cop's hand off his shoulder as striking an officer. His sentence had been light, but nowhere near light enough to save Matty from himself.

"There are consequences in this world, Pratt."

"I did the time for you."

"Two and a half years. Big whoop."

"Thirty-two months."

"How do you know I'm talking about *you*, anyway? A lot of people got consequences to pay."

Pratt looked down at the office floor. Unlike the rest of the warehouse, it needed sweeping. He tried to keep from tapping his foot, from fidgeting.

"It's usually easy money, this work we do. But then occasionally it's hard. Hard as a tomcat's little pecker."

"When you get caught, right?"

"It's what I chose. The reason don't matter. It's what Malloy chose." Bonne cleared his throat. Narrowed his eyes. "When people get caught, those are bad days. No arguing that."

"Who's Malloy?" Pratt asked.

Bonne coughed once into the hand with the big ring. "You'll know all about Malloy soon enough," he said.

"Why's that?"

"And he won't know about you until it's too late."

Here it was. Pratt was finding out what, exactly, to be afraid of. He said, "I don't want any of your money, Mr. Bonne. Easy or hard or any other way. No disrespect. Appreciate everything you did for me, but I don't want it."

"That's convenient," Bonne said, "because I ain't paying you. This is a favor between gentlemen."

Pratt watched as the wizened crime boss finished off his seltzer. He screwed the cap back on tight and, with no warning, tossed the bottle at the window behind him. Pratt jumped a little in his chair, expecting a crash of glass that did not come. The bottle flew outside, glinting in the sun before it spun out of sight and thumped in the dirt. Pratt hadn't noticed the window was open. All the sound from the world was muted on this side of the building. This was the edge of the property, peaceful green pastureland beyond.

"I never asked you to do anything too skilled, but I know you got a talent for it. Them Springstead guys that time, ones started mouthing off after the baseball game. Yeah, I know about that. I know what happened your second day in the pen, and I know the guy you did it to. Lavar Shaw. Pretty tough individual. I figure the training wheels are ready to come off."

"Lavar Shaw was survival."

"So's this, Pratt. You got no choice."

"So is what?"

"You ain't a kid no more," Bonne said. "You want to be done, you don't just breeze out the front door."

"We're even. I did my time." This was all Pratt knew to say, but he also knew it probably didn't matter what he said. Not probably—it didn't matter.

Bonne jammed the heavy ring up hard on his finger. "Nobody's even. There's guys I help and guys I hurt. You fall in that first bunch. I'm asking you to do something for me, and if you do it right and don't perform a full wop opera in my office, I won't ask you to do nothing else."

Pratt scoffed. His throat was dry and his mind was struggling to catch, like an old engine in the cold. He felt himself pushing down on the yellow armrests, his legs tensing. A flight instinct.

"Don't be stupid," Bonne said, and Pratt heard something a little desperate in the man's voice. "Don't even think about making us enemies."

Pratt was aware of all the bones in his body, his skeleton propped in the uncomfortable chair. The floor was moving, but the world outside the window was steady. Pratt focused on the tree—a bony hand straining up out of the earth. Groping in the sunshine and in the dark of night. Whatever it wanted, it would never get it. This old man who let the day's heat in the window to keep from shivering, who'd apparently given up cigars and Scotch for seltzer—this guy was still going to run Pratt's life. Asking, this time, for what exactly? Pratt knew, but didn't want to admit it. In the old days, Pratt had wanted nothing more than bigger orders from Bonne, but this was crazy. It was crazy, but Bonne was saying it like it wasn't.

"Malloy's my book-chef past year and a half. Past six months of that, he's also a premier client of Joe-Baby Jones, only Malloy don't know it." Here was Bonne's grin. It looked painful, like it was costing him something. "Joe-Baby has these remote setups—cops bust 'em up, no big deal. Calls 'em party supplies. So, Malloy's been laying husky bets at one of these. Joe put me wise. Got another egghead to check Malloy's math, old guy who's retired now... that report didn't bode too cheerful."

Deliveries. Tailing people for a night. Driving Bonne's cronies around. Sure, they'd had to talk sense into a dude now and then, corner a sloppy small-timer and explain a few things. All of it leading finally to the job that got botched, moving cars to the chop shop. It didn't add up, that Bonne would ask Pratt to do this. Pratt wasn't a darling—Nairn had that much right—but this? It could only be punishment. That was the only thing that made sense. Forced penance for Matty.

Bonne was still talking, saying Malloy started with him *after* Pratt went away, so he wouldn't recognize Pratt. In case Malloy was looking over his shoulder, he didn't want Roger and Nairn trying to sneak up on him. They had enough eyes on them as it was—more important eyes than Malloy's.

"End of the month," Bonne said. "Get familiar with the asshole's wheres and whens—don't do it till it's right. We don't need a circus. End of the month. That's no big rush."

"A murder?" Pratt heard himself finally say. "You want me to do a murder?"

Bonne's look was condescending. "They do something to your brain in there? You gotta keep up." He indulged in a sigh and told Pratt, patiently, that a lot of guys killed a lot of guys. He himself had killed four of them, in the early days. Four. Did Pratt think he was better than Bonne? "State of Florida fries 'em in the chair," he said. "US Army blows 'em up in the desert. Philip Morris makes a mint giving 'em cancer. Be glad you're on the right end of it. Your life's out ahead of you, so long as you can buckle down and do what you need to do. This one thing."

Who's making an enemy out of who? Pratt wanted to say. Whose brain isn't working right?

Bonne leaned his elbows forward on the desk and looked Pratt in the face, the old man's eyes a translucent, cataracted green. He stared at Pratt a minute, maybe waiting until Pratt seemed present, like he could truly listen. When Bonne's voice issued forth, it was in a strange whisper, and what it said was that Bonne wasn't going to let Pratt leave him.

"What?" said Pratt.

"Everyone else left me, and it ain't gonna happen with you. I ain't leaving that to chance. I'm not a gambler, Pratt. I'm the house."

Bonne was still staring right into Pratt's eyes. He looked both haunted and like a ghost. Pratt thought maybe he was starting to understand, or at least he wasn't totally lost now. If Bonne made Pratt do this, he'd have something he could always hang over Pratt. Not being able to leave probably meant a lot of things, and one of them was that he couldn't betray Bonne. Pratt was the next best thing to Matty, but without Matty around—Pratt was seeing this through Bonne's rheumy emerald eyes—Pratt was also dangerous. A person who knew too much. A person who might've changed an awful lot in lockup, made new friends.

"Insurance," Bonne said, as if reading Pratt's thoughts. "You can be free of the business, but we'll always be on the same side, you and me."

Pratt could feel his clenched jaw quivering. His knuckles were white, squeezing the plasticky armrests.

Bonne leaned back. His sweater had a pocket on the chest, and he dipped into it with two fingers and held a fold of cash out toward Pratt. It looked like five hundred.

"I'm not taking that," Pratt said.

"For walking around," said Bonne. "For milkshakes."

"I ain't taking it."

Bonne nodded his head sagely and slipped the money back in his pocket. "Well, what *are* you doing for expenses?" he asked.

"That's my business."

"You want a regular job, I can get you a regular job. Just for now."

Pratt didn't respond. There wasn't anything he could think to say that would've been helpful. He looked toward the window. He could hear wind gusting outside, but there were no leaves on the tree to show it. Bonne leaned to the side and opened the same drawer he'd opened before. This time he pulled out a gun and, along with it, a green bag Pratt knew contained ammo. He set it all in front of Pratt and told him with a quick scowl that this offering, unlike the money, could not be turned down. He slid a piece of paper across the table and waited for Pratt to take it.

"You'll get used to the idea," Bonne said. "Everybody gets used to everything."

And with that the old man raised himself out of his chair and stepped back over to the window, showing Pratt his back again—the whiskery nape of his neck and the heels of his leather shoes. Now the wind had something to blow against, rippling Bonne's sweater where it hung loose on him.

"I know I'm going a little nuts," he conceded, wiping his hand along the sill to dust it. "I lose you, I go all the way."

Pratt stood. He reached for the gun and dropped it into the bag with the ammo. The bag said WITHLACOOCHEE STATE FOREST and featured a winking raccoon. Pratt could smell gunpowder and oiled steel. He could still smell Bonne's aftershave. He could smell the odor of wet mulch wafting in from outside. He was nowhere near accepting that he might use this gun to end another man's life. It had been ordained to happen, but none of this felt real.

"I should've stayed in Z-hell," Pratt said, but this drew only a cool nod from Bonne, who still faced the window. Pratt would've needed to stay in there a long time, he knew—Bonne would never die and he'd never lose his marbles. Not really. Just this much. Just enough to turn Pratt's open destiny sideways.

"No more contact for us till the job is done," Bonne said. "No phone. Nothing."

Pratt was standing and had the bag and slip of paper in hand, but he felt like he shouldn't leave the office. Once he left, none of this could be undone. He wanted out of there, though. He wanted to breathe, and in just a moment he would soberly retrace his steps across the warehouse floor, then drive slowly off the grounds, and once he was out on the main road, he would yell out the window like a moron. That's what he would do. He could see it all already.

"Oh, yeah," Bonne said. "Get over to your storage unit. I didn't want a record of me still paying for things for you. Three more days, they can sell your stuff."

Back at the motel, in a grim trance, Pratt ran his finger down the want ads and called on apartments. One month. He'd pay for a place for thirty days. He sure wasn't going to stay in this shithole any longer than he had to, inhaling mildew and listening to strung-out couples scream at each other like cats. The first place he called on was taken. The second place wanted a background check and a fat deposit.

He opened the curtain wider, the corner lamp on its wobbly stalk doing almost nothing. He picked up the phone and dialed the next number—since it was long distance, he had to ask the woman on the other end to accept a collect call from "I'm interested in the condo."

The connection clicked through and the first thing she said was, "Collect, huh? I guess you *do* need a place."

Her name was Lulu. The condo she'd advertised as "very furnished, quiet neighborhood" had actually belonged to her deceased mother, and apparently it still had all her mother's stuff in it. Lulu was in Delaware and hadn't had a chance to come down and clean it out.

"*All* her stuff," Lulu emphasized. "I just want to prepare you. She, like, collected things. That's putting it kindly."

"That's no problem," said Pratt.

"You don't have furniture, do you?"

"Not even close," said Pratt. "I travel light."

"No kids, no pets—not that you could even *have* a kid in there. Other than that, I'm easy. I never did this sort of thing before."

"That's me," said Pratt. "No kids, no pets." He was circling Lulu's number over and over with a ballpoint pen, about to rip through the paper. There was a woman outside leaning against a cart, smoking. Probably waiting to clean Pratt's room, though to clean it properly she'd have to burn it down and bury the ashes.

"It's not exactly a bachelor pad," Lulu said.

"Well, there's all different types of bachelors."

"That's a fact," said Lulu. "I can vouch for that." When she laughed, she seemed older—a laugh that was part cough. "To be honest," she said, "I don't know what all's in there at this point. There's a second bedroom. You can pile everything in there if you want, to make space in the other rooms. It's a dust factory if you leave it all out, so do what you have to do."

"I'll manage," Pratt assured her.

"The key is taped to the bottom of the dolphin statue. The big one. Actually, two are big—the one with the green waves all over it."

"Green waves. Got it. Like Tulane."

"Like what?"

"Nothing. A baseball team."

"Look, I want to get off this phone because I don't know what it's costing me, but I'm trusting you to put a money order in the mail. Send it to the address in the ad. Last name Stamper."

"I'll have it out tomorrow morning."

"Don't let anything stop you. Don't get sidetracked."

"I won't."

"I'm putting faith in the universe and expecting to be rewarded for that faith. In other words, I don't want to deal with any bullshit."

"There won't be any bullshit," said Pratt.

"It's up to you," she said. "Humanity's good name is in your hands."

*   *   *

The next day, Pratt got his money order sent, then drove to the storage unit with his head in a fog, flinching every time a dragonfly walloped the windshield, the sky Popsicle blue and cloudless, the roadside flowers blooming madly in the color of spoiled butter.

He was still in a fog when he spoke to the terminally bored college girl—probably the owner's daughter unhappily home for the summer—and she informed him he had to pay for the whole current month to gain access to his belongings. The whole month plus a late fee. The girl said she didn't make the rules. Pratt had signed a contract with all this in it, she reminded him, and even though he himself hadn't signed anything, he didn't argue. His mind was twisted up in itself, trying to accept the extra reparation Bonne had dropped on top of his prison sentence, trying *not* to accept the details of that reparation. All he could focus his eyes on was the girl's tiny doll hand straining to lift her enormous bottle of Fiji Water, the dozen shiny bracelets on her arm tinkling with the effort.

His shoes squeaked loudly in the long, empty corridor—why were they called sneakers, he wondered, when they made noise wherever he went? The girl had given him the key to the new padlock they'd put on; he slid it in, heard the hollow click, then slipped the lock free and dropped it in his back pocket. He took a deep breath, preparing to face this next thing he didn't want to do. This next ordeal. He gripped the metal handle tight, ready to have to yank the door upward, but at the slightest pressure it rolled open smoothly, clacking softly until it couldn't go higher.

Pratt cleared away cobwebs and flipped on the overhead fluorescent light, which glowed immediately without a flicker. The unit before him was narrower than his cell had been, but deeper and with a much higher ceiling. It was mostly empty, except for a squat pyramid of five or six boxes stacked against the back wall. Pratt had avoided thinking about this place, this stuff, while he was locked up. The bill had been paid all at once, in advance, enough to cover the length of his sentence; Bonne had probably had a runner drop off cash. Pratt hadn't wanted to deal with any of it back then—his own things, his parents' things, whatever keepsakes had survived—and his attitude hadn't changed since.

He shuffled to the back of the unit, pulled all the boxes down to the floor. He started easy, digging through the one black-markered CLOTHES—more of his anonymous faded polo shirts and khaki shorts, a Puma sweat suit, seven or eight balled-up pairs of white socks, a long-sleeve T-shirt from some charity 5K Bonne had sponsored. Next was a KITCHEN box, out of which Pratt pulled a stained coffee grinder that must've once been his mother's; neither Pratt nor his father drank coffee, and his uncle had always gotten his from the gas station up the road. An apple corer, for his father's pie baking—Pratt remembered him bragging about his flaky crust that came from using real lard. Pratt's only sport coat, gray with yellow pinstripes, was in this box for some reason, heavily wrinkled and stinking of dust. Heck, maybe he'd get it cleaned. The nicest garment he owned. But then, where would he wear it? Who would invite him anywhere, except to a warehouse to give him unwanted orders he couldn't possibly follow?

Next was SPORTS. Who had even labeled these things? Pratt pulled the box open and found the expected mitts and baseballs, an ancient tennis racket—a collector's item more than anything usable—and a ratty football, flat. Graying tennis balls. A knee brace.

Two boxes left. Pratt knew which one held his parents' old souvenirs. It wasn't labeled, but it wasn't as heavy as the others and was taped more carefully. He lifted it up onto his lap and used the

LeBaron key to free the flaps. He paused, cocking his head to listen—he didn't know what for—and when he heard no sound from the rest of the building, he reached in and pulled out with two gentle fingers a photo. It was from some distant Halloween, of his parents dressed up like Bonnie and Clyde, his mother happy but very much out of her water, his father, in contrast, looking at home in the garb and bearing of a doomed outlaw, as if he truly might rob a bank in broad daylight. Beneath the photo, ticket stubs from an Al Green concert. Pratt's father's drumsticks and a yellowing poster for a short-lived band he'd formed—Some Cars Are Trucks, it was called. There were glass vials full of sand from different beaches; his parents had taken a trip to Southeast Asia to celebrate his mother's graduation from college, sleeping under the stars a few steps from the surf and eating street food. His father had started college, Pratt knew, but he never finished. Instead, he'd dropped out and founded a small magazine dedicated to county politics and local wetland preservation, paying the bills by working double shifts at a steak house. Farther down in the box, below his father's small-craft pilot's license, was a Mexican-looking doll with walnut shells for eyes, a back scratcher, and an amber-stone ring—there had to be a story to the ring, but Pratt would never know it. A wine cork, stained lavender at one end and scripted in French. Pratt did know *this* story. His father had stopped to change a woman's tire in the rain, a black Mercedes coupe, and her husband had turned out to be old sugar money. As a thank you, the couple had sent him a bottle of Bordeaux worth hundreds of dollars. Pratt remembered his mother lamenting that the people were too classy to send a check. The last thing in the box, stuck flat against the bottom, was a *New York Times* crossword, finished in ink. Pratt didn't know what was special about this one, because his mother did crosswords all the time—a steady type, goal-oriented. She was unsentimental, which was probably the reason Pratt had only one small cardboard box of her and his father's things. His father, on the other hand, had been adventurous, maybe a bit too much so, his plans too ambitious and half-baked to ever work out—but his mother, Pratt guessed, wouldn't have had half the fun she'd had in life without him.

Pratt pushed the box away and leaned back until his shoulders were flat against the cool cement. He removed the lump of the lock from his back pocket and rested it aside. The light overhead was buzzing now, the bulb too bright to keep his eyes open. After a moment, he could hear his father's expressive voice—a little Southern, a little thin—his father telling him, in a tone of awe, that Pratt's mother *never* nagged him. Never. N-E-V-E-R, his father had told him, and there was plenty to nag about. Pratt remembered a specific morning when his father had taken him out for omelets to let his mother sleep in. "For a lot of wives," he'd told Pratt, "complaint is their art. They never learned to play an instrument, so they take minor grievance to the level of New Orleans jazz." He'd told Pratt never to give his mother a hard time. Never in his life, because she didn't deserve it.

"They were amazed with each other," a friend of his father's had once told him. "They were permanently grateful." That same friend had told Pratt, the afternoon after the funeral and several Johnnie Walkers in, how ironic it was for his father to die on a tourist ferry. His father never would've taken a ferry except that Pratt's mother was with him, and he wanted her to be comfortable. If he'd been alone, he would've hitched along on a fishing boat, would've pitched in and helped on a charter just for the hell of it, because it might be interesting. He was a dying breed—at this the guy had cleared his throat, embarrassed at his choice of words. The kind of dude, he'd continued, who could throw his hand in on anything, make a little money here, a little there, enough to finance his next occupational fever. And he'd convince you his new idea was going to work. "I bet he never paid income tax in his life," the guy said admiringly.

Pratt, his eyes still closed, could hear a fly now, its noise competing with the buzzing of the light. He had never paid taxes himself. He hadn't been an adult that long, and he'd been in prison much of that time, but still. It was a trait of all the Zimmer men that they didn't thrive in normal jobs. Or maybe just couldn't handle them. Pratt's paternal grandfather had been a bush pilot in Alaska. His great-uncle had been a bartender in Chicago and supposedly invented a drink called the Yellow Jay, its ingredients lost to time. Pratt's mother, he recalled, liked to say of his father that she wouldn't sell him for a million dollars but wouldn't pay ten bucks for another one just like him.

Pratt sat up, blinking. One more box. His own stuff from when he was a kid. He knew even before he mechanically pulled the tape free that there was nothing important or special inside, and he was right. Plastic trophies coated in what was meant to look like gold. Report cards full of Bs, but with high marks for conduct—back then, he could behave when he needed to. A few stacks of now-worthless baseball cards, not a Hall of Famer among them. A little field guide he and his mother had used once or twice to watch birds down in the mangroves. A stub from *Return of the Jedi*. 1983. He'd been ten years old. It was all so anonymous. If a stranger saw this little pile, they'd have no idea who Pratt was. And if someone he knew saw it, they'd notice immediately that none of these things made any reference to the two biggest facts of his life: that his parents had drowned three miles off the coast of Naples, Florida, and that he'd done two and a half years—well, thirty-two months—in a state prison north of Tampa.

As Lulu, the daughter of the deceased owner, had promised, the condo Pratt had rented was as appallingly cluttered as the storage space was sparse, packed to the gills with the sum lifetime accumulations of a lonely old lady with an aggressive affection for trinkets and decorations of any kind. Pratt had never seen anything like it; each time he stepped through the front door, it took him aback. Corps of ceramic figurines marched over every flat surface—angels, farm animals, ballet dancers—all with the same vacantly satisfied expression on their faces. Bowls of seashells. Shellacked sand dollars. Wall hangings that read in ornate script I BELIEVE or IT'S NOT THE AGE—IT'S THE ATTITUDE. Needlepoint on the throw pillows. Baskets of painted pine cones. Tall round tins that had once held designer popcorn. The closets were jammed to capacity with extra bedding and small gadgets in their original boxes, coffee-table books of Irish landscapes that no longer had a place on the buried coffee table. Scented candles, never lit. Pratt would not need to buy cleaning products—there was a floor-to-ceiling cabinet loaded with detergents of all stripe, window and toilet and floor cleaners, antibacterial wipes, gallons of bleach, countless varieties of brushes and sponges and rags. In the kitchen, vast caches of canned food and breakfast bars and nondairy creamer. A dusty bottle of Bailey's and another of something called Frangelico. Pot holders and place mats and old pasta boxes crammed with fast-food condiment packets. Dozens of undersized spatulas that looked like a child's sand toys. And the refrigerator, which Pratt now gaped at in a bemused trance, was covered top to bottom and corner to corner with every conceivable brand of magnet. The fridge, but also two kitchen walls, which must've been slathered in magnetic paint, held magnets of travel destinations. Key West and Tarpon Springs and the Tampa Museum of Art; magnets stamped with the names of dentist offices and tax firms; magnets bearing jokes about how fulfilling shopping was or how useless men were; magnets of former presidents—Dwight Eisenhower and JFK and Ronald Reagan, Ike in his military uniform and the other two with their slick, dark, parted heads of hair.

Pratt carried the last box from the storage unit through the kitchen to the living room and burrowed out some space behind a glass-topped dining table whose surface was obscured by numerous plastic bags full of old receipts. There was just enough space to walk through to the bedroom. That was all he needed.

He went back outside and down the steps and crossed the parking lot, hesitating before he reached the LeBaron to look side to side and behind him. He opened the door and took a knee and fished the gun out from under the back seat. It had sat hidden under there when he'd driven to the storage unit and then to the condo, and now he was taking it inside his home—that's what this place was, temporary or not. It was Bonne's gun, but it also wasn't—not really. It surely had no official connection to Bonne, and Bonne had never fired it. It was Pratt's gun. That's who it belonged to: Pratt. It hadn't hurt anyone yet, and it was up to Pratt whether it ever would.

He carried it inside with its ammo and took it back to the bedroom. After pulling a collection of seasonal thimbles out of the way, he stashed the gun in the nightstand drawer, closing it up in what would be its dark, airless little lair. Pratt sat there a moment, just blinking. He pulled the drawer back open. The gun was still there, of course, cold and indifferent. Heavy-looking. Ready whenever Pratt was. It seemed to stare up at the ceiling with the same insane composure Pratt had seen in the faces of the lifers at the penitentiary. Just staring. No such thing as time.

He went to the kitchen and made a rum and Coke in a purple teacup. A single ice cube. A squirt of lime. He carried it out front, along with fixings to make a few more, to the modest porch that overlooked the parking lot. The dolphin statues stood sentry before a mountain of outdated newspapers still in their plastic, but this was by far the least cluttered area on the premises. The best place to think. There were bamboo wind chimes that tocked gently in the slightest breeze. A tiny cactus that looked to be doing fine. A rectangle of faded turf covering the concrete.

Pratt quickly finished his first miniature drink and made another, not giving the ice a chance to melt. He could hear the last golfers of the day out behind the building, a narrow spot in the fairway and a kidney-shaped sand trap. He could hear them hacking away, cursing the game they'd chosen to spend another late afternoon playing. Pratt took a deep breath of the heavy, vine-flower air. A slurp from his drink. Bonne's story was that he wanted to have something on Pratt so Pratt could never leave him, so they'd be linked even if Pratt scrammed the business. All right. That made a crazy sort of sense for a man who'd lost his family. His *real* family. But also, Bonne wanted assurance that Pratt would never talk about anything he knew, would never take up with a rival of Bonne's, would never... whatever. The old guy maybe didn't himself understand which it was, mostly love or mostly good business practice. He just saw the world taking everyone away, one by one. The same thing had happened to Pratt in his short life. Maybe Bonne was testing him, vetting him as some kind of heir, now that the rightful heir was resting in peace. Maybe he was giving Pratt time to realize that he didn't want to live the straight, paycheck-to-paycheck life, that he couldn't plod along with all the do-gooders, the law-followers. Maybe—a parade of maybes. Pratt threw back the rest of his drink and reached up and brushed the chimes with his knuckles, listened to them awaken to their clackety work and then settle back down. It didn't matter, Pratt understood. That much he could grasp. It didn't matter *why* the order had been issued. The why was recreational thinking. The why was something to indulge in when you didn't like the what.

Pratt thought of that long, stiff hug, the old man's stubbled cheek rasping his neck. Had Bonne been checking him for a fucking wire? Right after he'd done his time? Right after he'd tucked himself in a corner of the prison and stayed as quiet as a mouse? He thought of Roger and Nairn. Could Bonne really be looking to cool them off, when they'd been on the news the very day Pratt saw them—not really them on the screen, but their exploits. Roger had been with Bonne over ten years, Nairn maybe five. He'd never cooled them off before. Nairn. That redneck asshole.

Pratt watched an old man maneuver an enormous white Lincoln into one of the tight parking alcoves. Three-point turn. Five-point turn. The guy guided his fender into an oak sapling, tilting the young tree against the thin orange cords meant to steady it. Pratt knew he couldn't think any of this through yet, but he knew in the meantime he needed to start tracking this guy, this Malloy, needed to start the legwork even though he had no intention of following through on the job. He'd have to figure something out, something a lot smarter than saying no to Bonne. Until then, he needed to give the appearance of falling in line. Starting the legwork wouldn't hurt anyone. It was something he could do for now, something he at least understood. He was no closer than he'd been yesterday to seeing himself as a hit man, but a stakeout was nothing new. He had time. End of the month, that was three weeks. Time to find a side door before the house collapsed. For now, he'd go through the motions.

Bethuna Pawned. That was the name of Tony Castillo's shop, spelled out in Christmas-green letters in the front window. Pratt hadn't planned on seeing Tony. When he'd agreed to hang out, he'd figured he'd be gone by now. Gone forever. But he wasn't. And he liked Tony.

And besides having nothing better to do this evening than breathe the dust of a knickknack factory, Pratt didn't need anything else to feel shitty about—like standing up an old pal. So here he was, engaging in a social life.

Pratt entered the store, causing a bell to ding, and there was Tony, bent over in the main aisle, dusting his offerings of collectable beer and soda cans. Dress shirt. Bright white high-tops. Tousled bowl cut.

"I thought we were meeting at my place," he said, happy and matter-of-fact, straightening to full height but still a couple inches shorter than Pratt.

"I wanted to see if you had a pair of binoculars I could afford."

Tony stepped right over and gave Pratt a hug. Another one. Pratt was already busting his hug quota for the year in a twenty-four-hour period.

Tony stepped back and Pratt saw he was holding something the size of a cucumber in his hand—it was metal, with buttons near the base. Pratt tipped his head toward it questioningly. "That's not a toy for women, is it?"

"It's an electric pepper grinder," Tony said, "but I guess you could use it for all sorts of things. Once it's out of the store, it's not my concern."

Tony told Pratt to hang on and disappeared into the store-room, humming along to music that Pratt only now heard—the guitar-heavy riffs of Molly Hatchet. Pratt panned his head around, taking in the shop. It was impressive, someone his own age running a business—the guts it took to start it, the focus it took to make it thrive. The place was as packed as Pratt's condo, everything tagged with little orange stickers. There was a long shelf of teacups—Tony and Pratt's deceased landlady had that much in common, but beyond that, their inventories diverged. Everything from alligator luggage to bomber jackets to backgammon sets could be had at Tony's shop. Igloo coolers. Flashy hubcaps. Fishing poles on racks overhead.

Tony came back out and tossed a compact pair of black binoculars at Pratt, and Pratt caught them casually with one hand.

"That's why you played middle infield," Tony said, smiling.

Pratt raised the binoculars to his face and looked toward an old-timey wall map of Europe, the countries misshapen and Easter-egg-colored and crowded with cartoon symbols. He turned the focus knob until he could easily see the jewels in the crowns, the crests on the shields. Venice, Italy, had been its own little republic. Denmark had controlled part of Sweden.

Pratt lowered the binoculars and asked how much they cost, and Tony waved him off.

"Let me pay you *something*," Pratt said.

"They're a gift. I can't give the gift of second sight, but I can offer you exaggerated sight."

"I'll take any sight I can get," Pratt told him. "Thanks, man. And my wallet thanks you."

"What are they for, anyway? You got a hot neighbor or something?"

"This is Florida—my neighbors average about seventy years old."

Tony climbed into a restored Wagoneer with wood paneling and Pratt followed him a couple short blocks to his stucco rambler. They parked out front and walked past a colossal satellite dish with a bed of pine needles in its shallow bowl. Before Tony could get his key in the door, Pratt caught him by the elbow and told him he was sorry.

"Sorry for what?" Tony asked.

"Baseball," Pratt said. "And just... everything."

Tony gave a dismissive shrug. He was too good a dude to hold a grudge, but Pratt wanted to say sorry and Tony was going to have to put up with it. This might've been the whole reason, Pratt now saw, why he'd come to visit Tony—he owed the guy an apology. Long overdue.

"Sorry we bailed," he said. "Matty and me. It wasn't supposed to be like that. We were supposed to win states. We were stupid."

"Hey, it's fine," said Tony. "It's all good memories to me. If you guys weren't into it anymore, you weren't into it anymore."

But both of them knew that not being into it hadn't been the problem. It was what Matty was into *off* the diamond. Senior year, when Bethuna should've been a dominant squad, the team was missing its best two players. Tony had been a decent pitcher, but his defense and run support were off getting drunk and high, trying to get girls out of their halter tops instead of getting Tony out of early-inning jams.

"We should've at least said something," Pratt said. "Instead of just disappearing."

"We were kids, man. Water under the bridge." Tony opened the door and kicked off his high-tops as he led Pratt inside. "Anyway, we still beat Pasco. I threw a four-hitter."

Tony motioned toward a futon and Pratt lowered himself onto it. Tony still didn't drink, but he said he had a couple beers left over from a party, and Pratt accepted the offer. Pratt was stone sober—those three or four tiny rum drinks probably added up to one normal drink. Tony's living room was neat. Compared to the shop, it was as spartan as a monk's dwelling. There was a big-screen TV in front of one wall, and a framed *Jaws* poster hanging on another, the monster coming straight up from the depths for the straw-haired swimmer.

"The three of us *would've* won states," said Tony, returning from the kitchen with a beer for Pratt. "Me with my screwball, you turning double plays, Matty crashing into fences in the outfield."

"Nobody throws a screwball anymore. You were the last one."

"Now I *am* a screwball. Life imitating sport."

"You can say that because it's not true. You're a successful business owner."

"The shop's doing okay," Tony agreed. He sat down in a doughy La-Z-Boy but didn't lean back. He looked like someone propped up on a metal folding chair. "I sold a fancy stroller the other day for four hundred dollars, and a crib today for two and a quarter. I think it's a new market for me, designer baby gear."

"You're your own boss. That's the main thing. Nobody can tell you on a whim to do something... something you shouldn't have to do."

"True enough," said Tony. "All the dumb shit I do is my own idea."

Pratt drank his lager and Tony his Coke. Pratt knew that Tony's parents were alcoholics. They'd gotten divorced somewhere around middle school, and after the split they'd finally been able to get along.

"Remember that lefty slugger from Plant?" Tony said. "Sophomore year? Coach put on the continental shift. Matty was playing right because Plant had so many lefties. He walked straight into foul territory and stood there. First pitch, guy yanks it into the cow pasture. Second pitch, same thing. Matty hopped the little fence and climbed into the bleachers. Next pitch, dude hit it right to him, didn't have to move an inch—held up his glove, standing there in the tenth row."

"Classic," said Pratt. "I could never forget that." Baseball. This was the way to talk about Matty. Pratt felt thankful that Tony always seemed to know what to say, that he could find the needed words.

"He'd drink those protein shakes," Tony said. "His forearms would get like Popeye. Skinny legs and Hulk Hogan arms."

"Led the district in homers," Pratt said. "*And* strikeouts."

"Outfielders are the risk-takers. Pitchers are fiercely independent."

"Sounds like a horoscope," Pratt said. "It's true if you want it to be."

"Remember he brought those baby alligators to assembly?" Tony asked. "Like eight inches long. One of them clamped on to Lisa Thompson's shoe and she nearly pissed herself."

"Most excitement Lisa Thompson ever had."

"I guess the pitcher part is sort of right," Tony said. "I like people, but I do work alone and live alone. The question is the infielder. They're supposed to be practical." Tony leaned forward and dusted off his end of the coffee table with his hand. "You did play the percentages. You never ran through a sign. Always took on a 3–0 count. You were practical in baseball, but I guess baseball's not life. You're a little harder to pin down in life, aren't you?"

Pratt finished his beer and set the empty on the table. "I'm trying to be practical now," he said. "Find the safest play and make it. That's my plan."

"Here's to the fundamentals," said Tony.

"Yeah, the fundamentals."

Tony held his soda aloft a moment, then tipped his head back and drained it. He tapped the can over his open mouth, getting every drop, then hopped up and told Pratt to make himself at home, grab another beer if he wanted; he just needed to check his email quick and he'd be back.

"Turn on the TV if you want," Tony said. "Never anything on. I'm gonna have that dish removed and plant a grapefruit tree. Anyway, everything on TV will come over the World Wide Web eventually. Matter of time."

"Really?" said Pratt.

"Computer is smarter. It's already got a screen."

"There was a computer in the prison library," Pratt said. "I never went on it. You had to schedule a time and say what you wanted it for."

"It's come a long way in the past few years."

"I wouldn't know. I never went on it before prison either."

Tony had been drifting toward the hallway, but now he stopped and squinted at Pratt. "Are you saying you haven't *ever* been on the World Wide Web? Is that what you're telling me?"

"Um, I think I played that *Oregon Trail* game once. Is that the Web thing?"

Tony shook his head gravely, disappointment and concern competing on his face. "I guess you better come with me," he said. "Let's hope it's not too late."

Pratt arose and followed him down the hall and into an extra bedroom that had a computer monitor on a flimsy desk and a display of mint *Sports Illustrated* magazines from the eighties—a headbanded John McEnroe hitting a volley; Michael Jordan in the '84 Olympics, tongue wagging.

Tony sat down in front of the screen and Pratt pulled up a chair beside him. Tony flipped a switch and brought the screen to greenish life.

"Anything you're interested in," he said, his eyes widening, "there's a site or what they call a chat room. Everything you can think of and a bunch of stuff you can't. Like the Devil Rays—you can see all the stats, the schedule, where they are in the standings."

Tony pressed a few buttons and everything he'd promised popped up.

"I haven't been following sports lately," Pratt said.

"Let's see," said Tony, tapping more keys as quick as a secretary. "This one here tells you about all the new restaurants in Tampa."

"Can't afford restaurants right now. Especially in Tampa."

"Well, they got a million of them. People post local activities. Weather forecasts and boating information."

"Boats aren't really my thing."

Before Tony could try another site, a phone started ringing from another part of the house. Tony got out of his chair and told Pratt to move over and take a few swings himself, that maybe he'd have more luck, and then he strode quickly out into the hall.

Pratt stood, then gingerly sat back down in Tony's wheeled leather chair. He stared at the screen, absently moving the mouse around, typed a few random letters and then erased them clumsily with the Delete key. He had no idea what to look up. None at all. He held his fingers poised above the keyboard, then dropped his hands back onto his lap. That he had no idea what his interests were was only part of the problem—the other part was that Tony mentioning boats had him trying not to think about his parents. He'd thought about them enough for one day. Pratt hadn't been on a boat since they'd died. Not a glass-bottomed river cruiser. Not a shiny out-rigged fishing charter. Not even a canoe. What did people do whose parents died in car wrecks? They got back into a car because they had no choice and got over it—that's what. They drove where they had to drive.

Pratt stared at the keys. Hearing no sign of Tony, he pecked in, one letter at a time, *Jack Prescott New Mexico*. He hit Return and a message popped up telling him no results had been found. He sat stumped, again surveying all the letters and numbers and punctuation marks and all the other keys with symbols he had no idea about, and then he began pecking again. This time, he managed to get himself into a phone book, complete with the little logo of the fingers walking over pages. He again typed in *New Mexico*, which was where his uncle had to be; if he wasn't there, then Pratt had no clue. The name worked. There were, in fact, several Jack Prescotts listed, a few in Albuquerque and Santa Fe, the rest scattered in towns Pratt hadn't heard of. He got out of the phone book, went back to the screen where he'd started, and pulled up a map. Clicked around until he figured out how to see smaller and smaller towns, focusing on the north because that's where the mountains were, the high ground. Bingo—here was one to try. He listened again for Tony, heard nothing, then exited the map and tried *Jack Prescott Angel Fire*—that Jack Prescott, he learned, was an attorney, a guy not much older than Pratt who had the neat, parted hair of the presidents back at the condo and specialized in real estate trusts. He found another to try, this one in a place called

Chama, and the fact that nothing came up was actually encouraging. His uncle wouldn't list any information about himself on the Web, wouldn't even advertise if he had a business. Pratt typed in his uncle's name along with *survival tours* and *fishing guide*. Finally, with *trail guide*, he hit on something. It was a chat room for people who favored backwoods vacations, and when Pratt scrolled down, he saw a comment from BluffBum700 that Jack Prescott was the top guide in Rio Arriba County, that he knew the scientific names of every species in the area, could whip up a trail meal worthy of a Michelin star—whatever that meant—and could probably tell you where the first raindrop of a storm would hit. He was tricky to find, the review said, but worth the search.

Pratt felt like a sighted deer, which didn't make sense because he was the one hunting. Chama. Chama, New Mexico. His uncle was indeed halfway across the country, and it had taken about ten minutes to find him. People said you couldn't run from your problems, but it really seemed true now—if Uncle Jack could be found, anyone could. This machine was a big flashlight that would search you out in whatever attic corner you hid.

Pratt rummaged for a pen in the drawers of the desk, then wrote the word *Chama* on a pale-green jai alai betting envelope. He went back to the phone book page, pen poised, but now that he looked closer, there was no number. It just said UNLISTED. Eight letters instead of the ten numbers Pratt needed. Why have the name here if there was no phone number? What was the point? Just then he heard Tony's footsteps coming up the hall. He quickly reset to the starting screen and folded the envelope and shoved it in his wallet—no credit cards and not much cash, but now something much more valuable would hide in the faded leather. The town. He at least knew the town.

"Find anything?" Tony said, striding hopefully through the doorway.

"Not much," said Pratt. "Some people talking about hiking."

* * *

A hollow thwacking sound woke Pratt from a dreamless slumber. He'd been dead to the world for many hours, but it felt like twenty minutes. He opened his eyes and gazed up at the ceiling fan, lazily twirling. Air fresheners in lace baggies hung from the fixture, but Pratt smelled nothing but mothballs. Another thwack, and an exchange in gravelly voices that Pratt couldn't make out. The bedroom where he lay—the habitable one, barely—was at the back of the place, right above the golf course. After a minute, another swing. Then a cart whining away.

Pratt sat upright on the edge of the mattress and it sank under his weight, the springs creaking in protest. 7:04. He leaned and pulled open the drawer. Gun. Slip of paper Bonne had given him. There they were. Not a bad dream. Pratt moved the weapon aside and picked up the paper. He turned it face up and quickly read what was on it, then folded it twice. He wasn't going to touch the gun again, he decided. It had its spot now in the nightstand and that's where it would stay. Three weeks, Pratt thought, gently pushing the drawer closed. In three weeks, he'd know how to get away from that gun without firing it. It sounded like plenty of time, but it could also pass in a flash. Three weeks, and it started today.

Pratt had been in this convenience store the night before, when he'd walked the half mile and grabbed a few bags of snacks for the condo—snacks that hadn't expired five years earlier. *He'd* been up here, but his car had not, and he knew the kid behind the counter was going to make fun of it. And yes, Pratt could see as he pulled up to the pump, the same clerk inside, wristbands on his forearms and a wire-brush shock of dark blond hair perched atop his head. He even wore the same bowling shirt he'd worn the night before, when he'd given Pratt the business for being so pale, saying he didn't carry sunblock strong enough for vampires, saying he'd had a cousin who was albino and they'd sold him to a circus in Pula.

"What the hell's Pula?" Pratt had asked.

"Is city on coast," the kid had said, in a vague European accent Pratt never could've placed.

"What coast?"

"Adriatic coast. Is sim-u-lar to Gulf of Mexico, but water is blue, not gray. Beautiful ladies at beach, not pedophile with metal detector."

Pratt stepped inside the shop now and the kid's face lit up, his eyes perfectly round. Such a boring job, he must've loved it when someone he could razz came in.

"What up, super-gangster? Early bird getting worm. You get out in sun today, no? I tell you is good for you."

"Twenty bucks on pump four," Pratt said.

An old lady in a housedress stood at the end of the counter, peering at rolls of scratch-offs. An elementary school delinquent skulked around the magazine rack.

"*Sveto Svanje*, this your car?" The kid stared in glee through the front windows, gripping his thin gold chain with a thumb and forefinger. "Look like what pimp drive in July of Fourth parade. Down-on-luck pimp who living in Kansas."

"I'll take twenty in gas, and I'll take these." Pratt plucked a pair of flimsy sunglasses off a dusty, tottering tower. They were blue with little white manatees on the earpieces. None of the other pairs were any better.

"You pay cash for fuel," the kid said. "This make me sad. This because you no granted credit card. They no trust you with plastic."

"Don't want one," Pratt said. "They're for suckers." He grabbed two small packaged pies off a display. "These, too, I guess."

"You must think for health," the kid said, punching Pratt's order into the register. "Junk food again. Always the junk food."

"I been in here twice."

"Is enough. I know my customer."

"Do you ever do anything besides stand behind that counter and perform your comedy?"

"I stay on grind," the kid said. "Twenty-four and seven. Laugh to the bank. Stack paper."

"You sleep upstairs, you work downstairs," Pratt said. "Kinda depressing."

Without breaking eye contact, the kid whipped a small plastic bag from somewhere and rested the pies in it, along with a couple napkins. "I do jogging. I eat vegetable. You will have the diabetes soon, my man. I do not wish this."

"Never been sick in my life," Pratt said. "Never gained a pound I didn't want to gain. Never flinched at a line drive."

"Okay, homie, you fly," the kid said. "You fly."

"Damn right," said Pratt.

"You fly, Superman."

Across from Malloy's office and two stolen bases up the street was a car-audio shop, and next to that sprawled a weedy coquina lot where the cars sat waiting to be worked on. That, or the owner of the stereo place was a collector of loose autos, since at least forty of them were lined up in almost-neat rows, many a make and model that didn't seem likely to be graced with high-end amps and speakers. Pratt pulled around the far end of the lot and found a spot that was partly obscured by a trio of thriving devilwood trees. Suncoast Accounting Professionals. Pratt had a made-to-order view of the place. Perfect spotlight on the front door, the front windows. He peeled the stickers off the blue sunglasses and slid them on, slouching in the driver's seat. The object of his attention was a two-story building as plain as a cardboard box. On the second floor was a title company whose door must've been around back. The two outfits shared a red-lettered sign, screwed right into the cinder block: CIPER TITLE and SAP. He smirked. SAP—was this sign fucking with him? Pratt glanced at his mirrors. He looked up the street and back down, his view to the left blocked by the trees and an abandoned plywood booth that looked like it once sold hamburgers and lemonade. There was a community theater on one corner—three performances next weekend of something called *The Birthday Party*. Next to it was a dormant scratch-and-dent appliance showroom. This was one of those neighborhoods where no particular vibe had won out. It was all low-rung, grinding commerce and very affordable housing. Not particularly dangerous if you minded your own business, but nobody had any extra money either. There were a couple stalwart nursing homes nearby. Concrete-block houses with above-ground pools crammed into their sandy backyards. No white picket fences. Pratt remembered a boy he'd known in elementary school had been attacked by a Doberman over here. Years later, in eleventh grade maybe, he'd picked a girl up for a date a couple streets north. Date was a generous way to put it—the girl's older brothers had glared at him from the moment he pulled his fifty-thousand-dollar SUV onto their cracked driveway until he and their sister were out of sight.

The scene felt surreal. Harsh, slanting light. Dogs barking at different registers in the distance. There was nothing wrong with the place—it was probably Pratt that was wrong. *He* was the strange detail. It wasn't helping him feel normal that, for all he knew, he was being watched. He was supposed to be staking out Malloy, but there was no reason to believe someone wasn't staking out Pratt to make sure he was on the job. No use worrying about it. He *was* on the job. He was doing what he was supposed to. If Bonne wanted him watched, so be it. And if Nairn wanted to harass Pratt for fun, so be that, too—he wouldn't do it here, where it might jeopardize Bonne's objective. He'd do it right in the open, while Pratt was eating breakfast at a diner.

He could hear the LeBaron's engine ticking, cooling off. The hiss of air brakes down the road. A baby crying inside an apartment. He slid off the sunglasses and raised the binoculars to his face. He could make out the little placard by Malloy's door without strain. Opening time was nine, still over an hour away. Pratt hadn't worn a watch since before prison, but he probably needed to get one so he wouldn't have to keep lighting up the dash with the LeBaron's old battery. He was early, but this was the only way to do it until he knew the guy's schedule: beat him to the spot and be cool and wait. Nothing to see yet. Closed blinds. A long vertical crack in the stucco from the building settling, or from a sinkhole starting down underneath.

Pratt twisted the cap off a bottle of generic Sprite he'd unearthed from the old lady's cabinets, past its expiration date but still fizzy. He forced down a gulp, the carbonation burning his throat. Capped it tight. He reached over onto the floorboard for a newspaper he'd grabbed off the condo's front porch—only a few days old, so they were still being delivered. With a corner of his eye still on the office, Pratt unfolded the paper and discarded the Business section, no use to a person with no money. He tossed away Arts & Entertainment, since he wouldn't be going to any concerts or gallery openings. He browsed the headlines, the bold print, from horny Bill Clinton in Washington to toddlers getting abused at a day care ten miles from where Pratt sat. The environment was going to hell. Little kids in China were chained to assembly lines, malnourished, making Pratt's shoes. He kept flipping the pages and landed on the World Cup, which was about to kick off over in France. Here was a list of attractions if you were going to Paris for any of the games. Eiffel Tower. A cemetery that was overflowing with famous dead poets and Jim Morrison. Churches that had already been around for centuries when explorers started bumbling into Florida.

Pratt folded up the paper and tossed it aside, and it was then that a car came to an abrupt halt in front of the office building. Suncoast Accounting was too small an operation to have many employees, and shady bean counters wouldn't want partners—yes, Pratt knew as soon as the guy got out of the car that it was Malloy. The dude made a final spirited attack on his cigarette, three hard drags, flung the butt to the sidewalk and strode over it without bothering to put it out. Pratt could see the thin coil of smoke still rising from the ground as Malloy—hair a color that combined orange and gray, six feet at most, soft around the middle, spry and harried—fumbled for the key he needed and jammed it in the dead bolt, shoving the door inward and yanking his briefcase in after him.

Pratt had commandeered some stationery and a pen from the old lady's stash, a matching set, both embossed with the name and logo of an eye doctor. He bit the cap off the ballpoint. He turned the key in the ignition a moment to light the clock display, then clicked it back off and wrote down *8:13*. Not the crack of dawn, but early enough to be the first one in, to get a jump on things in case you needed to duck out unexpectedly. Or work on accounts you'd just as soon other people not see. Pratt lifted the binoculars to make out the license plate, jotting it down along with *Nissan Maxima, Green, Dirty, Sunroof*. He left a space, then added *6-foot, Nervous, Smoker, 35ish*.

A set of blinds flipped open, and Pratt could see Malloy's form inside. The silhouette slid across the room, and then the blinds on the other window winked transparent as well. Pratt got the binoculars refocused in time to see Malloy hurry into his back office, the door closing behind him, gone as quickly as he'd appeared. Pratt stayed on the door, peering—he could even see the round brass knob—but nothing happened, the place still as a painting. Five minutes. Ten. Malloy didn't come back out. Pratt saw viny plants dangling down from their hanging green pots. A coffee maker. Three computers, identical, to Pratt's eye, to the one he'd used at Tony's. Beige file cabinets. It was as standard-issue as an office got. Malloy had opened the blinds like a man with nothing to hide, then immediately gone into hiding. There was one of those gold-painted cats, like in a Chinese restaurant—that was one odd detail, at least. A poster of the Grand Canyon. A poster of goldfish.

Pratt settled in and sipped at his knockoff Sprite. He checked his rearview whenever he remembered to—if someone was watching, they were well-hidden. The LeBaron was half in shade now, the front windows rolled down for the cross breeze. Nothing to do but wait. Pratt rehashed his *St. Pete Times*, finding fresh fodder on the back pages, the parts of the paper old people liked to examine on park benches: pinpoint information on the tides, hutches and vanities and four-wheelers for sale, tools. Some prices were firm, some tagged OBO. Pratt waited. He scanned the obituaries—the Irish sports pages, he had once heard them called in an old-timers' bar.

About 9:20—key in the ignition again—Malloy's secretary showed up. Her hair was baled atop her head with crisscrossing sticks. Long skirt. Black canvas Chuck Taylors. She parked in the tight alley beside the building, strolled splay-footed up the short walk, and stepped lightly inside with a neat sack lunch and a paperback book. Binoculars up, and here she was inside. She called something out, maybe letting Malloy know she'd arrived, then she was at the Mr. Coffee, running the sink faucet. She crossed back over and reached high to water the plants with a drinking glass. Tapped the arm of the Chinese cat to get it waving. Would she? No, she didn't wave back. She knocked, waited, then opened Malloy's door. Pratt didn't have the angle to see inside. He could see only the woman, leaning halfway in the room and making breezy motions with her free arm. After a minute, she shut the door and sat at her desk and started doing what secretaries did—those impersonal, enviably mundane tasks. Typing, opening and closing manila folders, licking her finger and leafing through documents. She answered the phone twice, giving quick smiling answers, again using that one arm to talk. Pratt wrote down, as if it mattered: *Secretary—9:20, late 20's, Blue Chevy Cavalier, Casual w/ Malloy, no sign of affair.*

About ten, Pratt got out of the car and stretched. He jumped up and down, knees high, then did a set of push-ups, his palms pressing into the gritty gravel—still, a half hour later he was yawning in the driver's seat, fighting to stay alert, the warmth of the car, despite being engulfed in shade, overwhelming him, sweat slicking the back of his neck. As much as he didn't want to tax the LeBaron's battery, he again turned the key and this time punched the stereo button, bringing up the numbers 92.1. Just a couple songs to perk him up. He turned the volume knob and heard thick, prickly static. He hit the Seek button and waited for the tuner to catch—anything upbeat would do—but the numbers rose and rose and then ran too high, into the triple digits and on up, until they ran out of room and started back at the bottom and began another climb. Just the static, no variation whatsoever. Right past 92.1, where he'd started. Pratt remembered the pop channel everyone used to listen to... he found it and, no, nothing. The classic rock station his uncle preferred... nope. The sports radio he used to hear the Bucs on hissed at him. Pratt sat there in the seat and nodded philosophically, as if something predictable had been confirmed. He shut off the stereo and took out the key. Of course, the radio didn't work. What did he expect with this junker? In the new quiet, he could hear occasional rolls of thunder—low, deep punch combinations from above, the weather limbering up. He looked over and saw puffs of smoke rising from the car-audio building, one of the technicians taking a break. Over the course of the morning, the odd geezer in clunky orthopedic shoes had happened by on the near sidewalk, a too-skinny mother pushing a flimsy stroller, a defeated vagrant in a black jean jacket—none of them had noticed Pratt. He was lost to the world in this little pocket where he sat. Lost to everyone but Bonne, he thought.

After eleven, Malloy emerged. Pratt sat up straight, feeling around for the binoculars and the keys. Malloy didn't have his briefcase. Wasn't wearing his suit coat. Just lunch, probably. Before he was even in his car, he had a cigarette lit—got in and opened the window and blew out a long stream of gray smoke. With no preamble he pulled an immediate U-turn and was headed away from Pratt, his car jerking around in the lane like a bee had flown in, and Pratt fumbled to get the LeBaron fired up and bumped it down over the broken curb and gave the engine gas, straining his eyes in the bright sun to keep Malloy in view.

For three blocks, a big black pickup with a load of cut wood was between Pratt and the Maxima, but the truck pulled off and Pratt saw how close he was to his subject and fell back. Malloy led him past a tiny elementary school—the kids out at recess looking disconsolate, milling about in their primary-colored shirts like commuters at a bus station. Malloy drove past a small museum dedicated to the history of Hernando County, as if anyone gave a shit. A pest-control business. Suddenly the old trees gave out and huge strip malls loomed on either side of the road, as if they'd jumped ahead three decades when crossing Indiana Avenue. Malloy, without using his blinker and barely tapping his brakes, yanked a left into one of the vast parking lots and barreled toward a Publix. Pratt waited for an opening and followed suit, tracked toward where Malloy had parked but then idled past, four rows, five, and pulled the LeBaron up in front of a busy

AAA office. He pushed his door open and got himself to standing, making a visor with the flat of his hand, and searched out Malloy just in time to see him stride through the automatic doors of the big grocery store, his orangish hair fluttering.

Pratt stepped up onto a sidewalk that ran the length of the shopping center, probably five hundred yards. The AAA was slammed. Through the windows, he could see lines at every counter—old people getting maps for national park trips, exhausted moms prepping for Disney. Pratt strolled toward the Publix as slowly as he could, keeping his distance. He meandered in and out of a store that sold light fixtures and then stalled in a Polish deli, eyes trained through the front windows—and here the man was again, plastic bag swinging from his finger.

Pratt got back in his car and crept across the lot. He couldn't use the binoculars here; he had to park nearer than he liked and slump down and squint through his open window and through the closed windows of other parked cars. Malloy leaned against the back of the Maxima. He hoisted the little bag onto the trunk and pulled a tray of food out, chopsticks, sauce packet. Malloy sprinkled the sauce, then ate the food mechanically. Was it sushi? Pratt couldn't tell, never having eaten the stuff, nor having ever had the desire to do so. Malloy muscled down his lunch—nothing to drink. The second he was done wiping his lips with a napkin, he had another smoke going, and after a couple earnest hits he dug in his trouser pocket and came out with a bright yellow cell phone. Pratt didn't know what he was looking for—just Malloy's routine, and he was only looking for that until he figured out how to make it not matter—but at any rate this canary-colored device was intriguing. An oasis in the stakeout desert. Malloy pulled a page of newspaper from somewhere and spread it on the trunk, then dialed a number and began nodding impatiently. He moved his finger from one spot on the paper to another, gesturing and jabbering, still finding time for another puff. Yeah, he was saying. That's right. That's what I said. The white napkin still crumpled in his fist. Smoking. Talking. Nodding.

Pratt followed Malloy back to the office. Again Malloy got out smoking. Again, he flicked away the cigarette before stepping indoors. Pratt rolled past the office and back to his spot between the Yugo and the Suzuki. He left the engine on—enough neighborhood noise at this hour to drown it out—and let the air run, the vents aimed right at his face, until after five minutes it was blowing hot air. He got the pad out again. *Publix. Yellow phone. Doesn't know he's betting w/ Joe-Baby.* Through the binoculars, Pratt found the secretary where she'd been before—probably had lunch at her desk. He didn't feel like spying on her. *95 fucking degrees*, he wrote on the pad. *How the fuck did I wind up here?* he added.

Pratt finished the warm soda, somehow warmer than the car it had sat in for hours, then watched a stray cat slink through the weeds, batting at dandelions—even the cat didn't notice him. He sat up and pulled out his wallet. It was the same one he'd had before prison. Weird to think of it sitting in a locker for almost three years. What about guys doing fifteen to twenty? Or more than that? Their shoes and hats and rings sitting untouched in the dark, like in a time capsule. All these prisoners with no homes to return to, no money to speak of, their wives and girlfriends long gone, getting released and handed the ancient contents of their free-man pockets—keys that wouldn't open anything, good-luck charms that had failed.

Pratt pushed aside his cash and slipped out the folded jai alai envelope. Chama, New Mexico. There had to be a way to find a phone number, but Pratt knew he wouldn't dare contact his uncle while he was still tied up with Bonne. He had to get clear of all this. He had no credibility with his uncle, and deserved none. Jack Prescott was not a man sympathetic to excuses—not unlike Bonne, come to think of it—and in Pratt's case, in the case of the boy who'd spurned him, he'd be even shorter on understanding. Pratt could see him now, in the crisp white T-shirt and dark blue slacks he wore every day. He was Pratt's mother's brother, but much older than her. He'd moved down after Pratt's parents had drowned, and Pratt had lived with him from age eleven all through high school. His uncle had been in the Marines and had still looked like it, not enough fat on him to make a biscuit. He'd jogged five miles every morning, rain or shine, had drunk nothing but black coffee before lunch and water all afternoon and a solitary beer each evening that he called his "golden beverage." Uncle Jack had done an admirable job of convincing Pratt he'd wanted nothing more than to step into a different life with no warning and look after a kid he hardly knew, but in time Pratt realized this couldn't be the case. His uncle hated the hordes of old people in Florida, some not much older than himself, with their gossip and golf and outlet malls. He'd taken work as a watchman at a tool plant near St. Leo, banker's hours, herding junkies and vagrants away from the property and waving loitering vehicles up the street. A man who'd been smack-dab in the middle of unimaginable shit all over Southeast Asia and the Middle East. And for almost a decade he'd played security guard in this Land of the Never-ending Parking Lot instead of doing what he looked to be doing now—guiding the uninitiated into the beautiful, harsh wilds and showing them how to live properly. He'd tried to show Pratt how to live properly, but Pratt hadn't wanted the lesson, and his uncle had moved away from Bethuna the very day after Pratt's sentencing. He was a Marine, Semper Fi and all, and he'd stayed at his post until the mission was lost.

* * *

Another two hours, Pratt perspiring through his shirt and finally stripping it off, before Malloy emerged, suit coat draped over his shoulder and briefcase in tow. He unlocked the Maxima and dropped his stuff in the back seat, leaving the secretary to lock up. Windows down. Smoke lit.

Pratt got out on the road and stayed one stoplight behind the accountant. At one red he pulled his shirt back on, at another he recorded the time on the notepad. Moon Road. Flycatcher Road. Masaryk Road. It was good to be moving. Good to have air washing through the car. They passed a dirt road that Pratt remembered led to a swimming hole, a spring thirty feet wide and forty deep, an excuse to get girls into bathing suits without sitting in traffic all the way down to the beaches. They passed an abandoned produce market. A defunct law practice—a brother-sister team, still displaying huge roof signs for DIVORCE! and BANKRUPTCY! Then, around the next curve, the roadsides were mowed low and even, dotted with ornate lampposts. A Mercedes and an Audi whizzed in the other direction. Malloy had driven them out near the new expressway—it wouldn't be done for months, but already these mini-mansion communities were popping up one after another. Malloy slowed, and so Pratt eased up. Here were the white wooden fences, gleaming. The quaint walking bridges spanning old irrigation dikes. Heron's Roost was the name of the place, the sign a cobblestone edifice that Malloy turned past as he quit the main road. Farther up, near the iron gates, was a towering waterfall, eternally pouring its own product back into itself, all day and night. Pratt let the LeBaron drift onto the shoulder, brought it to a stop on the immaculate grass. The houses in view all had screened pool areas and artfully pruned trees. The mailboxes were miniatures of the homes, done in Tudor or Spanish colonial or whatever else. Pratt watched the gate swing smoothly shut behind the Maxima, saw the car roll around a curve and disappear from sight. He could see a golf flag in the distance—a classy course, not like the one at his condo. He was sweating again already, sitting still. He knew he could get into Heron's Roost if he wanted, complete this day of surveillance professionally, and he also knew the reasons he wasn't doing it—one simple, one less so. First, this wasn't nearly deserted enough a spot to do what he'd been charged with doing, so no use casing it. Second—and it disturbed him that he was thinking this far into things—if this poor asshole Malloy had children, that was nothing Pratt wanted to know. If there was a basketball hoop nailed above Malloy's garage door and Hula-Hoops tossed in the flower bed, those were details Pratt definitely wished to remain ignorant of.

Pratt turned the AC all the way down, nudging the plastic stem, then navigated to the cluttered kitchen and drank two full glasses of tap water. Catching his breath, he made his way to the enormous couch, listening to the air conditioner hump and heave. He leaned back and sank in, the Naugahyde creaking like a ship against a dock, and soon enough he was thinking of Kallie again. Every night since he'd been loose, in the motel and now in the condo, she'd been the last thing he'd thought about after everything went still in the world. He could hear her voice, husky yet quick, amused but also impatient. Her laugh, which was only a different kind of breathing. He was thinking of her frank brown eyes, the dark fleck in the white of the left one, her shiny hair the exact same color as those eyes.

When he thought he'd be leaving, all he'd needed was to see her. But now he wasn't leaving. She was another person he owed an apology to—it was like he was twelve-stepping, working a program—but he wasn't delusional enough to believe that the pull he felt toward her had more to do with expressing contrition than it did with simple, gut-level longing. Seeing her had been one thing. He needed to smell her. Feel her little hand on his arm. He needed her to look into his eyes, to help him, just with her presence, get his mind settled.

He rolled into Kallie's corner of Tarpley—pulling a few odd turns and slowing down on the straightaways to make sure he wasn't being tailed—in the deadest part of late afternoon, nothing moving but the dried brown fronds that hung down the palm trunks like brooms. He turned onto the correct street, found a parking spot not quite blocking a hydrant. The Fiero was in sight, so she was home. He crossed the road, not bothering to lock the car, and made his way up the front walk of the duplex, his heart now fully waking up to what was happening. The yard still wasn't mowed. The neighbor's side was still a mess, dominated by the old, undriveable Cougar. When Pratt reached the porch, Kallie's spoonbill statue making sly eyes at him, he noticed—tucked under a red bench she'd put out to enjoy God only knew what view—a big blue tub overflowing with toys. Playground balls, a plastic push mower, a fluorescent green sword. A quick wave of dizziness passed over Pratt. A kid? There was going to be a kid inside? This he knew nothing about. A sucker punch. He'd raised his hand for the bell, but now his arm wilted back to his side. A child. What else could it mean? Was it some guy's Pratt didn't know? Some stranger? Would that stranger be inside, behind the battered aluminum door? Or, even worse, was it some jerk who was long gone, some dude Pratt would have no choice but to hate? Who he might even need to track down? But maybe the toys were for a friend's kid, a cousin's kid. Pratt didn't remember Kallie having any cousins nearby. Wait, though. In another part of Pratt's brain, a different room, a competing department, he was doing other math. Simpler math. The father wasn't a stranger, and yes, he was long gone—off to a place where no one could ever be tracked. It would be Matty's kid. Of course. Hoofbeats equals horses. Matty, a father.

Pratt pulled his eyes away from the jumble of toys and pushed the bell. So, she had a kid. She had Pratt's dead best friend's kid—was it anything to crumple into a ball about? He waited, disoriented, hearing no movement inside. His eyes wandered to the neighbor's door—now he saw the overflowing ashtrays, three or four of them, a one-hitter and a lighter on a dusty glass table. Pratt rang the bell again, waited longer, then realized the thing was broken. Of course it was. He knocked, and now came footsteps, the peephole going dark, the scrape of the lock. The door opened and she was standing there, fast as that, head at a tilt, face pinched in puzzlement but opening into something brighter.

"You need a shave," she said. "I almost didn't recognize you."

"I keep forgetting to buy a razor," said Pratt. "There's probably twenty of them in the place I'm renting, brand new purple ones, if I could only find them."

"Oh, yeah?"

"Never mind," he said. "Not important."

She stepped back, beckoning Pratt inside, but he was still drinking in the sight of her. Her strong tan soccer legs. The thick scar on her chin—Pratt knew it was from pulling a record player onto herself as a toddler. Clear-painted nails. She wore a thin pullover that revealed her smooth collarbones. On her wrist, a clunky digital watch.

"If you want a hug, step on in here," she said. "I'm not into porch hugs."

Pratt did step in, received and returned yet another embrace, this the only one to make his chest tighten like a vice. Kallie's shoulders felt slight and hard, her ribs delicate inside the clamp of his arms. He smelled flour on her, the scent of baking. He held her until it felt too long, until he could feel her going slack in his grasp. He stepped back and closed the door, his eyes roving around the duplex. There were more bins of toys along one wall—inside toys, Pratt guessed—and against another wall, right in the living room, a narrow bed made up in military-neat sheets. The place needed a coat of paint but you could eat off the floor. No doubt anymore—a kid lived here.

Kallie led Pratt to the kitchen, and immediately a little boy tottered in from the hallway, a crayon gripped in his tiny fist like a ranch hand's spoon.

"So, here's my big news," Kallie said. "Guess you didn't figure I opened a day care, with all the kids' stuff. This is Joaquin, my handsome genius."

The boy wore a miniature goalie jersey and a diaper. He seemed neither impressed by nor afraid of Pratt, coolly sizing him up.

"Say hi," said Kallie, and for a second Pratt thought she was talking to him, frozen as he was at the sight of this tiny human being who had Kallie's detached yet curious eyes and Matty's rakish posture and seemed already wiser, somehow, than either of them.

Joaquin raised his crayon as if for a toast and made an optimistic noise.

"Hey, buddy," said Pratt.

He was probably supposed to go and shake the kid's soft little hand, but instead he stood still and watched the boy cross the room and latch on to Kallie's leg, and she guided him over to a plastic picnic table hidden behind the real table and got him all set to bring color to the animals of the African savanna. She said, "Lion," and Joaquin repeated the word. Giraffe. Gazelle. His face was placid, his chin pegged with one deep, familiar dimple. Matty's.

"Tea?" Kallie said.

"I'm still years away from that," said Pratt. "Despite my new residence."

She uncovered a dish on the counter that was fanned with pastries. "You won't turn this down," she said, straining her fingers to carry the platter to the circular table, basically the same table from Pratt's condo's kitchen. "There's guava in them, but you can eat around that—I remember how strict you are, avoiding fruits and vegetables."

"I ate some fruit just today, I'll have you know." Pratt sat with his knees almost touching the underside of the table, watching Kallie collect what she needed for her cup of tea. Her toenails were shellacked clear, same as her fingernails. Her feet looked a little bigger and paler than before. "It was in the middle of a pie from a gas station. I'm guessing this is gonna be a little better than that."

Kallie pulled out a chair and sat down across from Pratt. "They're from Daily Cubana. They took me back as soon as I could put Joaquin in day care. As soon as I felt okay leaving him for a few hours. He's with his *papou* most nights. That's when I work, officially—lately, it's just whenever they need me."

"I know you still work there," Pratt said. "That's how I found you. Sorry, I sort of stalked you. When you were actually there... I don't know, I panicked."

"I was kinda wondering," Kallie said, "but also I don't care. I'm just glad you're here."

"Me, too."

Kallie looked into his eyes then, a challenging look, and after a moment, she looked away. "They're pretty good to me at DC, but it's so hot in there. I eat nothing but bread and I've lost ten pounds."

"Well," said Pratt. "You look good to me."

"Exact same weight as before Joaquin—this just isn't how I wanted to do it. I wanted to train like I used to for soccer season. Those mini-triathlons all through August."

Pratt remembered watching Kallie's games, driving with Matty down to Countryside and Pembroke Prep to cheer from the stands as she ran circles around the preppy girls. Matty would berate the refs until he and Pratt got kicked out. Pratt thought of graduation, of how Kallie had looked in that silly hat and judge's robe. She'd wanted to help children who'd lost their parents. That was the career she'd wanted, what she planned to do with her life. Those plans were on hold, apparently. First Matty dying, then the baby.

Pratt carefully lifted one of the delicate confections and took a bite. It was the best thing he'd tasted in a long time, flaky and moist and not too sweet.

"I guess you prefer a hundred years of a Cuban family's culinary tradition," Kallie said, "to something mass-produced in Delaware and sealed in plastic."

She propped her elbows on the scrubbed tabletop and Pratt could see red burns on her knuckles. He wanted to take her hands in his and kiss them, but of course he wouldn't. Besides ruining what was between them and the guilt of being disloyal to Matty, there was the fact that Joaquin could do a hell of a lot better for a man in his life than a broke ex-con who spent the workday spying on people from the driver's seat of a cheap white convertible. Yes, this was why he was afraid of Joaquin. He didn't want to be some mere acquaintance of the kid's mother, and he couldn't be the boy's substitute daddy. He wasn't going to pretend there was a way this could work where he was important to the boy. Joaquin would remind Kallie of Matty every day for the rest of their lives.

"I'm sorry about when you came to visit," Pratt said. "I don't have an excuse. Not a good one."

Kallie pressed her fingertips together, then nodded.

"It wasn't that I didn't want to see you. You know that. I mean, I didn't right then."

"You don't have to explain," Kallie said. "I think maybe I didn't want to see you either. I had to try, but..."

"Right," Pratt said. "I know."

"It was afterward. That's when I got worried. After I, you know... the second time. I started wondering if I'd ever see you again."

"I guess that's what I'm saying sorry for."

"I started having a hard time picturing you out, just free, still the same you. With Matty gone and Joaquin here, it felt like a different life started."

"It did," Pratt said. "A different life did start." He looked over at the boy, whose cheeks were scrunched in concentration, sketching something in the sky that didn't belong there. "It's a different life. I can't tell if it's the same old me."

"I wouldn't mind that," said Kallie. "The same old you has at least one fan."

"One's a start. It's not a club, but it's something."

"So, where you staying?" Kallie asked.

"How do I describe it? It's basically a two-bedroom trinket warehouse that still smells like the old lady who died in it."

Kallie smirked at him. It wasn't a humorous smirk.

"If I'm lucky, a golf ball might hit my roof one day for a little excitement. Bethuna. Edge of town."

"Got me beat on bedrooms." Kallie gestured toward the hostel setup in the living room. "If we're in the same room, he keeps trying to talk to me. Wants out of the crib. Once he does fall asleep, I feel like I can't make a noise. Can't even roll over. Out here I can at least read or watch TV. I have to keep the volume so low I can barely hear it."

The teapot whistled. Kallie stepped over to the counter and poured the steaming water, then sat down again. Her cup had a big chip in the rim where the white showed under the yellow enamel. Kallie never used milk or sugar or lemon or anything. She'd been drinking tea since high school—used to bring it in a thermos. It didn't seem weird now. It suited her.

"Does he know?" Pratt asked.

"Does who know what?"

Pratt nodded toward Joaquin. The boy was sitting on the bench, his plump legs rocking below. He was coloring energetically now, way off the paper.

"Oh, him," Kallie said. She licked her finger and reached over and collected a few crumbs Pratt had dropped. "I don't want Joaquin in that life. I hate that you're in it. I hated that Matty was in it. You guys didn't really have a choice, I know. But I want my son clear of all that."

Pratt shifted his weight in the kitchen chair and the squeak was like the complaint of a living thing. His back ached from sitting in the car so long, and from the old lady's mushy bed. Did his body actually miss the prison cot, the austere firmness of it?

"So don't tell him," Kallie said. "I don't want him to know. Matty didn't have a clue, and Mr. Bonne couldn't pick me out from any other girl Matty ran around with, I'm sure. Not at this point. It's not like they were always having Sunday dinner and inviting me over."

Pratt wanted to say Matty hadn't run around with all that many girls, but Kallie knew the truth. "I won't tell him," he said, looking at Joaquin. "You're not going to get an argument from me."

Kallie blew into her cup and sipped, staring at Pratt. "You've seen him?"

Pratt shrugged.

"It's none of my business," Kallie said. "Everybody's gotta do what they have to. I got enough of my own business. I don't need to worry about yours."

Pratt felt his stomach souring. He wished he could tell her everything. He watched her twist her bulky watch around and around her thin wrist, the way some women twirled their wedding rings.

"Matty didn't know?" he said, putting the ball back in her court.

Kallie kept staring at him. Her eyes stayed sharp, but the rest of her face went slack.

"I'm sorry," Pratt said. "I didn't mean to—"

"I wasn't showing yet," she said. She swiped at her face with the soft of her palm and wiped the hand on her sleeve. "I was building up the courage. I was afraid I'd tell him and nothing would change. He would've put on a big smile about it, but he would've gone on acting the same way. Doing whatever the hell he wanted."

Joaquin stood up from his work station, his crayon broken in half and hanging by the wrapper. He ambled toward Kallie, saying something over and over that sounded like "nook," and she collected herself with a shake of her head and smiled down at the boy.

"You want milk?" she said. "You can have some milk."

She stood and foraged for a kiddie cup in the fridge. Once Joaquin was in possession of it, he sank to his backside and fell to slurping.

Standing tall, Kallie gathered her hair behind her head and pulled a rubber band from somewhere and twisted it on tight. "Being in love with him was easy. Everyone was in love with him. Living with him—now, that's another story. Maybe I'm wrong. Maybe he would've shaped up."

"No," Pratt said. "He wouldn't have. He was running on fun and luck. He didn't know anything else."

"His best piece of luck was having you around."

Pratt clenched his jaw. He could feel the good, grounding pressure in his back teeth. He'd been in love with Matty, too—what else would you call it? He let the guy get away with anything. He didn't stand up and say enough was enough, didn't protest, not really, when after high school Matty started hanging out with absolutely anyone who was holding—slang-talking transplants from Long Island, music-festival girls with their cheap acid, trailer-park meth heads.

"He always had that Cheshire grin," Kallie said. "And you always had your poker face."

Pratt looked at Kallie's teacup on the table, its contents getting cold. "Do I still have it?"

"Exactly like before. Can't tell if you're pissed off or bored or want to get away from everybody or what."

"I been away from people enough. Or at least I couldn't choose what people I was around."

"I guess so," she said.

Pratt felt a perk of anger inside him. Not at Kallie, but at the fact that she was still connected to Bonne. Pratt hadn't gotten clear, and she hadn't either.

"Fuck, Kallie, I'm sorry," he heard himself saying.

"Again? Did something else happen you think is your fault?"

"I'm sorry about all the... well, I wasn't always honest with you. The covering for Matty I did. I'd make stuff up when he was, you know..."

"That's what you're worried about?" Kallie said. "You haven't been able to do anything wrong for three years, so you're dredging that up? All you guys did that crap. Hell, sometimes us girls did."

"No matter how many people were doing it, I'm still sorry. It would be nice, now, to know I'd never lied to you."

Pratt watched Kallie step over and pick up her tea, annoyance on her face—the aggravation of being brought into someone else's stubborn guilt.

"I never meant to have a poker face," he said. "I wound up with it because I never had a good hand."

Next morning, Pratt was waiting at Bethuna Pawned when Tony pulled up. Pratt held the door like an usher while Tony carried in a few cardboard boxes of still-packaged action figures. Captain America. Wonder Woman. A green one that looked like a lizard.

"Breakfast?" Tony said, pointing at a Tupperware that was tucked under Pratt's arm like a football.

Pratt let the door swing closed and proffered the container, and Tony pulled one of the pastries onto his flat palm and cupped his other hand under his chin for crumbs.

"Jesus, these are delicious."

"They're a day old. Should've had one yesterday."

"I need this every morning," Tony said. He took two more greedy bites, his eyes narrowing. "You've spoiled me. I'll never get over this."

Tony finished the first pastry and slid out a second, and as he chomped it rapturously, he glided around the shop, turning on lights and adjusting the AC and pressing buttons on his stereo that brought the music of Jefferson Airplane, or somebody like that, back into the world.

"Well," he said, twisting a dial that illuminated his showcases, "you're not here this early just to raise my blood sugar."

"I'm in the market for a watch," Pratt admitted. "One with an alarm. Not too pricey. I don't care what it looks like. Whatever nobody else'll buy."

"A watch. Alarm. Fashion not a consideration. Anything else?"

Pratt set his Tupperware on a rare open parcel of shelf, between a stack of Hardy Boys mysteries and a vintage toaster. "If you have any tapes. Music tapes. The car I bought doesn't have a CD player."

"I actually prefer tapes," Tony said. "You can throw them against a wall and they still work. CDs? You have to treat them like Fabergé eggs."

"I'm gonna pay this time," Pratt said. "I'm not trying to freeload your whole inventory."

"Those morning cakes I ate are worth more than any cassettes. Why don't you take a couple of those as a favor to me, and you can pay for the watch."

Tony didn't wait for an answer. He shuffled into one of the far aisles and after a moment emerged holding a shoebox of colorful plastic cases. "Take what you like," he said. "I'll peruse the timepieces."

Pratt watched his friend sidestep the counter displays and kneel down out of sight. He heard drawers scraping open and closed, the false bottoms of the cabinets sliding free. He turned his attention to the thirty or forty offerings in the shoebox—big band, Elvis, a smattering of college fight songs, and a fairly thorough survey of '80s hair metal. Pratt didn't know one loud glam band from another. He pulled out four tapes at random—W.A.S.P., Cinderella, Rough Cutt, and Autograph.

When Tony sauntered back, he had one hand concealed behind his back and a mischievous grin on his face. "Hope you found something," he said.

Pratt displayed his selections and Tony nodded, his grin unchanged.

"Need something to keep me awake," Pratt explained.

"Ear-splitting androgyny," Tony said. "It's got its place."

"Guess I'm gonna find this hilarious," Pratt said. "Whatever's behind your back."

Tony broke, releasing the loose end of a laugh. He moved his hidden hand into plain view, a shiny gold band clinging taut around his splayed fingers. It was an oversize and comically fake Rolex, winding knobs as big as somebody's fillings plugged into the brassy housing, a constellation of sparkly diamonds crowding the face.

"Yup," Pratt said, "that is funny."

"I had a few normal ones last week, but they sold. This *looks* expensive—I guess that's the whole idea—but it's cheap. It's basically worthless."

"I did say I didn't care what it looked like."

"You said that. I heard it."

"Then I guess this is my new watch," Pratt said, stoic.

"You can just have it," Tony said. "I wouldn't feel right charging you."

"You know what, I'm not going to argue. I wouldn't feel right paying for it."

Tony dangled the item from two fingers and Pratt put out his hand to accept it. Instead of giving his amused benefactor the satisfaction of seeing it on his wrist, he stuffed it in his pocket.

"Halloween is only six months away," Tony said. "You could go as Puffy Combs."

"A rapper, right?"

"Something like that."

Tony took back the shoebox with the rest of the tapes. Gave them an absent shake like ice in a cocktail. "Now I need to ask *you* a favor," he told Pratt.

"That watch was a favor?" Pratt said.

"I need something from you," Tony said. "The priceless Rolex notwithstanding."

"Okay, shoot."

"Listen, I play in a men's baseball league. Okay? It's baseball, not softball. Real pitching. Hear me out."

"I can hear you."

"Our infield is Swiss cheese," Tony said. "These guys play like they're wearing oven mitts. I'm talking comedy of errors to the point where it ain't funny."

Pratt shrugged, and this made Tony talk faster. He was saying there was nothing like those sounds—the ball whapping into the mitt, the ping of the bat. With these guys, he had to throw two strikeouts an inning or they couldn't win.

"I'm pretty busy right now," Pratt said.

"I'm busy, too," said Tony, "but, you know… it's every Friday night at seven. Houston Park."

"Maybe in a couple weeks," Pratt said. "I'm still finding my feet. See, before right now, I never even knew what time it was."

"I'm serious. I need you out there."

Pratt was saying a couple weeks, but he didn't really think he would play. He said it again—it seemed a good way to stall.

"Okay, two weeks," Tony said. "Fourteen days. I'll hold you to it."

"Appreciate you asking," Pratt said.

"I know you don't," said Tony, "but I'm gonna ask again anyway."

This time Pratt was later and Malloy earlier, so they arrived only ten minutes apart. Pratt got into the same spot behind the low-crowned devilwoods, Malloy the same parking space right in front of the door. Same suit coat but different tie, this time electric orange, like the hats hunters wore up in Citrus County. Blinds, then the vanishing act into the back office. Like yesterday, nothing else until the secretary showed up. She watered the plants. High-fived the portly cat. The same lady from yesterday pushed her stroller past—her black rubber shoes like people wore canoeing, her turquoise earrings that looked painfully heavy. It was only day two, and Pratt knew the script. This was how life was. Same thing yesterday, same thing tomorrow—it either bled you dry slowly or else whatever you used to break the monotony did you in a lot faster. Even people's lives that weren't boring were still predictable. Matty's life had ended predictably. Kallie was in the position you wound up in if you gave yourself to someone like Matty. Malloy was in there drifting toward a tragedy that he himself had painstakingly built.

The sun climbed. The car heated up. Pratt strapped on the watch. Might as well get used to wearing it. It was like a costume prop, so big it made his wrist look girlish. He turned the key and watched the lights come on, set the watch's alarm for ten minutes so he'd remember to turn on the engine and rescue the battery. The first cassette he grabbed had a robot hand on the cover, an eclipse occurring in the background. He guided the tape halfway into the slot and let the player pull it the rest of the way. Spun the volume low so the opening notes wouldn't blast across the quiet lot. Pratt listened to the first song with an open mind and no expectations, and he couldn't understand a word of it. It was certainly loud. It was raucous. Three hard-to-tell-apart songs, run the engine a while, then shut it back down. Pratt tried the next tape. The first song began slowly with ominous church bells that were soon drowned out by shrieking guitars. The second was propelled by a whomping bass line and pounding drums. Tony's soundtrack was at least serving its purpose. He was alert, bolt upright. The short hiss and then another song—wait, Pratt knew this one. He knew the Janis Joplin version. One of the songs Pratt's mother had played when she cleaned. Pratt could almost smell the bleach and Pine-Sol. He could hear his mother asking, as if genuinely concerned, whether Pratt and his father had been housebroken, or did she need to make an appointment for them? All the windows would be open these days, even if it was sweltering out, the curtains moving dreamily in a weak breeze—the same breeze that now lisped through this lot of second-rate cars. Just a stupid, regular day with his parents. Nothing special happening. What Pratt would've given for one more stupid, regular day. One more day eating peanut butter and jelly and taking an afternoon walk. After the last lingering note of the song, Pratt ran the LeBaron's engine again and gave the stereo a rest, not in the mood for more music, sweat starting to bead on his forehead, aches pinching his back.

Lunchtime. Publix again. This time Pratt didn't get out of his seat. He parked where he had a clear sight line and waited until Malloy came out of the store to dine on his trunk. Meatball sub this time. Again the yellow phone and the sports page. Again placing bet after bet. He looked like a tropical reef fish, with that phone and his orange tie and brushfire hair.

Same afternoon scene back at the office. Same heat for Pratt to endure—an effort required to bully the air in and out of his lungs. He picked up the binoculars for the first time that day. The secretary was laughing, the phone pressed to her head, rolling and rolling her gum. Pratt tipped his view upward, leaning forward in the seat. The title company on the second floor might've been out of business. He scanned over until he found the theater. In the drab lobby, a young woman spoke to a very old man, explaining something, pointing to a schedule hanging on the wall. Pratt kept panning around. Everything seemed stained and cracked, softened by the humidity and dried out by the sun. The crows on the power lines were as jaded as city workers on a smoke break. Pratt found the notebook. Why not? *Publix again. Yellow phone again. No idea what to do about this again.* But he couldn't get antsy. It was only day two. Early days of a job he'd never complete. The way out would appear—he just had to stay patient. Had to resist the panic inside him, the shallow-buried wisdom at the back of his brain that knew how day two turned into day three into day four, and then suddenly you were counting in weeks. Time was slow on the inside, fast out here.

Pratt couldn't face late afternoon in the old lady's condo. There was a hole-in-the-wall bar up the street from the complex, and he decided to walk there, past a mirror-windowed tanning salon and a Bible shop whose door was propped open to the sinful air of the world with a bucket of dried concrete. He could have a normal-size drink, maybe hear some music other than men in heavy makeup shredding their voice boxes. Certainly no one would know him. No one from his old life would visit such an obscure establishment. Cheap, by the looks of it—another plus.

Outside the bar, a line of shiny-chrome motorcycles. Inside, a half dozen customers—overweight, leather vests, patchy beards. The bartender was a wiry man with protruding veins on his arms, his black tank top tucked into stiff-looking Levi's. Wire-rim glasses gave him an incongruous scholarly look.

"Do you for?" he asked, tilting an ear toward his new patron.

"Rum and Coke, please." Pratt had the feeling—maybe he'd had it all day—that he was *too* sober to think clearly, that the world was too vast and too bright to process with simple, dry thoughts.

"Got a darling, far as rum goes?"

Pratt looked around the big room, much bigger than it had looked from outside. "Priciest one you got must still be pretty cheap, right?"

The bartender's face tightened, like a disappointed coach. "Making fun of this place?" he said. "If you didn't belong here, you wouldn't be here. That's a fact."

"Sorry," said Pratt. "Just a joke." And he did, to his surprise, feel genuinely contrite. He hadn't expected the guy to be sensitive.

"You're okay," the guy said. "Just don't make fun. That's all I ask."

Once Pratt's drink was prepared—a nice heavy pour with the liquor, he noticed—the bartender walked down to one end of the bar and immersed himself in a colossal and use-limp paperback that looked to be eight hundred pages long. Pratt took himself to the other end, where he was out of the way and where less smoke hung in the air. Old R & B songs were playing at an incidental volume, bass lines you could feel as much as hear, men talking syrupy sense into the women they loved. There was a Buccaneers poster from when they wore Creamsicle orange. A poster of a chopper with its handlebars on fire.

This was better than the condo, hands down, but Pratt wondered if he'd wanted to come to a bar because it was something he could do now that he was out, something free people had a right to. As far as anybody in this bar knew, he *was* free. As far as the state of Florida knew. Pratt had gone from having no privacy to having a secret he couldn't get rid of. Prison was full of cramped spaces, starting with his cell, but the LeBaron was confining in its own way. So was this town. He was avoiding company on the outside the same as he'd done inside. For two years he'd steered clear of the persistent religious and support groups. He'd made a studied effort to be left alone, and most of the time it worked. All except once, really—Lavar Shaw, a jumpy meathead who'd started his sentence with the idea that he needed to knock someone cold his first day in Statesville. He'd chosen Pratt—young enough, sorta tall but not too big, white. Shaw had done him a favor, because after that day Pratt was left even more alone. He'd signed up for the grounds crew, a job where no one tried to talk to you over the roar of the mowers. He'd been good at it, which, with landscaping, means you don't get so bored you mess up easy details. It means you can handle the sun. It means you can handle solitude and tedium.

When Pratt set down his empty glass, the bartender headed his way, this time bringing his book along with him and keeping his eyes trained on one of its dense paragraphs. With one hand, and without looking up, he refreshed Pratt's drink—ice, liquor, cola, lime—his blind arm relying on its own training and intelligence. Plato. He was reading Plato. Pratt didn't know people actually did that. He didn't say thank you, not wanting to interrupt, watched the bartender stroll abstractedly back down the bar and rest the tome on the wood and lean over it.

Pratt turned his head and caught his own reflection in a framed Miller Lite mirror. He was practically scowling, scowling at himself, his forehead bunched and jaw torqued. The bartender was right: Pratt belonged in here. He didn't need to be out inflicting his surliness on innocent people. He'd been tricked into thinking he was an affable guy because he'd always been attached to Matty, but now he saw the truth. On the outside, without Matty, Pratt wasn't the same. Because of Matty, he'd never known what a shit he was—the kind of guy who tried to hide from people, and who, when he accomplished this, would not be missed.

He slurped away the top of his drink. Set it back down soundlessly on the glossed wood. He remembered when he'd found out Matty had died. He'd been walking through the common room on his way to checking in for morning lawn work. At that hour the radio was always on; afternoons, the TV replaced it. The woman's voice was soft like a kindergarten teacher's, like she was breaking the news that there'd be no ice cream today. Matthew, she'd called him. Matthew Bonne. Son of well-known Hernando businessman Arthur Bonne. The neutral way the woman related the facts, it was like she had no idea who the Bonnes were. Maybe she didn't. Maybe she was new to the area. The information had felt unreal to Pratt for less than a minute. It made too much sense. What it did was make Pratt feel old, like a lifer. This is what happened to people with long sentences—they got big news on the inside, where there was nothing to do with it but carry it around like stones tied to your neck. Bonne already knew. So did Kallie. They'd known since the night before, but Pratt was finding out with the general public. The common room was empty, oddly, and Pratt stood in it for several minutes. Not wanting to break anything. Not wanting to run away. He remembered the creeping feeling on his spine that something aside from Matty's life had ended. Something Pratt wasn't ready to have end, like maybe his youth. Something he *was* ready to have end, like being an asset of Bonne's. It was the only time he hadn't shown up to work, and his super let him off without a cross word.

* * *

Pratt was standing on an open swath of carpet eating a bowl of baked beans when he was startled by a sharp ringing. He stepped around a waist-high stack of welcome mats to where he knew the old phone was—its big square numbers, the extra-long cord pooled on the floor beneath the rattan end table. The old lady must've been hard of hearing because the thing called out like a train whistle. Three rings. Five. Pratt took another unenthused bite of beans. After seven rings, the answering machine clicked on. An old woman's voice, scratchily high-pitched and overly pleasant. "Edith Warner's answering machine is broken. This is her fridge filling in. Tell me the message nice and slow and I'll write it down and stick it to myself. Is it cold in here or did somebody leave me open?" Then the shrill beep, followed by a distracted telemarketer who sounded a week out of high school, rushing through a script that promised a complete line of quality financial products—reverse mortgages, rental management, no-commitment appraisals. The kid left his name and contact info. Probably one of his last calls of the day, after hours and hours of machines and hang-ups and senile women thinking he was their grandson.

Edith Warner. Yes, Pratt had seen it on bill stubs and insurance forms in this drawer or that. Different last name from the daughter. He hadn't thought the phone would still be on. He carried his bowl over and rested it in the sink, then opened a cupboard in the laundry room that contained what must have been a decade's worth of North Suncoast phone books. Ran his finger down the spines for the most recent edition, though it likely wouldn't have mattered. He carried the book to the kitchen and let it fall open on a chopping block, located the number for Edith and wrote it down on a slip of paper adorned with a drawing of an elephant and the caption "Remember not to forget," secured the slip in place with a pornographically curvaceous pewter statue of a Weeki Wachee mermaid. He could give the number to Kallie and Tony, he supposed, and just leave the outgoing message as it was. No one besides the two of them needed or wanted to get in touch with him.

He picked through to the bedroom and collapsed on the mattress. Stared at the popcorn ceiling, the sprinklers out back chut-chutting. He heard an old man's bellowing laugh, the laugh of the fat and happy. What he didn't want to do right this minute was think about Kallie—that was a bad nighttime habit he hadn't figured out how to quit. Had to head those thoughts off. Had to get to sleep without lying there for two hours like a lovesick dunce. Pratt leaned his weight and half-rolled, reaching out for an antique-looking radio on the nightstand—the other nightstand, not the one holding the gun. He didn't expect the thing to work, but as soon as he pressed the switch, a woman with a lilting voice could be heard issuing warnings about overwatering, about deficiencies in the Florida soil. Pratt turned the dial. It was AM, so it was all talk. Politics. Fishing. Politics. At the far end of the dial was a guy with an old-fashioned Southern accent—patient, thoughtful, a touch sad. He spoke of the ancient Aztecs, their system of learning and pastimes and what they ate. He said they built a civilization of great advancement and endurance, and then with no surprise or scandal in his voice, as if speaking of Catholics taking Communion, he delved into the various bloody sacrificial rites they performed to appease their fickle gods. Pinning hummingbirds to sticks and brandished them still living like children's pinwheels. Piercing gushing holes in their own tongues. Pricking infants with thorns to offer up their innocent cries. The Virginian paused to drink. You could hear it, the single ice cube clinking and his hard swallow. He explained that once a year the Aztecs elected a handsome young man and dressed him in fine raiment and fed him the ripest fruits and most succulent meats and placed four nubile women at his disposal, and each afternoon this pampered soul would stroll the streets playing a flute of rosewood while the citizens bowed to him and kissed the ground he trod upon. At the end of the thirteenth day, dust would be raised all over town as young and old and rich and poor gathered at the foot of the sacred hill to watch the chosen—healthy and sated and cleansed of all complaint—bid goodbye to his family and to the teary-eyed beauties he'd spent night after night with and rest his flute on a flat stone and begin scaling upward to turn his smooth body over to the priests.

Salmon-colored tie. In fact, through the binoculars, it *was* a salmon. A necktie made to look like a colorful, slender fish. Cue the stereo shop opening up. Cue the secretary, whistling up the walk, a spring in her step—if this was a movie, she would've had a great date last night with the man of her dreams. Plants. Cat.

Pratt listened to the final song on the W.A.S.P. tape—or sat through it, at least. When he pressed eject, the button gave way too easily and didn't make a click like usual. Like it wasn't connected to anything. He pushed it a couple more times—loose as a piano key. Pratt listened as the player automatically flipped the tape back to side one. The hissing. The obnoxious opening notes. He hit the useless button again, again, but to no avail, not even a hiccup in the sound coming through the speakers. Pratt jammed his finger in the slot and could feel the edge of the cassette inside. He tried to force it farther in, tried to jimmy it loose. The singer was caterwauling about the thoughts sweating inside his head, promising to howl in heat, then delivering on the promise. Pratt turned the stereo off, then back on, but still the device would not release its hostage album. He nodded. Okay then—no music.

*   *   *

Fried chicken today. A little foam side tub, probably potato salad. A woman with four kids pulled into the space next to Malloy's, and Pratt watched the accountant help her lift a stroller out of her trunk, help her hoist a rucksack of a diaper bag up onto her shoulder. Then he got in his car. No yellow phone. No sports section. Okay, back to the office. Back to Pratt's spot in the sweltering shade.

Cue the skateboarder. Cue the fat white guy with a shaved head walking a pair of Chihuahuas.

Pratt sat up straight. Malloy was coming out early, two o'clock, all his stuff with him. Pratt got the LeBaron moving casually, old hat at the route to Heron's Roost, but when Malloy made a left at the end of the block instead of a right, Pratt had to cut in front of a delivery van to follow. Some place other than work, Publix, home—Pratt would take it. He kept his mark in easy sight all the way out Blue Cove Extension to Route 19, the old, slow state road that the new expressway would make obsolete. Nineteen was a grand showplace of decrepit, sleazy strip malls, the traffic thickening as they headed south. A vast, red-lighted intersection every third of a mile. Boat-equipment emporiums. All-you-can-eat buffets. Malloy kept swerving, looking for a stronger current in the river of cars, and Pratt kept him close without leaving the center lane, following him down into Pasco County, past a stream of catchpenny breakfast places, a half dozen depressing titty bars, a mall that had bottomed into a permanent flea market. Bayonet Point. Holiday. In North Pinellas, Malloy branched onto Alternate 19, a sleepier thoroughfare, and the traffic thinned. They drove past chalky limestone side roads and over short bridges that spanned mucky canals. Pratt stayed two cars back. He knew Malloy was headed to one of Joe-Baby's places—he could feel it.

He quit Alternate 19 just past a three-story fish restaurant with nets hung all over its outside walls. Pratt hung back, watched the Maxima motor up the narrow frontage road and pull around the back of a long, stark, mostly abandoned strip mall, the stucco discolored where signs for businesses had been removed. He watched Malloy negotiate the potholed back alley and park behind a stand of palmettos as big as a Fotomat, his green car obscured by the thousand dusty fronds. Binoculars up—Malloy strided, hands punched into his pockets, to an anonymous back door that had once been white. He knocked, waited. Probably chewing his cheek in need of a smoke. Door opened to a dark interior. Black guy in shiny sweatpants and undershirt. Malloy followed him in and the door shut behind them.

Stillness now. This was mostly what Pratt spent his time doing: watching quiet, unmoving doors. He swiveled in his seat and looked behind him, suddenly anxious. Nothing there. No one around. Birds warbling in a French-sounding language. Cars on a road in the distance, seeming to move without effort or sound. He wanted out of the driver's seat but stayed where he was. Malloy's impatience was in him now, pulsing, like too much caffeine. He peered through dusty-trunked pines toward a trailer park stashed away behind the shopping center. A girl in a sombrero dug in the sand with a plate. An old woman waited for her dog to do its business.

It wasn't really the heat. It wasn't even impatience, because where the hell did Pratt have to be? What was plaguing him was that Bonne, like always, was right. Pratt did owe him. There'd been nothing greater in Pratt's power to accomplish, nothing else to make his existence worthwhile, than keeping Matty alive. Nairn had said as much at the diner, and goddamn it, he was right. Pratt had shielded Matty from trouble until he thought he was invincible, had shielded him instead of really helping him. Criminals were wise when it came to blame. Bonne could sense frailty, even his own. It was a fact that both Bonne and Pratt had killed Matty, Pratt the point man, and it certainly felt like a fact that Pratt was Bonne's for the keeping. They were bonded. Pratt had no identity other than belonging to Bonne, and at the moment, he couldn't even think straight. If he couldn't think straight, how was he going to outmaneuver a mastermind?

He squeezed his keys in his hand. He felt a crazy urge to help Malloy, to run him off the road as soon as he left Joe-Baby's, grab him by the lapels and shove him against the hood of his car and make him understand he had to quit gambling, had to throw himself on the hard floor of Bonne's office and beg for mercy. Blubber for it. Kiss the old man's shoes. He needed to get on a payment plan for life like some asshole taking out a mortgage he couldn't afford. He needed to make a case for himself, needed to make Bonne see him as something other than an irredeemable degenerate.

In the next breath, Pratt knew he was thinking like a child. He was imagining what would be good for *him*. For Pratt. It was too late for Malloy. His life was in default. Foreclosed. Pratt pressed the meat of his palms into his eye sockets. Slumped down into the seat. Stealing wasn't like anything else. Stealing, for Bonne, was its own category. The man's bird dogs, back when he used to hunt, had one tooth each capped in sterling silver, so no one would take off with them. His house was built eight feet off the ground to accommodate the reinforced concrete bunker underneath.

No, Malloy wasn't getting out of this.

And no, Malloy wasn't the guy Pratt needed to worry about saving.

Kallie was still wiping sleep out of her eyes when she jerked her Fiero through the parking lot of an out-of-business gas station, cutting around the intersection at 41. She hit her blinker and mashed the gas to make a left, waving at whoever she'd pulled in front of. She'd overslept her afternoon alarm, and now it was rush hour. Five hours, that's how much sleep she'd been allotted this day, and her body had rejected that plan and taken six. She caught a green light by the discount golf course, a green light at the Italian deli. She had an eighth of a tank—she could wait until after the day care to fill up. She'd get a little time with Joaquin—an hour and a half, at best—feed him, then drive him out to her father's trailer so she could do the whole thing again, the overnight shift, the heavy baking for the next day. She hadn't gotten out of DC until almost ten this morning, two hours later than she was supposed to, because the owner's daughter, fresh out of business school and sporting a perfect Rachel-from-*Friends* haircut and designer leather pumps, was moving all the bookkeeping and accounts to the computer. From what Kallie could gather, the advantage of going digital was that less paper would be used. The disadvantage was that no one, including the owner's daughter, knew how to use the system, and even when they did everything right, the computer would malfunction on its own.

Kallie saw blue and red lights flashing two cars behind her. She let off the gas, even though she wasn't speeding. She would've been speeding, but the traffic wouldn't allow it. The car behind her pulled onto the shoulder and the police car roared up close to Kallie's bumper. She eased onto the brake and began to drift to the right, hoping the cop would speed past on his way to something more important, but as she slowed the cop slowed. She brought her car to a stop next to a bent guardrail that overlooked a swamp dotted with foam cups and empty cigarette packs.

Kallie slipped her license from her wallet and extracted the registration from the glove box, already accepting that her time with Joaquin was shot. She'd whisk him through a fast-food place and ask him about his day on the way to his granddad's. She spied the cop sitting in his car behind her. Looking at a clipboard. Talking on his radio. What the fuck was he waiting for? Finally, he took a last sip of his soda and drew himself up out of his cruiser, looked around the scene appraisingly before strolling up beside Kallie's window with a bored and slumpy air.

When he saw Kallie, his manner changed. He stood up straight and sucked in his gut and forced a smile that was supposed to be friendly but came across as smug. He rested his forearm on top of the car and slid off his sunglasses.

"Do you know—"

"Seat belt, right?" Kallie interrupted, more coolly than she'd planned. The voice in her head urging her to act nice was being drowned out by the voice that wanted to tell this clown to hurry up and do whatever bullshit he had to do because some people in this world had places to be.

"Well, yes, miss—that's right," he said. "Is there a reason you weren't wearing it?"

"Just a busy day," Kallie told him. "Do you need these?" she said, holding her license and registration out the window.

The cop's face tightened. He didn't like being rushed through his performance. He took what Kallie offered but didn't look at the documents, just held them in his free hand, which looked as soft as a child's. He leaned down closer, his sunburned face and spiky hair filling the window.

"I understand being busy," he said. "We all have busy days, but there's always time for safety. You'd rather be late than in the hospital."

Kallie nodded—not too impatiently, she hoped.

"I'm on special duty this week," the cop explained. His name tag said Greun. He was late twenties, not much older than Kallie. He smelled like Irish Spring and syrup. "I'm on the city's Safety in the Details initiative. We're trying to reduce serious injuries from auto accidents by twenty percent."

Fundraiser, Kallie thought. Perfect time to get shaken down for an involuntary donation.

"I'm not the bad guy," Officer Greun said. "I'm trying to help. I've seen too many people get hurt."

Kallie saw him glancing down at her hands. His eyes had traveled over the rest of her, and now they were taking stock of her ring fingers.

"I want to make sure everybody's taking care of themselves. People need help with that sometimes. They need someone to look out for them. We all do."

Kallie again forced a nod. Sometimes there was no saving men from their clumsy attentions—you just had to weather them.

"Now, look, if I believe my stopping you has made an impression, good or bad, that's the point. I want you safe, that's all. Beautiful woman like you—I don't like to think you're putting yourself in danger out of absentmindedness. I wonder if there's anybody at home to make sure you keep safe. Make sure you're looking out for yourself."

Jesus, Kallie thought. Just give me the damn ticket.

Officer Greun rearranged his weight. He settled his elbow down on Kallie's window frame and propped his red face on his fist. "A court date isn't the only kind of date, you know. There's other kinds of dates that are a lot more fun."

The cop looked at Kallie expectantly, proud of his line even though it didn't make sense—you didn't get a court date for a seat belt violation. She took a steadying breath and, strangling all inflection out of her voice, told Greun that she needed to pick her son up from day care an hour ago, so if he was going to ticket her, please go ahead and proceed with that.

"I already sighted you," the cop said, grinning, and when Kallie returned line number two with a stony glare, he sighed and stood up to his full unimpressive height, shoulders slumping like when he'd first gotten out of his car, pulled a ballpoint pen from somewhere and scribbled on his clipboard, recording Kallie's license number and the time and whatever else, driver after driver whooshing past on the nearby road.

"You want a ticket, I'll give you a ticket," he said, acting like Kallie had been rude, like things had been going fine until Kallie had insisted on being uncivil.

"How much is it for?" she asked him.

"Call the number at the bottom. They'll provide any information you need."

"I'm just wondering if this ticket is going to chew up the entire shift I worked last night."

The cop tore the narrow yellow sheet at its perforation and handed it through the window. "Call the number," he said, trying to act as cold to Kallie as he thought she'd been to him.

As soon as she was back on the road and out of the cop's sight, Kallie thumbed the button to release her seat belt. Childish, but it made her feel better. She was in the throes of rush hour now, driving behind an old lady whose white curls barely fluffed up above the headrest and who was sure to stop at every yellow light until Kallie could get off this two-lane logjam.

It had stuck in her mind, that idiot's question about whether Kallie had anyone to look out for her. Because the answer was no. She had her father, who had never lifted a finger to help raise her, and who now, three nights a week, looked after Joaquin and bathed him and practiced his numbers and letters. She was glad he was a good grandfather, but it still angered her that he'd found these skills so late. In fact, this babysitting arrangement helped him more than it did Kallie. It enabled her to make more money, but Kallie then turned around and kicked in four hundred dollars a month for her father's expenses—the upkeep on his trailer, his diabetes supplies. He'd recently started drawing social security, but the amount was a joke because much of the work he'd done in his life—and he'd done a lot, Kallie couldn't fault him there—had been under the table. Landscaping. Scraping boat hulls at the marina. Life had bullied him and now it was bullying Kallie. That cop was a bully. They were everywhere, a whole world of bullies.

And then, Kallie thought, finally hanging the left on Gadd, there was Pratt. She should not have been thinking about him as much as she had these past two days. But, to be fair, they'd once been so close and he'd been gone three years and now here he was, popping back into her world. To what *degree*, she had no idea. She didn't understand Pratt, never really had, but that alone kept her mind landing on him over and over. He was the one that got away, even though she'd never hooked him in the first place. He was the opposite of a bully. Always had been. She remembered back in high school, some scumbag white trashers had been harassing a skinny freshman every day on his way home from school, throwing his book bag in a tree, dumb shit like that. Pratt had, for no special reason, walked the kid home for a whole week, until the assholes had moved on to some other deviant diversion. She remembered senior year, when, very drunk and smarting from a fight with Matty, she'd come on to Pratt, pawing at his zipper. She'd told him it would be their secret. So embarrassing, to think of it now—you weren't supposed to be able to recall things that happened while you were messed up on vodka, but Kallie recalled. She remembered him holding her tight until she gave up the cause and rested herself harmlessly against him. Kallie knew things had gone the way they did only because Pratt was a good guy, not because he didn't think she was pretty or something, but it still stung her to this day that he'd resisted, whether she was sloppy drunk or not. And then the other day, at the duplex—the fact that he thought he needed to apologize for covering for Matty. It was maddening, really, that Pratt was so good and all he could do for her was say sorry for something she didn't care a bit about. That's it. That's all he could do.

Kallie was on a bigger road now, a half mile from the day care, but both westbound lanes had stalled because of some problem up ahead. The exhaust was making her lightheaded. When the traffic came to a complete stop, she closed her eyes and rested her head back. She'd thought nonstop about Pratt for forty-eight hours, and scarcely a minute about the guy she was supposed to be dating. The guy she *was* dating. Who was quite good-looking, objectively—better looking than Pratt. Who had money. Who knew about wine and spoke three languages to Kallie's one and a half. Until Pratt appeared, Kallie had been maintaining a positive attitude about Ferris. She could still like the guy. But Kallie wasn't crazy about how strong he came on with Joaquin, like he wanted to get close with the child as a way to get close with the mother. She didn't love the way he was overly gracious to waiters, to the guys at the car wash, like he felt bad for them or was making amends for something. Kallie didn't know what he had to make amends for—maybe only the fact that nothing bad had ever happened to him that his parents couldn't fix. With Pratt, Kallie knew what he'd been through. She'd been through some of the exact same things.

Pratt rang Tony's doorbell three times before he appeared. He wore a rainbow-smeared smock, goggles pushed up on his forehead.

"Paintball?"

"I'm losing," Tony said. "Want some pizza?"

"I do."

"Don't you want to hear what's on it?"

"Not really."

"Grab a slice. I'm on the back porch."

Pratt followed Tony into the kitchen, stacked a couple slices onto a paper plate, then proceeded into a screened room floored with lime-bright Astroturf. A big ink press sat on a heavy wooden table, stencils lying all about, and a long clothesline was strung along the ceiling, seven or eight shirts hanging from it. One said SITTING DUCK. Another, MIDDLE SISTER. And another, NEVERNUDE, its first N crossed out.

"One store's already agreed to carry them," Tony said.

"Is it Bethuna Pawned?"

"You go it."

Tony raised and pinned up the one he'd just finished: FRESH IS AS FRESH DOES.

"Like *Forrest Gump*," he explained.

"The movie?"

"Stupid is as stupid does."

"I'll take your word for it."

"Jesus," Tony said. "You're like a control group for the effects of pop culture." He peeled off his goggles, his bowl cut no worse for wear.

"Favor to ask," Pratt said, swallowing hard to get down some pizza crust.

"Anything but roofing," Tony said. "I don't get on roofs."

"I need your car. The Wagoneer. I need to trade. I'll have it back in a day or two."

"What, are you helping somebody move?"

"Something like that."

Tony pursed his lips. "The favor isn't letting you drive the Wagoneer," he said. "It's me driving that divorcée road trip car."

"Cruise is broken and there's no music. I also wouldn't mess with the convertible top."

"What happened to the tapes?"

"The concert is canceled. No makeup dates either."

The next day, Pratt watched Malloy from the comfort of the Wagoneer. Luxury was an unintended benefit—really, he didn't want to spend the whole week in the same car, sitting in the same place, especially after following Malloy to Joe-Baby's in the LeBaron. But intended or not, the Wagoneer had copious legroom and a lofty ceiling. Pratt could run the air full tilt if he wanted, parked in the full sun.

Black tie and white shirt for Malloy, like a waiter at a New Year's party. The secretary was late, then very late, then she never showed up at all. Day off, Pratt supposed. Not like she had much to do when she came in. There were zero walk-ins. So far that week, a couple envelopes had been delivered. A pest-control guy had come around and sprayed with his little metal wand. A Culligan man had hauled in a jug of water and the secretary had signed for it. She must've known Malloy was dirty—not that he was cheating Bonne or even that Bonne was the one he was cooking books for, but she had to know something was up. Malloy probably had a couple old clients he kept for appearances, and the secretary's job was to tell everyone else who called that he wasn't taking on new accounts. She did her sparse work without asking the wrong questions, and likely got paid well for it.

Pratt had taken the time that morning to pick around under the old lady's scraggly azalea bushes, where the delivery boy preferred to fling the newspapers, and laid hands on that day's edition—not a month old, not a week old, not a day old. June 11, 1998. Looking at the date on the front page made him think, for the first time in days, about his parole appointment. His first check-in was that afternoon, and here he was stalking a fellow citizen at Bonne's behest. That's what lawyers said: that you were doing something at someone's behest. Pratt had no idea what to expect from the check-in. Your parole cop was supposed to make sure you weren't on drugs, and Pratt wasn't. Your parole cop was supposed to make sure you were looking for work, and Pratt guessed he'd have to be evasive about that. Your parole cop was supposed to make sure you didn't wind up right back in prison, but from what Pratt knew, most ex-cons *did* wind up back inside. If they didn't, it had nothing to do with their PO. The only thing Pratt was truly worried about was the guy—if it was a guy—asking if he'd seen Bonne since his release. Fraternizing, it was called. With known criminals. Did he want to start off his second life lying to the authorities? Neither of them benefited from being connected to the other. And if Bonne found out Pratt had given up their meeting, that would be the same as refusing his order. If asked, lying was the only way. If he got caught in the lie, Bonne couldn't consider that his fault. If he got caught in the lie, he'd tell the PO he was afraid to tell the truth, afraid of Bonne—that *wouldn't* be a lie.

Pratt opened the newspaper and skimmed the headlines—unavoidable disasters, disasters due to negligence. An article about middle school kids eating angel's trumpet flowers for the free high, then winding up in the hospital. On the front page of the North Suncoast section, a story about a man who'd been hanged from a bridge in Citrus County. The guy had gone off his rocker on meth and, to keep his three-year-old daughter away from his ex-wife, had dropped the girl off the same bridge, breaking the child's back when she hit the dry creek bed below. The police had been looking for the man for two weeks, the paper said. Someone other than the police had found him and administered the due punishment—stripped him naked and shoved his own socks in his mouth and duct-taped his wrists to the girder. The "someone" who had found him was no mystery. The sorry soul had been hanging there half the night, his shoulders wrenching slowly from their sockets, deerflies feasting on him, trucks loaded down with tires and frozen pizzas and roofing supplies thundering overhead with no idea he was there, until the tape finally gave out.

Time to get it over with. It was true Pratt had no idea what to expect, but when he saw that the county had put his PO's office in a trailer in the middle of a sun-beaten limestone lot, he didn't think this particular civil servant would be in a gleeful humor. The trailer was one of a couple dozen labeled with plastic signs tacked to their doors. The one Pratt was looking for, and found in the second straight row, read CORRECTIONS—COMMUNITY SUPERVISION. He knocked and interpreted the grunt that issued forth as an invitation to open the flimsy door and step inside. Like in most mobile homes, the floor felt like it might give way under Pratt's feet. At the far end of the cramped space, an air conditioner groaned. Behind a desk that his hulking form dwarfed was a red-faced guy as stout as an ox. He made a perplexed face as he spoke into a phone that his beefy neck held in place without the help of a hand. He motioned for Pratt to sit down in the black molded assembly chair, and Pratt obeyed.

"It *is* a new mouse," the guy said into the phone. "Your buddy brought me this one day before yesterday." While he listened, the PO's round horse's eyes rolled vacantly around the office, never alighting on Pratt. "I did that already," he rejoined. "It's whenever I try to actually *put in* the charge. I can type it on the screen, but I can't put it in."

Lipiski. The name was on a placard resting cockeyed on the desk. Someone had thrown the nameplate together in five minutes with a label maker from Office Depot.

"Yeah," Lipiski said, chuckling archly. "Windows would be nice. The only window I got looks out at the next frickin' trailer."

The officer begged off the call and took a wheezy breath. He adjusted himself laboriously in his overmatched chair. Oxygen did not feel abundant in the trailer. Pratt could see the cop's blocky, medical-looking sneakers under the desk. On the other side of the computer were an open bag of Twizzlers and a Diet Coke.

"I got sixty-seven of y'all," Lipiski said. His eyes looked strained, his head the size of a beach ball. "The other guy retired last year. Think they replaced him?"

When Pratt saw that Lipiski wanted him to answer, he said no, he didn't think the man had been replaced.

"That's correct," said Lipiski. "They didn't replace him. They gave his load to me. None of these old deadbeats want to pay taxes, and then they complain about the crime."

Pratt nodded, trying to seem dismayed at what he was hearing.

"The situation we find ourselves in, Pratt Zimmer, is that of the classic squeaky wheel."

Again, Pratt nodded.

"But in this case, you want to *avoid* the grease."

"Yessir," said Pratt.

"You do *not* want this grease."

"No, sir."

"You gotta be back in that chair one month from now. Four-thirty p.m. Is that complicated?"

"No, sir," said Pratt.

"Are you being a smart-ass with this 'sir' stuff?"

Pratt paused. "No, not at all."

"No, not at all, what?"

"No, not at all, sir."

Lipiski reached around and took a sip of his Diet Coke. It looked like a little tomato juice can in his kielbasa fingers.

"If I decide I want to, for any reason, I send you two doors down for drug testing. Take a piss in the plastic shot glass. Any reason I want. My slightest whim."

"Yessir," Pratt said.

"You find work yet?"

"I'm close. It looks like I'm gonna get on with a lawn company."

"Honest-sweat kinda work. That'll be good for you."

"Yessir."

"Next time we talk, you'll bring contact info for your supervisor."

"Absolutely."

"If not, the grease."

"I understand."

The gigantic officer took another dainty sip of his soda. Pratt braced himself to be asked about Bonne. Lipiski was thinking about something, distracted, gazing off. Bonne had to be the next topic.

"You can tell by looking at me," the big man said, "that it's hard for me to get going."

This Pratt did not answer.

"Know what else is true, though? Bet you can guess. You're a good guesser."

"Once you get going," Pratt said, "it's hard to stop you."

Lipiski smiled, looking jolly but a bit demented. "You're gonna be a natural at this, kid. Being a parolee. Not that it's all that difficult. At least in theory. People sure do *make* it difficult."

Lipiski downed the last of his beverage and dropped the can on top of a bunch of others in a small metal bin. Perhaps his spiel was over, but Pratt resisted asking if he could go. He might be getting out of this without any mention of Matty, Nairn, or Roger. Maybe this guy didn't know or care who he was—was that possible? Maybe all this guy's charges had complicated histories. Maybe he wanted to let Pratt become the new person the state wanted him to be, rather than reminding him of his mistakes. Was any of that possible?

"Well, it's quarter to five. You're the only thing between me and an unnamed number of Heinekens. That's not a desired position."

"No, sir," said Pratt.

"No, sir," repeated Lipiski.

When Pratt walked into the corner store, still feeling buoyant because the parole officer had seemed not only disinclined to ride him, but disinclined to give him another moment's thought for the next thirty days, the clerk blurted out, "Ice the wrist, player." His face could barely contain his goofy smile.

"Igloo stitches," he told Pratt. "Bling bling."

After a moment, Pratt realized he'd forgotten to take off the ridiculous watch. He'd used the alarm because the Wagoneer was so comfortable. He'd parked Tony's vehicle around the corner from the convenience store to avoid fielding questions about his change of transportation, but had neglected to remove the fake Rolex, had worn it to the meeting with the PO.

"Moving up in world," the clerk said. "I shall fetch finest malt liquor?"

Pratt had an impulse to slip the watch off and put it in his pocket, but that would only make things worse. He grabbed another pair of sunglasses off the same rack as the other day, then pulled a couple frozen ham pockets out of a flip-top freezer. The old lady's microwave was accessible, but the regular oven was stuffed with office supplies.

"Again shades?" the clerk said. "You purchase here and sell on streets?"

"I left them somewhere," Pratt said. He picked a sleeve of salted cashews off their rickety rack, then spotted the outrageous price.

"Just buy. Flipping cheddar like you—couple bucks nothing."

"What's your name?" Pratt said.

"I am Josip."

"Joseph?"

"No, Jo-seep."

"I'm Pratt," Pratt said.

"Prott."

"No, *Pratt*."

"Prott. I know. Rhyme with cool cot."

Pratt sat taller in the Wagoneer than in the LeBaron—even though he knew where Malloy was going, it was nice to be able to see him far ahead in the traffic. Same route, 19 to Alternate 19. Same approach to the building, same parking spot in the stand of palmetto, same goon in sweatpants letting him in the back door.

This time Pratt kept his cool while he waited. All seventeen minutes. Malloy striding back out to the Maxima, crumpling an empty pack and shoving it in one pocket, pulling a fresh pack from another and slapping it against his palm. Back out to the main drag, smoke chugging from Malloy's car window like a locomotive. Pratt followed half-heartedly most of the way back to Bethuna, the traffic tightening with the time of day, and lost him somewhere near the Christian high school. Pratt let it happen, let the Maxima pull farther ahead until it hopelessly blended in with dozens of other sedans. He'd settled into a routine, Pratt had, like any work week, Monday to Friday, and now he was knocking off early. He was doing all this for appearances, he had to remind himself. He was doing the work of the mission to figure out how *not* to complete it. If he wanted to let Malloy head home without an escort, if he wanted to skip the security gate and the relentless fluoride-laced waterfall, he could do that. If he wanted to melt seamlessly into the Friday afternoon rush, all these drivers sick of their jobs and ready to forget them for forty-eight hours, he could do that. He could pretend he had a party to go to later that night. Could pretend boredom was his trouble.

Back at the condo, he slid open the drawer of the nightstand and lifted out the gun. He held it in his hand like an exotic fruit some stranger had handed him. It was cool to the touch, like a vise in a basement workshop. His fingers felt dumb against it. You could ask this thing a million questions and it had one answer. He'd said he wouldn't touch the thing again, but here he was rubbing his fingertip over the nub of the sight. Like scratching an itch. The click of the safety, back and forth. Pratt remembered feeling powerful with a gun in his hands, the few times he and Matty had fired them with some redneck Matty had briefly befriended, out in the scrub pines somewhere. It had been bracing, swinging a big pistol around and hearing the noise that came from every direction and stopped the world for a moment, usually missing but once in a while turning a Budweiser bottle into a scatter of amber glitter on the sandy ground. Back then, Bonne had forbidden them from owning guns.

Pratt placed the weapon on the nightstand. He looked out the window into the steady golden glare of the tropic sun. He thought of his parents, how they would've viewed this mess he was in, and felt a dull, familiar irritation—not shame, exactly—that radiated down from the back of his head. His parents hadn't particularly respected the law, but they'd respected right and wrong. They'd trained their young son not to depend on anybody's Bible or anybody's trite maxims—he was a good guy, and he needed to do right by his gut. Never argue away your own right impulses, they'd told him. Never talk yourself into the easy road. When Pratt's mother spoke of these things, she meant conducting himself with decency; when his father spoke of them, he meant making himself of use. They'd known Pratt was a good little dude, or at least hoped it, and never could've imagined what he would become.

Pratt slumped limply down onto the mattress and shut his eyes and allowed himself to indulge in the memory of going fishing with his father. They would drive out toward Anclote, through what felt like a hundred miles of desolate marshland but was really about ten, a big eerie nest topping every tree that had managed to stay upright—ospreys, eagles, hawks. They'd park behind an abandoned boat graveyard and hop a fence, toes poking through the chain-link, then trek a half mile through hot woods. His father always knew the winding, secret ways to get places they weren't supposed to go. Startled armadillos tottering off into the high weeds. Battalions of dragonflies diving past. There was a certain bend in a certain arm of the tributary, beyond sight of the guard towers at the hydroelectric plant but close enough that the water was artificially warm. They would cast through three dozen shrimp in an hour, pulling up amberjack and sheepshead one after another into the sunlight. The fishing was easy. The toil was in getting to the spot.

Afterward, on the way back to town, his father would stop off at one of the dreary concrete bridges where people without cars dropped lines for their dinners, and he'd give away every fish they'd caught—a low-rent Florida miracle. Buckets empty and back on familiar roads, his father would say, heel of one hand propped against the steering wheel and eyes concealed behind dark shades, "Some people say the beauty of fishing is in the contemplative quiet. The timelessness of a classic pursuit. The connection with the eternal life-giving waters that enable civilization. Me, I kinda like pulling out a shitload of whoppers till my arms get sore."

Pratt could hear his father's voice too clearly. He sat upright and opened his eyes to the bright window, a chill zipping down the knuckles of his spine. It echoed in his head, that voice—resonant but not authoritative, prepared to mock its own assertions if they sounded pompous. With the edge of his hand, Pratt brushed the gun, like someone clearing crumbs off a dinner table, down into the open drawer, where it landed with an echoless thunk.

If Malloy went to the office on Saturday, Pratt would know nothing about it. He had pined to see Kallie all week, but sitting and spying on Malloy had put him in the wrong mood, made him feel sneaky and ill-used. He called Tony on the old lady's phone and Tony said he was catching a ride down to Clearwater Beach to see the sandcastle artists, but he'd leave the keys to the LeBaron in a rubber boot by his front door. He said he made a lot of new friends driving Pratt's car, mostly at the beauty salon. Said he'd already joined a bridge circle and a book club.

Pratt went and exchanged the cars, and of course the LeBaron was filled to the line with gas. It even seemed cleaner, but that may have been Pratt's imagination. The morning sun was diffuse and watery through the windshield. When Pratt got on County Line and aimed the car toward Tarpley, light flooded in, and he felt around blindly and soon understood that he'd misplaced yet another pair of sunglasses. They were in the Wagoneer. He was too far away to turn around for them, so he squinted all the way to Kallie's, past the medical complex and past pastures of spindly cows and past the twenty, forty, sixty churches that lined the route.

Pratt stopped partway up Kallie's crumbling front walk, taking a moment to visibly shake his head at the mess on the neighbor's side of the small property. He was carrying two cardboard boxes. He set them down on the porch and knocked on Kallie's door, now hearing the insistent bass thump of the neighbor's stereo. When the door opened, the thumping grew louder, coming through the floorboards at 8:45 in the morning.

"You get evicted?" Kallie joked, jutting her chin at the boxes.

"I don't think I could get evicted if I tried. Just lost in the clutter and never heard from again."

Kallie bent down and pulled back one of the flaps. It was a load of nonperishables from the old lady's reserves. Cans of beans and stewed tomatoes and bags of rice.

"There's hot chocolate powder in there," Pratt said. "There's a bunch of popcorn, too, the microwave kind. I figured somebody ought to use this stuff."

Kallie thanked Pratt without much conviction and told him to put the boxes on the kitchen table. She smelled like bread again and had flour on her eyelashes. She'd worked last night and hadn't showered yet. She wore a tattered Tampa Bay Rowdies T-shirt and turquoise soccer shorts.

"Don't bring anything else over here, okay? I appreciate the thought. It's nice. But I don't like being a charity case."

"Okay, sure," Pratt said, a little stung. He wanted to say that he was more of a charity case than she was at this point, living off his fast-dwindling savings from before prison. He wanted to ask who *gave* a gift of old groceries except a charity case. "You want me to take them back?"

"Don't be like that. They're here now. We can use them." Kallie looked down at herself, like she just realized what she was wearing. "A phone call would've been nice. I do occasionally look better than this."

Pratt bit his tongue. He didn't want to say he'd trade the world to kiss one of her hips. Instead, he mumbled, "I don't have your number."

"I know. I forgot to give it to you. You just always had it before. Here, I'll write it down."

"I got one, too. A phone number. Newly discovered."

Kallie brought out a pad and pen and set them down on the table between the boxes.

"We can call each other like normal people," she said, writing for a moment, then tearing the sheet in half. She'd written K, Pratt saw, not Kallie—a slight, meaningless intimacy, but nonetheless it gave him a little jolt. He wrote the old lady's digits on his half and they traded, and in the quiet, not altogether comfortable moment that followed, the neighbor's speakers became prominent again, thudding their way through another identical song.

"Let me ask you something," Pratt said. "Does your duplex-mate over there ever clean up his side?"

"How do you know it's a he?"

Pratt gave Kallie a look.

"Clean up?" she said. "It's all I can do to keep him from waking Joaquin up at all hours."

On cue, Joaquin walked around the corner wearing a construction helmet and blue superhero cape. He had something in his hands and brought it over to Pratt, offering it upward. "Fix?" he said.

Pratt accepted the toy, some kind of fighter jet that was supposed to light up, without looking Joaquin in the eyes. "Let me check the batteries," he said. He unscrewed the plastic panel with his fingernail, popped out the AAAs, got them installed in the right direction. He felt like an asshole being standoffish with the kid, but he would've felt the same if he acted like his pal. He still didn't have his mind around the fact that this was Matty's flesh and blood. Bonne's flesh and blood. When he handed the ship back, Joaquin mashed a button—video game sounds blared and the boy ran off with a smile on his face.

"You're not going to make it as a Christmas elf," Pratt told Kallie.

"His grandpa put those in," she scoffed. "You were never great at being funny, were you? That hasn't changed."

"I'm still trying," Pratt said. "But I won't quit my day job—once I find one."

Kallie had been working on a cup of tea when Pratt arrived, and she reclaimed it and sat at the table. Pratt slid the boxes aside so they'd have room and took the chair across from her.

"June's not cooperating," Kallie said.

"June the month?" said Pratt. "I'm not a big fan either."

Kallie took a long gulp from her cup. Pratt supposed she rarely drank tea that wasn't lukewarm at best.

"Raised the rate at the day care," she said.

"Can you use a different one?"

"Not unless you want old ladies chain-smoking on the playground. The young ones' boyfriends stopping by half drunk."

Pratt nodded.

"Car starts up about every third time I try it. I leave it running in the parking lot when I do errands, so I won't get stranded."

"Somebody's going to steal it," Pratt said.

"They can have it."

"If you ever need a ride, just call. Now that you got my number."

"I'm thinking of picking up one day a week at the dry cleaner up the road. I talked to the guy. I'd be losing the one day I hang out with Joaquin."

"I'd trade cars with you, but it wouldn't be much of an improvement." Pratt felt heat building at the back of his neck, the same as when he thought of his parents. The fact that Kallie had to scramble and worry. The fact that he had no money to help her, no connection to offer that she wanted anything to do with. He didn't like hearing all this—it even made him a little angry at *her*, though that didn't make sense.

"What I need to do is start sleeping with a mechanic," she said. She gave a little laugh, but Pratt's whole body tensed up.

"Sorry," she said. "I guess I'm not funny, either. I guess we're not going to sit around and laugh, you and me." She looked into her teacup. Stood and took it to the sink and ran water in it. She leaned forward and gazed out her little kitchen window.

"This is my view right here," she said. "Perfect angle. Can't see the neighbor's old tires under that tarp. Can't see the landlord's cinder blocks. Can't see the highway because of the high fence. Swaying palms and puffy clouds. Jacaranda blooms—they'll be gone any day. This is my spot. Right here."

From his low seat at the table, Pratt couldn't see anything of the view but a slice of cobalt sky. But he preferred what blocked the view—the delicate, curving bones of Kallie's shoulders under the thin material of her shirt, the lustrous hair pulled up off the back of her neck, the way her calves flexed to keep her leaning weight steady. Her tiny heels—one of them would fit in his palm. Pratt needed to get out of Kallie's house. He'd seen her and spoken to her and smelled her and now he needed to let her rest. He needed to get out of there before he did something stupid. She hadn't asked him over. Hadn't asked him either time he'd shown up.

Outside, Pratt made it to the street but then, on further reflection, doubled back. He glanced at Kallie's front windows to make sure she wasn't looking out. In quiet strides he went into the neighbor's side of the yard, took in hand a garbage bag that wasn't blowing away because it had a few beer bottles in it, and began placing in more bottles, gently so they wouldn't clang, fifteen or twenty of them. He worked around the crippled Mercury that probably had squirrels nesting on its engine. He emptied all the ashtrays and stacked them one inside the next. Picked up the grease-stained fast-food bags and loose cigarette boxes and some losing scratch-offs.

Pratt heard a door open. Thinking it was Kallie, he turned that way. It wasn't her. It was the neighbor. He was an inch shorter than Pratt, about the same age, neck tattoo, wearing flip-flops. The guy came down off the porch asking Pratt who the fuck he was, and Pratt put a finger to his lips.

The guy chuckled nervously. He stopped his approach just out of Pratt's reach. "Fuck you doing in my yard, dude?"

"Glad you came out," Pratt said. "You can finish up. Seems like maybe you got started at some point, because the bag was out here. You got called away on important business, I guess."

"Fucking jokester," the guy said. He was looking around, toward the street, trying to grasp where Pratt had come from and whether he was alone.

"I'm a friend of Kallie's next door," Pratt explained.

"Then why don't you go back on that side where you belong?"

Pratt took a half step forward. He smelled cheap weed. Nothing Bonne would move. Something grown in a spare bathroom. He looked the guy straight in the eyes. "Look, champ, I'm gonna need you to keep your voice down. In fact, you don't need to say anything else. Just listen."

The guy was smirking, trying to think of a clever retort, not wanting to give any ground, when Pratt snatched him by the collar, a handful of T-shirt and gold chain. He pulled the guy close so he couldn't take a swing, so close their foreheads almost touched. "If you keep playing your music loud, I'm gonna walk in there and carry those speakers out and throw them in the retention pond across the street. I *want* to do that. I look forward to it."

Pratt knew as he was threatening this guy that it was a bad idea, that he should be keeping a low profile in light of both his current illegal assignment and his status as a recently freed ex-con. But something had snapped in him. It happened once in a while—his brain turned off and his blood turned to Texas chili. He could tell, standing eye to eye, that this idiot knew it, too. He had a survival instinct. He wasn't going to issue a formal apology, but he wasn't going to mouth off anymore.

"I want your garbage can neat, right up next to the house," Pratt told him. "And you see that little tree over there? You see the one? I'd like a bird feeder to hang in that tree, and I want you to keep it stocked with seeds. When I come back over here, I don't want to see an empty bird feeder."

The guy was as stiff as a board, trying not to get manhandled. He had a sore at the corner of his mouth.

"Say okay," Pratt said.

The guy nodded stoically.

"Say okay, dude. So I can leave."

"Fine," the guy said. "Okay."

Halfway home, the adrenaline from scolding Kallie's neighbor wore off, leaving Pratt exhausted. He drove in a midday weekend trance, the whole county quiet, the sun a mean, warped disk straight overhead. Nobody was on the roads but those aerodynamic little buses that carried old people to the malls. Churches, churches, churches, passing them going this way now. More churches than homes—each man could have his own religion, his own aluminum cross to mutter prayers under.

When Pratt pulled into his usual spot, a man dressed like someone from *Miami Vice* was leaning on a government Crown Vic a couple spaces down, a pleasant expression on his face. He was older than Pratt but still three decades too young for Cypress Plantation Distinguished Residences. He didn't know who the hell the man was, but he was here to see Pratt. He shut off the LeBaron and walked over to the Crown Vic, acorns crunching beneath his sneakers.

The man looked Pratt up and down, appraising him in an instant. He took his weight off the car, smiling with perfect teeth. "Pratt Sajak. My man. You actually live in this hospice fantasy camp?"

"It's growing on me," Pratt said.

The man stepped forward and shook Pratt's hand, his fingers long and palm cool. He introduced himself as Detective Gianakos. He didn't bother flashing a badge, but he didn't need to—he had that cop swagger, both entitled and prepared for resistance. Gianakos looked like he got his hair trimmed once a week, had it combed straight back, thick as a helmet. Pastel shirt and black suit. Alligator shoes. Serious timepiece—a toned-down and genuine version of Pratt's fake watch, which thankfully was inside the condo and not on Pratt's wrist. Gianakos' sunglasses, which he now slipped off and hung from his collar, probably cost more than all the clothes Pratt owned.

"Invite me onto the porch for some casual chitchat," he said. "This isn't a social call, but we can lend it that air. It's the weekend, after all."

They scaled the six or seven steps, Pratt trailing his new companion and breathing in his Drakkar Noir. He asked if Gianakos wanted a rum and Coke, and Gianakos said he was reasonably certain Pratt's liquor wasn't up to his standards. He sat in one of the patio chairs and caressed the big dolphin's back, petting it like a dog he was trying not to rile up. Pratt went ahead and sat in the other chair. Whatever this was, he had to sit through it. A bug zapper was keeping busy on a nearby porch. Farther away, mellow Cuban-sounding music with a lot of horns.

"Not sure where to begin my narrative," Gianakos said. "This county has been fucked up for a few hundred years, way before it was a county at all. Guess I'll just start somewhere around the particular fucking up that concerns you."

"Okay," Pratt said.

"You look tired," said Gianakos. "Getting enough sleep, I hope."

"I spent the morning beautifying a duplex."

Gianakos leaned forward and casually wiped one of his reptilian loafers with a pale green handkerchief that matched his shirt. Lifted his foot to examine the job he'd done. "I want to make sure you're educated. Make sure you're equipped to make informed decisions about your future. That you don't fall prey to misapprehension and delusion."

"That *would* be a change," Pratt said.

"I'll be your guidance counselor." Gianakos shimmied off his jacket and draped it over one leg. "You didn't have one when you needed one, a guidance counselor. That, or you didn't listen."

Pratt could see that Gianakos' upper body was muscled, his chest lean. He was taller than Pratt, or maybe just had better posture. He was a perfect third baseman—enough height to cut off the line, twitchy enough to react, and by the looks of it a strong arm.

"Not sure you noticed since you were locked up at the time, not sure how much attention you were paying to the outside, but a couple months ago two warehouses were torched—same night, same method. Whoever burned them didn't particularly mind the two being linked. Didn't take particular pains to hide it being arson. Didn't mind a bunch of firefighters risking their lives."

"Yeah, I did hear about that," Pratt said.

"Who does all that sound like? To you?"

Pratt shrugged, and Gianakos allowed himself a hint of a smile.

"He's got this taco truck," the detective said. "Opens it on weekends, uses it to scrub some of the winnings—that you're aware of, too, right?"

"I *hope* it has some other purpose than the food," Pratt said. "The tacos suck. I tried it once. The guy put radishes on everything."

"I wouldn't know," Gianakos said. "I don't eat things out of trucks." An iridescent beetle buzzed down onto Gianakos' shirt. He looked at it calmly, then flicked it back into the bright day. "I have an old friend on the Board of Health," he told Pratt. "I have a wealth of friends. That's because of my optimism and sincere eyes. This particular inspector, this buddy of mine, he happened to be cracking down on unsanitary food trucks. That was his most recent crusade—he's probably on to something else now. We all have our pet projects, right?"

Please don't let me be this cop's pet project, Pratt thought. He was sitting in the shade, but his legs were jutting out into the sun. He could feel the skin on his shins tightening.

"We were gabbing one day, and he let it slip he was pulling a surprise visit to that very taco truck. Of all the trucks. Barrio with Blinkers—what a stupid fucking name, right? He had a tip on it from somewhere. Can you believe it—right after the warehouses burn, he's going out to Bonne's truck?"

"That *is* curious," Pratt said. He noticed the potted cactus near Gianakos' feet. He'd forgotten all about it, but it looked as healthy as it had the day Pratt moved in. He hadn't watered it a drop or moved it into direct sun.

"Yeah, I decided to tag along, keep him company."

"Naturally," Pratt said.

"Good luck that day." Gianakos gave a little whistle. "Gas cans. Gloves. Matches. Even ventilators—what's he worried about, OSHA? All of them the same brands Bonne sells at the supply, stashed down in this custom compartment underneath the truck—secret compartment." Gianakos ran his hand over his mold of black plaster hair. "My guess is they weren't done. There's a couple more warehouses I think were marked for catastrophic overheating. Bonne backed off those once we visited the truck."

"Smart way to get around a warrant? Is that the idea?"

"Oh, I'm smart. It's not *all* luck. Not sure what I can get into court, but I'm not too worried about that right now. There's been so much corruption, nobody can say where this is going."

"It was the inspector's idea," Pratt said. "He happened to mention it to you in passing, during one of your social interactions."

"I got Roger and that asshole Nairn sans alibis. Nairn claims he was whacking off to a Sears catalog. Roger says he was reading James Joyce or some shit. Sure, I got plates off a company car to and from where they keep the truck, but really, the arson is only a start. A jumping-off point. I know the old man isn't used to having to hide, isn't used to being slick, but the times they are a-changing, as Bruce Springsteen says."

"Dylan," Pratt said. "Even I know that."

Gianakos shrugged affably. "An encouraging first chapter, but I'm going for the full unabridged novel. I'll get what I want. If I was a horse, you'd go all in on me. You'd bet the farm."

"Why would you tell me all this?"

"Why not? Bonne knows I'm after him. He doesn't think any-thing will come of it. Thinks he's untouchable. What else would he think? Nobody stays untouchable forever, though. Forever's too long. I mean, you have to die to get to forever."

A breeze moved through thinly, and the wind chimes produced sheepish applause. Pratt heard the thwack of yet another driver.

"You want me to turn on Bonne because you found some stuff in a truck? More or less? That's what this is all about?"

Gianakos' face was calm. "I've got some other avenues. Wide ones. Narrow ones. Not going to lie, though, Pratt—testimony from you could be very helpful. Wherever this is going, your testimony could be, well... valuable. I'm going to take the old dude down. I know you don't really want to work for him anymore. Thought it made sense to pay you a visit."

"Why would you say that? That I don't want to work for him?"

Gianakos made a broad gesture encompassing the fixed-income, elderly settlement Pratt resided in, then a more specific gesture toward the LeBaron. "You're flirting with poverty, my man. It can be hard detaching yourself from these sorts of outfits, I know."

Pratt tried not to show anything in his face. He tried to make a mirror for Gianakos to look into. The detective was right that Pratt wanted through with Bonne. Hopefully he had no idea why that wasn't possible at present.

"You know all kinds of shit, Pratt. Don't sell yourself short. A lot of these fashionable boulevards and winding dirt roads, they lead right to your vicinity. See, people are going to wind up on the correct side of this, and people are going to wind up on the incorrect side. I'm trying to figure out who wants to be where—seating arrangements for the courtroom. I'm doing you a service, yes, but I'm not doing it selflessly. It ain't alms for the poor around here."

Pratt didn't want to hear any of this. He wanted to go back in time twenty minutes and pull into the bar down the street instead of being here, listening to this pitch.

"I did three years for the guy," Pratt said.

Gianakos grinned tolerantly. "Exactly," he said. "You did *only* three years. Thanks to Dunfee, that drunk mick."

"That's a hurtful stereotype."

"Three years for that whole building full of cars, a known organized crime operative with a previous record. Evading. Striking a cop. Fuck me. Dunfee was so far down in Bonne's pocket, he went through the wash a couple times."

"Organized crime operative. That's a pretty fancy name for someone who drove some cars around, delivered some packages."

"I agree. Thug-in-training is more apt."

"Thug?" Pratt said. He looked down at his wrinkled shorts and old polo shirt and scoffed.

"Ask yourself something," said Gianakos. "How'd your little high tea at the parole trailer go the other day? Let me guess—no mention of Uncle Bonne? Lipiski, that rhinoceros. It's like a joke: Bonne's Irishman and Bonne's Polack walk into a bar... You've been handled with kid gloves, Pratt, and you're not a kid anymore."

"Listen," Pratt said. "You have a talent for public speaking, no question about it, but listen for a minute." Pratt leaned forward and pulled his feet underneath him. "I'm trying to leave all this shit behind. You're right—I'm trying to be done with it. Trying to see what life is like without breathing Bonne's stench all the time. Okay?"

Gianakos clicked his tongue. "If Dunfee was still around, maybe you could do that for free, but Dunfee's not around and I've taken it upon myself to clean up this shithole. Hasn't been right since Cortez started poking his fucking nose in."

"And things would be worse without Bonne," Pratt said. "You know that's true."

"Once Dunfee got ahold of you, was flipping even mentioned? Once he came and personally took over your case, was the subject even broached?"

Pratt didn't answer. Gianakos already knew. Dunfee had made sure to say the words for the record, loud and clear for the camera, then had let the notion die a quick, untheatrical death.

"They graduated the same year from Bethuna. Played football. Bonne's family moved down here when he was in tenth grade and it was love at first sight. Dunfee was quarterback, and Bonne fullback. Soon as they graduated, it switched—Bonne was calling the plays, Dunfee doing his dirty work." Gianakos had been playing it cool, but now Pratt saw sweat beading on his upper lip. "You've already been in," he said, growing irritated. "Whatever I pin on you now, you'll do a lot more than three years. Not threatening you. Just telling it how I see it." Gianakos unfolded his jacket enough to extract his handkerchief. He whipped it open and wiped his face. "Not yet," he said. "I'm not threatening you *yet*."

"That's reassuring," said Pratt.

"It's going to be messy for you either way. Might as well be on my side for it."

"Where'd you get the tip from? To look in the taco truck?"

Gianakos refolded his hankie but didn't put it away. "A lot of people tell me a lot of things," he said. "The ones that tell me the right things at the right time, like before it's too late—things usually work out for them."

Pratt was hot, parched, annoyed, but he managed to keep his cool while Gianakos stood and slapped him on the back and handed him a business card embossed with the Hernando County seal and its blue heron gliding across a picturesque orange sunset. The detective took a greedy breath of the humid air and surveyed the complex—the low, sprawling live oaks whose roots buckled the walks, the plastic flamingos staked in the flower beds. He descended the stairs with a bounce and fired up his Crown Vic and slowly rolled out toward the main road without a backward glance.

Alone, Pratt spat the word "fuck" under his breath. He stared at the chair where Gianakos had sat, wanting to throw it off the porch. The air reeked of his neighbor's honeysuckle and the cop's cologne, and Pratt felt dizzy. He fished his keys out of his pocket and let himself into the condo and sat on the kitchen's one accessible chair. He picked up a ceramic napkin holder shaped like an old country pickup truck and turned it in his hands. His mind raced to make sense of what had been dumped on him, and he was almost glad it couldn't. When he figured all this out, he'd know how bad it was. Turn on Bonne? Now, after doing the time? What the fuck? Also, a good way to wind up dead, if Bonne got wind of it before the curtain dropped. On the other hand, what other chance would he have to get out from under the man? To really get free of him? Pratt didn't trust Gianakos an ounce, but the idea that Bonne's time was coming was not, he had to admit, completely ridiculous. His pool of allies was drying up. With the new expressway, Bonne's territory was growing in value, unwanted value, by the day. What Pratt didn't have a handle on was whether he'd be *forced* to help Gianakos. He didn't want to know the answer to that. Honestly, right now he just wanted to keep following Malloy and stay loyal to the devil he already knew. Or *be* the devil he already knew—a pawn and a henchman but not a traitor. Gianakos didn't have much yet, not enough to take down a guy as established as Bonne, but without the cops on a leash, maybe Bonne wasn't as established as he used to be.

Pratt set the little truck back down on its black-painted wheels, slipping Gianakos' card beneath it. He stood, the chair stuttering against the linoleum. Went over and pulled a thermos out of the cabinet and filled it with water from the tap and guzzled fast, spilling it on his shirt. He didn't want booze. He filled the thermos again. Emptied it again. The message stamped on it read OF COURSE I TALK TO MYSELF, SOMETIMES I NEED EXPERT ADVICE. Gianakos had no idea what Bonne had told him to do… Pratt wondered now if this was the reason Bonne wanted something on him, something bad enough that Pratt couldn't turn on him. Maybe the old man thought Gianakos was a credible threat.

Pratt shuffled into the living room and stood there in the center of the condo for a long minute, in the dim, dusty light that forced its way past the closed blinds. He couldn't hear the Cuban music, not with the windows closed. Just the combined, strained hum of countless air conditioners. A creak in the floor when he shifted his weight. He was stuck between the closest thing he had to a father and a slick cop looking to make a name for himself, probably sighting down a promotion to Tampa. They were both asking him to do things he didn't want to do, both trying to use him, to limit his options.

Surprising himself, Pratt stalked over and yanked the boxes from the storage unit onto the floor, whipping them into the open by their flaps—one, two, three, all of them. He gathered his balance, took a hard step past a plastic bin filled with greeting cards, a noise escaping him that he didn't recognize, and punted one of the boxes high against the wall, where it knocked down two frames that clattered to the baseboard, pairs of balled-up socks flying out and getting lost amid the junk. He turned and kicked the next one into the TV, the flat football and a few discolored tennis balls spilling onto the carpet. Feeling a strange exuberance, he swung his leg a third time—his stupid old report cards fluttered out, an alligator skull tumbled into some bolts of fabric leaning in a corner. Next was the box he really wanted to have a go at—the one with his parents' old crap in it. He took a stiff stride and drew back his leg, stood that way a moment, arms out like a tightrope walker, but then his resolve ebbed and his shoulders slumped. His foot came to rest on the floor. He was trembling, standing in the midst of a disorder that he'd only made worse.

He lowered himself to the carpet. Pushed the box away gently with the sole of his sneaker. Bowed his head between his bent legs. His parents. His fucking parents. Why did they have to die? Why did they have to do this to him? If his parents had been around all this time, he'd never be in this position. He'd have a normal job, maybe a promotion by now. A mortgage. He and his father would still go fishing. He'd help his mother with her crosswords. Pratt ground the heels of his hands into the rough roots of the carpet. He knew his predicament was his own fault, but it wasn't *only* his fault. The first rule of being a mother or father—you had to be there. You had to be around. For everything Dale and Natalie Zimmer had done right, they'd failed at the most fundamental part. Pratt had an uncle in

New Mexico who probably never wanted to see him again. A woman across town he wanted and couldn't have. He could smell the carpet, musty and earthy like all carpets in Florida if you didn't clean them often. Above him, the fan sat still, its circular light fixture as dim as a forgotten moon, and Pratt sat still below it, feeling like nothing good was going to happen to him for a long time.

Monday morning found Pratt at the library fifteen minutes before it opened. Four or five homeless guys waited by the door, so he parked at the far edge of the lot and ate a granola bar and drank his orange juice. He'd replayed his encounter with Gianakos, sitting around the condo staring at the walls. He kept seeing Gianakos' shiny watch in his mind's eye. His pricey sunglasses. It was possible Gianakos didn't really need him, that he was taking a wild shot and would desist when Pratt didn't respond. It was also conceivable that the guy was desperate for him, didn't have much without him, needed a star to greenlight the whole production. Did Gianakos really think it meant something that Roger and Nairn had bland alibis? What were those two supposed to be doing in the middle of the night on a weekday, attending a soiree at City Hall? Nairn. Pratt hadn't seen the fuckface since the diner. It wasn't good fortune—Pratt's fortune had never done him any favors. If Bonne wanted Pratt checked on, Pratt realized, he'd never use Nairn for that. Keeping a low profile wasn't Nairn's specialty. More likely, Bonne had ordered Nairn to stay clear of Pratt because he was working on something, to go the other way if they crossed paths. Nairn wasn't keeping tabs on Pratt, but for all he knew, Gianakos was.

Pratt looked up and saw that the sign had been flipped. He watched the homeless guys drag themselves inside, and after that a pair of mothers with small children. He joined them and wandered over to the desk and told a young librarian with a perfect smile that he was looking for information about the warehouse fires from a while back. Like he'd hoped, she knew right away what he was talking about—besides what Bonne ordered to happen, there wasn't much big news in Hernando County. She asked if it was for a school assignment, probably thinking Pratt attended the community college, and Pratt nodded and said it was. He followed her to a cabinet with a bunch of tiny film strips in it, then over to a bulky machine with a green-tinted screen and a big knob on either side. She loaded the film, got it in focus. *St. Pete Times*, North Suncoast section. Pratt was becoming a newspaper connoisseur. Soon he'd exhaust the current year and need to dig back into 1997. He thanked the woman, gave her a slight grin that reignited her own big smile, then watched her walk back toward her desk with prim steps in her black penny loafers, wondering how it was that every librarian he'd ever seen seemed like she never could've been anything else.

The article, for a double arson, was buried, nowhere near the front page of even this regional section of the paper. Pratt put his fingers on the knob and scrolled the text, running his eyes over the short, straightforward paragraphs. Mascotte and Claverton. Okay—he knew these places. Mascotte was mostly Mexican, a place migrant pickers lived during the season. Over the years, more and more taquerias had popped up, churches that did service in Spanish. Claverton was the place many of the pickers did their picking, a stronghold of Old Citrus, abandoned when the trees were bare of fruit. Both warehouses had been unused for years, at least officially. One, back in the day, had been a clearinghouse for heavy grove equipment. One had once held remaindered and damaged medical supplies, whatever that meant. They'd both been owned by the same industrial real estate firm, Sun Baron Holdings out of Lakeland. Pratt had never heard of Sun Baron, had never been to Lakeland except for a baseball tournament when he was thirteen. Mascotte. Claverton. What they had in common was that people didn't go there.

Pratt leaned back from the machine. An announcement was made over the PA that story time would begin in five minutes. Over by the atlases, a man scratched his arms and fought to sit still, probably needing his fix. In the kiddie section, a blond toddler in a checked dress pulled picture books off the shelf, three and four at a time, and piled them on the floor.

Pratt scrolled down again. The police suspected arson but no suspects had been identified. No motive. No connection to any greater pattern. Nothing to go on except that the warehouses were owned by the same entity, but that wasn't much because most companies that owned warehouses owned a bunch of them. None of Sun Baron's other warehouses in Oldsmar or Temple Terrace had been damaged. The Bethuna Fire Rescue had arrived on the scene in eleven minutes, but nobody had called them until the structures were piles of smoking drywall and red-hot aluminum—some teenagers had driven through the smoke on their way back from a party in Orlando. No collateral property damage. No insurance claimed, Pratt imagined.

There was no doubt Sun Baron was a dummy company somebody was using to secure unwatched storage space. The whole thing was crime-on-crime, someone moving into Bonne's territory and getting a clear message to move out. It was the exact kind of thing local cops had never spent much time on, especially if no one got hurt. Gianakos was the part of the equation that seemed out of place, but maybe Pratt, and Bethuna, just weren't accustomed to a cop wanting to do his job, to beat Bonne instead of benefiting from him. And how else was Gianakos going to distinguish himself? Bonne was the only game in town. That's what the fires were all about—keeping it that way.

* * *

Malloy was already at the office. The library research had delayed Pratt, and then at the last moment he decided not to park by the stereo shop, the temperature ticking up a degree each day as it would the whole month of June. He found a shady lot a few blocks away. Put on his sunglasses and an Eckerd Drugs cap he'd come across in the condo. That, and the fact that he'd finally shaved, were as much as he was going to muster in the way of a disguise. You took a disguise one step too far, it had the opposite effect.

He took a meandering route toward Malloy's office, walking past a low-roofed day care with a sad jungle gym in the side yard, cigarette butts strewn in the patchy grass—the kind of place Kallie didn't want to take Joaquin. He passed an old sweets shop that Dunkin' Donuts had put out of its misery, its lot pocked with anthills as big as ladies' church hats. He saw the Maxima—that was really all he needed, to make sure Malloy was where he expected him. As he strolled across the street, he saw the secretary at her desk, her hair in ringlets now, the fingers of both her hands wrapped around a pink coffee mug. Pratt went down and circled an oily-surfaced retention pond—every neighborhood had one—and walked around some cracked basketball courts with no nets on the rims, the hoop posts leaning this way and that like doddering drunks.

He moved the LeBaron to a side street and waited for Malloy to pass on his way to Publix, and like clockwork here the man came. Up the main drag. Left into the Publix parking lot. In the store and out. Sushi, like last Monday. Yellow phone. Paper. A recurring dream. After lunch, Pratt found another weedy lot, this time south of the office, where he had a view up the alley and would know when the Maxima moved. No need for the binoculars or notepad. Out of habit he back-cranked the key and turned on the stereo, and was quickly reminded of the lodged W.A.S.P. tape. He stuck a pen in the slot and jabbed and jiggled, but it wasn't coming out. Pratt listened instead to the noise of the no-frills summer around him, mostly droning insects and whining cars. He peeled off his sweaty shirt and hung it out the window. Still as a stump, sticking to the seat's upholstery, he watched the minutes move robotically on his gaudy watch. They were all the same length, he thought. No matter how you spent them.

The next day, Pratt again parked elsewhere in the neighborhood, going on foot patrols to monitor Malloy. In the afternoon, halfway back to his car, Gianakos pulled up beside Pratt in the Crown Vic and offered him a ride. The detective wore the same black suit, or maybe one like it. A different shade of pastel shirt. He was finishing a smoothie, slurping at the dregs.

"No, thanks," Pratt said. "Stretching my legs."

"Come on, Pratt Morita. Walking in this heat?"

"Is it warm out? I hadn't noticed."

Gianakos glanced into his rearview, primping his oily black hair. "Did you walk all the way over here from your nursing home?"

Pratt shrugged.

"A walkabout? Like Crocodile Dundee?"

"Bingo."

Gianakos slid his sunglasses onto his forehead. His eyes were unhostile, younger-looking than the rest of his face. "Well, just bum around with me. I'll drop you off right back here. Enjoy some of this air conditioning your tax money pays for—not *your* tax money, but somebody's. Mine, come to think of it. Let's talk."

"I thought we already did that," Pratt said.

"Well, that's not nice. You make it sound like a chore, spending time with me."

Pratt knew he didn't have a choice. He wondered how long Gianakos had been following him, or if he'd honestly just been driving by.

He was glad he hadn't parked across from Malloy's office. He made his way around the long hood of the car and got inside. The promised AC was ice cold. It blew inside Pratt's collar and up his sleeves.

"I was a little ungracious the other day," Gianakos said. "Everything I said was true, but I could've taken a more cordial tone. I could've stressed the carrot, not the stick."

Gianakos turned off the radio, which had been broadcasting an elaborate weather report that included dew points and wind speeds. He pulled away from the curb and cut over to a potholed road that wound alongside Bethuna's slow brown mile of river. It was lined with run-down houses supporting leaning carports.

"What I should've said was that I envision a bright future for you. Hard to see it right now, but it's there. Someplace better than this. You must be sick of Bethuna. I picture you with a significant wad of currency in your pocket, big enough to make you limp. There you go, down a sun-dappled avenue where no one knows you. College even—it's not too late. Dumber guys than you do it all the time. Not that I know yet exactly how dumb you are."

"What would I study?" Pratt said.

"At first you major in girls. Figure out the rest later."

When Gianakos came to Masaryk Pike, he went on across, onto a smooth blacktop that sliced through acres of scrubland. A CD case was strapped to the visor above Pratt—Dave Matthews, Blues Traveler.

"What's going to happen," said Gianakos, "will be the end for some people, and I don't mind saying I'd like for Nairn to be one of them. I'll put that right out there. He's a foul-smelling redneck—one fewer makes the world a better place. I'd like it to be a beginning for you. I know your story. Who wouldn't root for Pratt? Who wouldn't wish another chance for you?"

"Are you talking about witness protection? Federal witness protection like in the movies? Is that what you're talking about?"

"No, nothing with the Feds. Witness protection is outpatient prison. It's lifetime parole—real parole, not whatever it is you have."

"Enough rope to hang myself," Pratt said.

"That's every man's right. To hang him*self*, not have someone else do it."

Gianakos let the car lose speed. He turned onto the Starkey Crossover, which wasn't much more than a dirt track through pine lots scattered with old sheds and barns—impossible to tell the houses from the outbuildings. They were heading back toward where they started, making a loop. The Crown Vic smelled like Gianakos' Drakkar Noir. The floorboards were completely clear of debris. The car's only imperfection was a six-inch crack in its windshield. Pratt wondered if it got there thanks to someone's head.

"Tell me if this statement is wrong: You can't move on with your life until Bonne is out of business." Gianakos turned the air a notch higher. If his hair wasn't a papier-maché cast, it would've been blowing around in the artificial gale. "You can't. You can't tell me that's wrong. See, there are some new elements about who've grown tired of the old patriarch. It's not only me. It's people a lot meaner than me, who don't have to play by the rules like I do."

Pratt wanted to ask what new elements, but it was a pointless question. There were always new players trying to come up. The world would never run out of them. "Why are you telling me you want Nairn to go down?" Pratt asked instead. "What do I care about Nairn?"

"What you care about Nairn is that if you don't get on board soon, I go to him. Whether I like it or not. Then you're on the outside looking in."

"Why not Roger? Is Roger too loyal or something? Too much integrity?"

This amused Gianakos. It earned Pratt a mellow smile. "I wouldn't say it's loyalty, exactly. Roger has resigned himself to his life. Resigned himself to his life and, how to put it... dedicated himself to curating it just so. He thinks a lot about his personal dignity. Right and wrong, as he sees them."

"Sounds like loyalty to me," Pratt said.

Gianakos gave an assenting tip of his head. "Yeah, okay—maybe loyalty. Anyway, Roger's down the list."

Gianakos cut a hard left and then a soft one. "Oh, I almost forgot," he said buoyantly. "I have a little stroll down memory lane for you. Something that might spark up nostalgia, as the Fresh Prince says."

"I can't wait," Pratt said.

"It involves a lemon."

Pratt waited.

"And bird-watchers."

"Bird-watchers?"

"Let's see," Gianakos said. "You would've been right out of high school. Boyish and fun-loving."

"Yup, that's me."

"You weren't a central character in the story, but the guy who told it recalls you being there. You and Bonne's kid, may he rest in peace. Six, seven years later, this dude still has a bone to pick. Lives elsewhere now—can't tell you where. Did a good job getting lost, that's for sure. Scrapes barnacles off dock posts for eight bucks an hour. Lives under a fake name in a weekly efficiency, eating beans out of a can and drinking Mad Dog. You could say he got out with his life, but geesh—it's only a life in name. Anyway, getting the absolute shit kicked out of you for an hour straight, something like that sticks with a person."

"I wouldn't know," Pratt said. "I never seem to get the shit kicked out of me."

"Because you're a super badass?" Gianakos asked.

"Because I don't make the badasses mad."

Gianakos slowed the car at an intersection so two kids on low-rider bikes could cruise past. "He's got a couple other stories, this guy. He hasn't had much going on to distract him from the past."

Yes, Pratt knew what the detective was talking about, and Gianakos knew he knew. Bonne had sent him and Matty out to the woods to see what happened in grown-up business when you deviated from best practices. The two youngsters had stood there ten feet from the action, trying not to make eye contact with the poor sap tied to the tree, trying to pretend it wasn't shocking to see Nairn in his fingerless gloves turn the guy's face into rare prime rib. The guy had information Bonne wanted, at least that's what Bonne thought, but no matter how many haymakers Nairn threw, the dude wouldn't give up a thing. When the guy's lips were busted in a dozen places, swollen roadkill, Roger had walked over with the candy-yellow fruit and shoved it in the guy's mouth, causing him to blubber and almost pass out, trying to speak but only drooling all over himself. Pratt remembered Roger's line. He'd said, "You missed your cue, buddy. You were supposed to say this stuff a half hour ago." Bird-watchers? Is that who those people were who came along with their reaching, hushed strides, a dozen strong—Pratt could see them now, all with binoculars around their necks. The unwitting middle-aged hobbyists were headed right for the scene. There'd been nothing to do but slip away and let the avian enthusiasts make the most exciting discovery of their forest-going careers.

Whatever stupid thing that guy had done, he'd been smart enough to clear his beaten carcass out of town immediately, the moment his canvas-vested guardian angels untied him, smart enough to change his name and find a new industry to toil away in and hope, quietly and anonymously, that he wasn't important enough for Bonne to search for.

"The moral of this story is about loose ends," Gianakos said, as if following Pratt's thoughts. They were back near where they'd started, rounding a long curve that described the retention pond. A white egret stood out in the middle of it—the whole thing only a foot deep. "It's impressive, actually, to have your shingle out as long as Bonne and have so few of them, but eventually some asshole like me comes along. Somebody with a throbbing hard-on for you."

"This is good right here," Pratt said.

"Okey dokey," said Gianakos. He heaved a good-natured sigh. "Back to your walkabout, Prattrick Ewing. I guess it's exactly what you need right now. So much to think about."

He slowed the Crown Vic, drifting near the curb and to a stop, and didn't look toward Pratt again—just sat there with a faint smile, patient, smug as the *Mona Lisa*, then accelerated away briskly as soon as Pratt was out of the car, leaving the street empty and hapless, like a little Western town after the train had pulled away.

Kallie drifted in and out of sleep on the cot in the living room, Joaquin at day care, the duplex eerily quiet, like the guy next door was sick or something. Kallie was cozy in the peacock blue robe her father had given her that past Christmas, but for some reason couldn't manage to fall into a deep slumber. Her fingers ached. Her feet ached. Countless seasons of soccer and her feet had stayed strong, yet standing on the concrete slab at the bakery for ten hours at a clip had ruined them in a year.

She'd had good news today, for once. The owner of the bakery had pulled her aside and thanked her for tolerating her daughter, with all her new ideas. The old woman had said the bakery couldn't afford to lose Kallie, whether her daughter knew it or not, and she'd given Kallie a two-dollar-an-hour raise. It was good news, of course—money is good news—but what Kallie didn't need to be doing right now was calculating what the humble influx of cash would mean for her. It wouldn't mean much. It'd help keep the car running. It'd go toward day care price hikes.

Kallie could hear cars shooshing past over on the highway, sounding like one of the settings on Joaquin's noise machine. Distant calls from birds. The rough hum of the air conditioner. Two dollars an hour. She should be happy. She rubbed her feet together gently. Nestled her head into the pillow. She could feel her breathing evening out, falling into a rhythm.

Next thing, she was massaging her smarting knee. Her body had jerked upright on the cot, heart pounding. Something had startled her just as she was submerging into dreams, and her leg had flailed into the wall. She pulled her robe closed, blinking, sitting cross-legged with her hair over her eyes. Here it was again, the phone—the phone ringing from the kitchen. She had to answer it—she always had to answer it because it might be the day care, something going on with Joaquin.

Kallie slipped off the cot and fumbled into the next room, steadying herself against the wall, brushing hair away from her face. She groped to grab the receiver off the cradle.

"This is Kallie," she huffed.

"And this is Ferris," the voice on the other end replied, playfully matching her breathlessness.

"Ferris?" she said.

"In the flesh. Well, not in the flesh, but, you know..."

It wasn't the day care. It was the guy she was dating. Or seeing. The guy she was trying to like because there was nothing wrong with him. Maybe she liked him. On paper, she liked him. She'd told him not to call in the afternoon like this, but she had to admit that didn't leave him a lot of options. She worked more nights than not. In the afternoons, she slept, or tried to, and then shuttled Joaquin around.

She'd tried dating a couple other guys in the past year, and it had always fizzled pretty quickly. She honestly couldn't tell if she was too busy for a boyfriend, or if she just didn't like these guys enough to *make* time for them, to carve out space in her crowded little life.

"Haven't heard your voice in a couple days," Ferris said. "Had a few minutes here, thought I'd check in."

"Oh, great," Kallie said. "I should be sleeping right now, but we can talk for a minute. You can wish me sweet dreams."

"I like to picture you getting in bed," Ferris said. "I like to picture you doing all sorts of things."

"Yeah, yeah," said Kallie. Ferris had said he had a few minutes, but Kallie figured he had more than a few. She could hear the breakers rolling onto the shore through the phone. He was sitting on his neat square of balcony, out behind his Gulf Harbors condo. It was Tuesday. On Tuesdays he didn't open his store. The condo was an investment. When he needed something bigger—he'd told Kallie this suggestively, lowering his sunglasses at her and then shifting his eyes toward Joaquin—he'd rent the condo out and buy something bigger, something inland near the new expressway. This after they'd known each other only two months.

"I won't keep you," he said. "I just wanted to make sure we were still on for Saturday. Jessie said the boat is all ours. It's got a grill on it. Full kitchen, actually. Full bedroom, too."

"Sounds amazing," Kallie said. "It sounds awesome, but I'm still not sure a hundred percent I'll be able to make it. Sorry—it's my stupid schedule. But it sounds incredible."

"You're not sure you can make it?" he said. There was concern in his voice but something else, too. Frustration.

"I probably can," Kallie said. She walked with the phone over to the kitchen window. Her little view. An old man jogged past on the backstreet in Velcro sneakers. "It's just that it's only Tuesday. Things have been crazy with me lately. I don't want to say I can go and then not be able to. That would be too disappointing. For me."

Kallie heard Ferris trying to suppress a sigh. She didn't expect someone like him to understand. He had a manager that ran his store on the weekends. When he did go in, the place was open ten to six. Mostly he drove around and met vendors, had lunch bought for him.

"I hope everything is okay," he said. "This is the second straight time you're backing out of plans."

"I'm not backing out. I'm just saying…"

"You canceled Sunday afternoon. I had that cabana rented on St. Pete Beach. I'm starting to wonder if… you know, I'm wondering if there's a problem."

Kallie picked at a thread in the silky sleeve of her robe, then stopped herself. "We've been really busy at the bakery," she said, which was true. "And my dad flaked on me twice last week for watching Joaquin," which wasn't true. "My AC's been on the fritz, so I had to deal with that." Sort of true.

"What does all that have to do with Saturday? If you need a babysitter, I'll pay for a babysitter."

"I told you, I'm hoping it will work. I think it'll work."

"You're hoping. You think."

Yes, his tone had gone frosty. Kallie could hear him bite into an apple. It was true he'd done nothing wrong, but now that he was being chilly to her, she couldn't help thinking about her stupid two-bucks-an-hour raise. Two dollars an hour would mean exactly nothing to Ferris. His car had twenty thousand miles on it, not two hundred thousand. When he took it to get worked on, that meant upgrading the stereo.

"Look," he said. "What I'm asking for is an open dialogue. Whatever's going on—if we don't communicate, we're doomed."

Now Kallie was the one sighing. "I'm a little overwhelmed over here, okay? Don't take it personal. It's not you. It's got nothing to do with you. You're wonderful."

"Well, I'm glad you realize that," he said. "You're not the only woman who thinks so. I'm a nice guy, Kallie. I shouldn't be treated badly because I'm nice. I'm great with Joaquin. If you'd let me meet your dad, I'd get along great with him, too."

"Sounds like you're great with everybody," Kallie said. "Sounds like I should be grateful to be with somebody who's so great with everybody."

"Why not?" Ferris spat. "I'm grateful to be with you. You're the one who doesn't seem excited enough to make an effort. What am I supposed to think?"

Kallie could feel her shoulders tensing. She could feel the linoleum sticking to the soles of her tired feet. It made no sense for her to be cooling off on Ferris because of Pratt. Nothing romantic was going to happen with Pratt. Nothing romantic *should* happen. It might've been weird dating someone who wasn't Matty while Pratt was around. That was stupid, too. The bigger problem was obvious: the depth of her feelings for Pratt threw into relief her shallow feelings for Ferris. Mr. Sit-on-My-Balcony-and-Look-at-the-Waves-on-a-Tuesday-Afternoon. When you were a kid, it was okay to date people for the hell of it. But when you *had* a kid, it wasn't such a hot idea. She wouldn't be able to escape the facts. She liked Pratt's hands better than Ferris'. She liked the way Pratt walked. Pratt would never, she knew, ask her to have an "open dialogue" with him. He would never try to convince her that he was "great"—in fact, she liked that he wasn't. But Pratt was a dead end. As far as love went, a dead fucking end.

Kallie went numb as she listened to Ferris speak. She needed to figure out what she wanted, he explained, and she needed to do it by this weekend. There were other women who wouldn't hem and haw at lounging with him on an Italian-made cabin cruiser, eating T-bones paired with a Napa cabernet. They were both adults, so he felt he could be honest about the situation. He liked her a lot, he said, and she, even if she'd forgotten it, liked him, too.

Kallie agreed with all this. Before she hung up the phone, she had an impulse to say she was sorry—it was because she had already figured out what she wanted, and didn't want. She'd figured it out, she supposed, the minute Pratt had appeared. She wanted to say sorry. But sorry, in her experience, didn't do a whole lot of good.

It was pitch dark in the old lady's bedroom. Clouds had shuttled across the night sky and blotted out the moon, a patient Gulf storm that might not drop its rain until tomorrow or the day after. Pratt flipped the switch on the old-fashioned radio. The Southern gentleman—he recognized the voice immediately, the wise and evenhanded tone, the lack of salesmanship. The man called this his Tuesday Talk. He thanked his listeners, who might've numbered a million or ten. This episode, the Mongols. Pratt, lying on his back like a man on a raft, lost at sea, listened as the gentleman detailed advancements in psychological warfare like he was reading the instructions for a new toaster. Hostage-taking—someone had to invent it. The use of human shields. The killing of the heads of rival clans in symbolic ways, like rolling them up in their own priceless rugs until they suffocated. The Mongols would cut off the feet of slaughtered enemy soldiers and deliver them in barrels to the enemy capital. There were no commercials. No guests. The host was probably in a shed in his backyard, sweating, sipping bourbon. He'd probably keep doing this week after week even if his equipment broke and his only audience was himself. He claimed that the Mongols had conquered one quarter of the world's people, and most days hadn't even needed to fight, terrorizing their opponents by razing farmland, by poisoning rivers, by catapulting diseased corpses over city walls.

Pratt shucked his shirt to the floor, peeled off his socks. A week since the last time he'd listened to this show. A week in which he'd seen Detective Dimitri Gianakos twice and Kallie only once. A week in which he'd met his less-than-conscientious parole cop. In which he'd grown accustomed to living in a sad dead woman's house, to using the same little pathways through the hoarded detritus that she herself had used. A week in which he'd grown expert about the daily routine of a walking dead man.

The Southern gentleman cleared his throat and wished whoever could hear a pleasant journey through their modern American life. After a few moments of static and several strange clicks, a woman with a lilting voice and no accent at all began listing the temperatures of European cities, a pause between each, as if you might want to write the information down. Amsterdam, 61. Barcelona, 73. Budapest, 69. Kiev, 68. London, 60. Naples, 70. All these and a bunch more, places that may as well have been make-believe, places with weather so mild—not hot, not cold—it wasn't weather at all. Places where not a solitary soul had ever heard, or ever would hear, of Bethuna Pond, Florida.

Low gray skies in the morning. No rain yet, the clouds aching to let it go. There was no sun to deal with—that was a blessing. Pratt called for a cab and sat waiting on the front porch, eating an energy bar, nodding to old ladies across the way who were having coffee in quilted housedresses and slippers. He went to pick out a newspaper from the pile, then decided against it—he'd concentrate on his own problems today.

The cabbie was Caribbean, and except to ask where they were going, didn't speak. He played something on the stereo that sounded like INXS and drove Pratt over to Dade City, to a rental lot that had once been a bank and still had those drive-through chutes sitting right in the way. As a goodbye, he told Pratt, "Be good, but not too good, mon."

Pratt suspected he'd be following Malloy out to Joe-Baby's that afternoon, but mostly he wanted a different car for some other business he had planned for later. This place cost twice as much as a regular car-rental shop—their cars were far from new and you weren't supposed to leave the state in them, but they let you put down a cash deposit instead of a credit card, the only place around that still offered such an option. Pratt and Matty had used them before—well, Matty really—when they had running around to do that nobody needed to know about. Matty pulling little deals off his dad's radar, or wanting to visit a girl with a Second Amendment–loving boyfriend. Today Pratt picked out a Dodge Neon, pale gray in color, the most forgettable vehicle available, and the rental guy walked around the car with a clipboard, taking note of tiny scratches and pings so he'd know they weren't Pratt's doing. The guy had long, thin sideburns and an eyebrow ring—something Pratt had never seen before being locked up.

"You might as well get the *in*surance," the man said. "Then you don't have to worry."

"No, thanks," Pratt told him.

"Be smart, man. You never know what'll happen out there."

"I don't use insurance," Pratt said. "It's, like, a principle of mine."

"You don't want peace of mind?"

"How to put this?" Pratt said. "Damaging this car is the least of my worries."

* * *

Sure enough, Wednesday, so after lunch came the field trip to Dunedin. The Dodge was cramped and sluggish, but it had cool air and the radio wasn't jammed useless with an '80s lipstick-rock album. The gray day—still hot, even more humid than usual—seemed to calm people, to subdue them. No one whipped back and forth in the lanes, no one blew their horn or revved their engine at the lights. Pratt wasn't concerned about losing Malloy; he knew where the guy was going. He just wanted to make sure Joe-Baby's was indeed the destination, to confirm there wasn't anything else to know about this poor sap. There wouldn't be. He wasn't having an affair. He didn't have a secret family. Wasn't into drugs. He smoked cigarettes and gambled. Smoked cigarettes and gambled. It wasn't smart, being this much a creature of habit. Bonne had taught Pratt and Matty this. While Pratt's uncle had been trying to instill discipline and routine, Bonne had been warning him about making grooves in the weeks. Only family should know where you're gonna be and when, he'd said, including Pratt in this designation with a sweep of his eyes.

Trouble Creek Road. Flora Blanca Avenue. Poisonwood. Bonita. Finally, Alternate 19. The Eagle's Nest Bar. The Channel Marker Bar. The White Tarpon Bar. Rich and poor, everyone wanted a bar. Pratt didn't follow Malloy behind the building. He was paying for this virgin car, and still he didn't want anybody to see it—wanted to *keep* it virgin. He passed Joe-Baby's strip mall and got off the frontage road and made a left back onto Alternate 19. Back up north. Back onto regular 19. Past Possum Lake and Salt Lake. The beginning of rush hour. Still no rain. The sedate, spent mothers sweating in their hatchbacks. The bearded war vets smoking pipes in their Buicks.

Back near Bethuna, Pratt pulled through a Checkers and ate in the parking lot, dropping french fries on the floorboard, and then drove next door, where he'd spotted a pay phone in front of a bowling alley. He stepped onto the curb with a couple quarters in hand. The phone book was lashed to the booth on a short metal chain, so he had to awkwardly prop it on his knee to flip through it. He wanted a general switchboard at the police station, rather than the direct line Gianakos had given him, and here it was. Quarter in the slot. Numbers punched. After four rings, a woman with a flat Midwestern accent asked what she could help with—when she had her answer, she said to hold and she'd connect Pratt, and immediately he heard ringing again. Just like that, as if he'd been waiting with his hand on the phone, here was Gianakos' ready-for-anything, slightly put-upon, wisecracking voice. Pratt could hear it just in the way he said his own name, gregarious and impatient at once. Pratt hung up. Gianakos was there. For once, Pratt knew where the detective was instead of vice versa. He was five minutes away from the station if he hurried. He dropped the phone book and hopped back in the Dodge, sped out of the parking lot and onto the streets, taking corners hard, straining the four-cylinder engine. He whizzed past a strip mall that was once a dairy farm, another that had been an orange grove. He slowed when he neared the police station, cruising toward the rear of the place on a quiet lane that would've been heavily shaded if there'd been any sun today. He parked at the roadside in front of somebody's Section 8 rental, close enough to have a view of all the dormant cruisers. Pratt gave it a minute, checking to see if someone would come out of the stained dwelling to accost him. No one did—nobody home, or whoever was home didn't care about Pratt and his Dodge. He rose out of the car and shut the door softly. Hoping to seem neutral, like any regular guy who had a right to take a stroll—and failing at this miserably, he knew—he walked by on the opposite side of the road behind some low-scraping live oak branches and trained a side-eye on the five identical Crown Vics. One, two, three. The fourth one, there it was—the six-inch crack in the windshield, barely big enough for Pratt to see it, a little luck, finally, the deep flaw in the glass straight as an arrow except for a frowning downturn at one end. Pratt about-faced and gave up the casual act, strode back to his car and climbed inside and lowered his visor. Reclined the seat. He could see the noses of the Crown Vics in a not-quite-even row, like sprinters at a finish line.

For the next half hour, Pratt sipped his Coke and watched clip-on-tie desk jockeys putter out of the lot in their Accords and Jettas, watched fresh-faced officers pull away in their squad cars, watched on-the-make lawyers steer reluctantly out into the disappointing world on the bouncy, worn shocks of their twelve-year-old Cadillacs. The Crown Vics were too far away to see who was getting into them, but twice one of the dark-fendered front ends backed out of view and then the car appeared at the exit, old guys both times, slumped posture, guys who'd risen as high in the force as they ever would and were waiting to retire. A UPS truck pulled past Pratt. A slow, bleating procession of about thirty motorcycles. A mosquito control truck, hissing out its noxious fumes.

Another Crown Vic slipped backward out of view. Pratt leaned forward, waited for the car to emerge—finally, it was him, the ambitious Greek, eating a peach or nectarine, bobbing his head to whatever college band he was listening to. Without coming to a full stop, he tossed his pit out the window with one hand as he wound the steering wheel with the other. He accelerated toward the stop sign at the end of the block—tap, tap, brake lights blinking through another rolling stop. Pratt waited until Gianakos was barely in view before he pulled out. It would be better to lose him than get made tailing him. Getting made would not only win Pratt more of Gianakos' attention; it would also mean he could never follow the guy again.

Three blocks through the dingy grid of the Timber Palms neighborhood, then the Crown Vic skirted a tiny county park that had been ceded back to nature, kudzu blanketing every tree. The right number of cars were on the road—enough to blend into, not enough to box Pratt in. Down 4 Mile. Down Perry Farm. All the way out along the train tracks and over to the outlet mall, which loomed up hugely out of nowhere, sprawling.

Gianakos went on past it, driving dissolutely now, taking turns with no hurry and leaving behind the lights and buzz of the mall for standard, weedy, sun-whipped inland Florida. Another minute up the road he hit his brakes abruptly—Pratt was forced to pull into a gas station or risk getting funneled up too close. Around the air pump and vacuum, he could still see the Crown Vic. He watched it pull into a trailer park and start creeping down the main drag, pulling a low wake of dust up behind it. Pratt got back on the road, waited for the light to change, then approached the trailer park himself, Gianakos' car out of sight. He partook of a deep breath. This wasn't going to be his smartest move, but he'd come this far so apparently he was doing it anyway, starting down the dirt lane, his tires tracing the tracks Gianakos' tires had made. Gianakos didn't know the car, he reasoned. Visibility was bad. He closed his windows and crept along, crept along, peering into the colorless early evening.

The trailer park was odd in that each unit had its own half acre of pine-picketed property. The place was landscaped. Tidy. Like no one wanted to let the other residents down. Pratt went deeper, farther from the entrance, letting the car roll without hitting the gas, far enough behind his mark now that the dust had settled. Flower beds in full bloom. Little flagpoles saluting from the tiny porches—Gators, Seminoles, the Marines, the Canadian maple leaf. No sooner did he begin to round the first curve in the long drive, and here was a car coming straight at him, the headlights glaring—yes, it was the Crown Vic. Eighty yards off, not quite the length of a football field. Pratt swore he could see the windshield crack. Sixty yards. Pratt felt his heart clunking around in his chest like something carelessly tossed in a box. He had just enough time to pull into the next right-side driveway, blinker and all, and pull too quickly up the drive and brake as smoothly as he could and pose stiff in the seat, the unremarkable back of the Neon facing Gianakos as he neared, hoping the detective didn't happen to detect that the small gray car contained someone he knew. Pratt held his breath. Slid down in the seat. What the hell would he say if Gianakos pulled in behind him? Jesus. Without moving his head, he put his eyes on the rearview and saw the detective very clearly as he passed by, his attention absorbed by something down on his lap. The Crown Vic made the same waist-high curtain of dust as before. Its small, saucer-like hubcaps. Its second and third antennas, jutting tall out of the trunk. Gianakos with his black hair and black clothes. He hadn't even glanced in Pratt's direction. Right in, right out—barely time for hello and goodbye. It was a pickup. Of what, Pratt had no idea, but it was some kind of pickup.

He blinked hard, pacing out a ten-count in his mind. He sat back up in the seat and put the car in reverse and drove through Gianakos' settling cloud. He didn't want to lose him. He made the turn onto the main road and went fast in the left lane for a quarter mile, floored the poor Neon to catch a yellow, swerved around a minivan hauling a pop-up camper. There was the Crown Vic, idling at a red light at one of the windblown intersections that served the outlet mall. Pratt followed the detective west, all the way back near Bethuna proper, then they veered north, never getting out from under the steel-colored ridges of cloud that lit up when the silent heat lightning flashed, up past the reptile-infested Croom Woods, past the Fox Chase projects. The Lighthouse Tabernacle, an enormous ministry of snake-handlers that targeted only the most downtrodden and desperate. Pratt knew where they were going. It was a pocket of the county known as Jonesville—Pratt had no idea its real name—that made the neighborhood of Pratt's after-prison motel look like Palm Beach. Nothing else was out this way. This was where junkies went to score and runaways hit bottom—no laws, no tax base, no borders except the one that separated it from decent, or at least pretending-to-be-decent, society. Politicians didn't even pay lip service to cleaning it up anymore, and it was beneath the dignity of a crime outfit like Bonne's. There was a hut where they fried whatever mudfish could be caught in the drainage ditches. A hut where somebody sold cheap port wine and expired cough medicine. Old boarded-up depots from an unimaginable era of pluck and optimism, now windowless brothels. Meth. LSD that was mostly rat poison. People stumbling around like zombies or leaning against walls. Pratt recognized these streets, and he also recognized the particular establishment Gianakos pulled into, unlicensed, renting rooms by the hour. The place was familiar because Pratt had accompanied Matty out here a couple times, Pratt waiting in the car and watching to make sure nothing bad happened to his pleasure-seeking friend.

This time Pratt watched from across the street, and watched his own back in the mirrors just as hard, as Gianakos stood up from his car without his jacket, chirped the alarm, and bounded up the concrete staircase at the corner of the building. Back erect, a knuckle dragging along the rusted railing, he strode all the way to the other end, to the last door, and with no preamble began pounding on it, one-two-three-four, with the meat of his fist. A moment, then one-two-three. When the door opened a crack, he shoved it inward and barked instructions that Pratt couldn't make out. Seconds later, a half-dressed man stumbled forth, trying to button his pants, his shirt in his teeth. Gianakos shouldered him to the side and stepped into the doorway, and Pratt spotted a woman—blotched skin, knobby knees, some kind of bustier on her upper half. Gianakos plucked the cigarette right out of her mouth and tossed it toward the man he'd evicted, who was hopping around on the walkway, trying to get shoes on his feet. Gianakos stepped inside and closed the door behind him, and the other man was left to drag himself down the stairs to his beat-up Oldsmobile, sling his socks and hat bitterly inside, collapse into the driver's seat, and gun the engine until it finally caught.

Twenty minutes later, Gianakos descended from the motel room in no hurry. Fastened his seat belt. Picked out a CD from the sleeve on the visor. This time he led Pratt to the coast. It was full darkness now, a night of thick, jungle air that condensed on the LeBaron's windshield, the wipers doing little to clear the view. Pratt was going to burn half a tank of gas following this prick all over Hernando County—lots of business in the service vehicle, most of it in service of Gianakos himself. One thing for sure, the guy's mission in life was *not* to transform Bethuna into a gleaming bastion of contemporary morality. Across 19, into a web of sharp-cornered lots and manicured canals. The houses getting bigger. Few American cars in the driveways. Screened-in pools. Private docks dwarfed by the mini-yachts they moored.

Gianakos pulled off onto a smaller road, then turned again onto a tree-lined drive that led to a parking lot adjoining a pearl-white condo building. Pratt had his window open and could hear and smell the Gulf. This was a condo building, yes, but it bore no similarity to Pratt's place, no shared DNA. Through his binoculars, he could see BMWs and Audis and Porsches resting in their numbered spaces. On the first floor, the glow of a lounge and bistro. Pratt could see through the glassed-in lobby to the crystal-blue swimming pool. A doorman—or whatever rich people called them—sat behind a teak desk next to a pair of elevators. Pratt watched Gianakos walk past him with a dismissive wave and head up, and then Pratt waited, watching the windows of the high rooms until—there it was—lights coming on in the corner unit on the fifth floor, at the top of the building. Gianakos' silhouette against the sun blinds, probably moving around the kitchen, pouring a drink. Gianakos either lived here or, more likely, got his mail elsewhere but had free and easy use of the place. Either way, unless the guy was sitting on family wealth and wore a badge for a hobby, these digs were way above his pay grade. Pratt kept watching, but Gianakos was probably out on the spacious back balcony now, enjoying the shushing music of the sea, propped up on patio furniture that cost more than what most folks had in their living rooms.

Thursday morning, the buttery sunlight searing through the closed blinds told Pratt the clouds were gone. They'd slunk off during the night without delivering what they'd promised. In ten minutes, Pratt was in the Neon, squinting behind his sunglasses, headed toward Suncoast Accounting under a sky of perfect glass-blue that magnified the heat.

He parked in his old spot and cranked the AC, munching honey-roasted peanuts in small handfuls until nothing but dust was left in the one-pound bag. The trees, even the weeds, looked dried out, let down, leaves shriveled and flowers pale. Here came Malloy. Now his secretary, in a plaid skirt and an old-fashioned men's hat, something a private eye would wear in a black-and-white movie. Pratt had a radio and turned it on. It told him that out in the world, people were going on strike for a living wage, armies were bombing each other in parts of the former Yugoslavia he had never heard of.

In the afternoon, Pratt set the alarm on his watch. Although he was weary and strung out, he never really came close to nodding off. There wouldn't be a trip to Dunedin today, which was a relief. He'd been out of the pen only a couple weeks and already, like everybody else, he dreaded his commute.

He kept watch until three, and then with a dry throat and aching eyes he drove across town to that same pay phone at the bowling alley. Main switchboard. This time, when the woman connected Pratt to Gianakos' desk, the phone rang five times and a machine clicked on. Pratt hung up. He waited a few minutes, until a sullen guy in a *Mystery Science Theater 3000* shirt finished his own call, and this time when he tried the detective he altered his voice—deeper and gruffer, a manlier version of himself. The five rings. The answering machine.

Without high hopes of a sighting, Pratt headed out toward the fancy condo building in light traffic—the young still at work, the elderly avoiding the worst heat of the day. An animal hospital. A muffler shop. Across 19, into the other world. The pristine boats. The styled pineapple palms, fronds shooting heavenward like punk haircuts. Workmen installing sprinkler systems. Roofers repairing Spanish tile. The neighborhood was teeming with activity, but the people who owned the houses—them you never saw. No trace. Inside starting cocktail hour or gone to their summer places on Cape Cod and the coast of Maine.

Pratt pulled off into the weeds, partially hidden by a winking wall of vine, and a pulse of confidence spiced his blood when, through the binoculars, he saw movement in the top-corner unit, Gianakos' third-baseman's frame gliding here and there behind the window screens. He was gone for a minute, then back, his tall silhouette the only sign of life in the building. Gone again. Pratt lowered the binoculars. Gianakos was here—he just had to wait. What he did best. Pratt checked the mirrors. He turned the radio up three clicks—classic rock, the best he could hope for. A get-the-Led-out block. "Whole Lotta Love" and "Heartbreaker" on the way, the DJ promised. A small gray spider lowered itself from a high shelf in the foliage and landed on the windshield. Pratt tapped his knuckle lightly, and without hesitation the creature began quickly pulling itself right back up.

There was movement in the lobby, and Pratt got his binoculars up in time to confirm who it was. He got the car started and waited until he saw the Crown Vic roll out and take the first corner. He was good at this, Pratt allowed himself to think—he'd pinned a tail on this cocky cop two days in a row.

He followed his mark three miles south on 19, the countless strip malls blending into one, until Gianakos pulled into Murtaw Muscle Company, the meat-market gym where the Long Island transplants went to pose and grunt. Pratt watched Gianakos strut into the place, then waited forty-five minutes—dully tracking tank-topped meatheads and booth-tanned women with long, fake nails to their Mustangs and Jeeps—until the detective reappeared, showered and in a different shirt, and pulled out the back of the parking lot, avoiding 19, into a labyrinth of narrow streets lined with identical tiny villas, speed limit fifteen, each residence with a decorative light post and cramped parking space. Beige stucco and brown trim. This is where they kept old people who didn't even have enough money to live where Pratt did. Building after building, Gianakos wended his street barge, back tires clipping the grass of the corner lots. Soon both cars were out of the maze and into territory Pratt knew. Little Sam Road—the stretch with all the guns-and-ammo shops, the army surplus stores, the taxidermists.

Gianakos hung a left into a grid of sandy lots and aging, sprawling ranch houses, doorless sheds, leaning fences that wouldn't keep anything in or out. He made another turn, and when Pratt got close to the corner, he saw a dead end sign. Instead of following, Pratt drew up the binoculars to see which house Gianakos chose, then advanced a block and turned left and rolled up and up, ten yards at a time, until he had a one-street-over view of Gianakos—he saw the tall figure step up onto a front porch, saw a light come on, barely detectable in the sunny late afternoon. The chosen estate included a half dozen log cabin outbuildings scattered about the grounds. Big dogs kept in the side yard by high chain-link, the first fences in good repair in the neighborhood. A glossy black Range Rover, notably out of place, sat in the circle drive.

Eyes pressed to the binoculars, Pratt watched Gianakos type a code into a keypad. Watched him pivot his head coolly, scanning the street behind him—an impulse, a habit, no nerves in his movements. The door opened—Pratt couldn't see who was behind it. The detective stepped inside, the door shut behind him, and in his absence everything went still. The pulse of satisfaction that had run through Pratt earlier now had a dark edge. He was getting close to something, something worse than the police because the police had to follow rules, or at least pretend to, something worse than Bonne because Bonne knew him, cared about him.

He glanced at the cubic-zirconia-encrusted face of his watch to make sure the seconds were still ticking, then eyes back up. The outbuildings were quiet. The dogs were suddenly gone. Pratt backed up the Neon, getting the car mostly off the road. He kept the sewing-machine engine running and the parking lights off, dusk beginning to find its way down through the crowns of the trees. Gianakos didn't come out for ten minutes, twelve. Pratt kept the radio quiet. He could only sit here for so long, the scene getting eerier. There was the distant thump-echo of a basketball on pavement, no rhythm to it, disappearing for minutes at a time, then returning louder, the daytime noises it competed with—cars and children and legal labor—dropping off. He could smell hot grease on the air. He thumbed his notebook open and recorded the name of the street he was on, one over from Gianakos' rendezvous. He scanned with the binoculars and couldn't find a house number anywhere, but he wouldn't forget the house.

He panned wider and took in the neighbor's house—a mailbox hatch wagging open, a pickup weighed down with fifty-gallon drums, a pair of black boots hanging on a power line. Pratt saw something moving in an empty lot catty-corner to where the Crown Vic and Range Rover were parked. Closer to Pratt than to the house Gianakos had entered. It was a person. The cherry of a cigarette, that's what had caught Pratt's eye, and now Pratt could see the form in the last thin light, huffing the thing down until he could barely hold it. This guy made Malloy seem like a casual weekend smoker. He was staring in the same direction as Pratt, the wrong vantage if he was supposed to be a lookout. He wasn't a lookout, though. Pratt watched him rub his face hard with his palm and twitch his head around like horseflies were after him. This wasn't a person anyone would trust with security. This was a junkie, or close to it. He was keeping out of sight in a copse of heat-beaten hardwoods, shuffling in a tight circle, scared to cross the street. Cutoff jean shorts. Black Orlando Magic T-shirt.

Pratt checked the house again. Nothing going on. He surveyed the street where he was parked, down to the cul-de-sac and then back behind him, in the mirrors. He tucked the pad and the binoculars under his seat, cut the engine. The basketball had gone quiet, the crickets tuning up. He stood and eased the driver door shut. He looked around again, then walked between the two houses nearest him, along a plastic fence that came up to his waist, past an orange tree that had dropped its rotting fruit, and into the tangled greenery of the empty lot. He didn't want to sneak up on the junkie, and so made no effort to muffle his steps. He emerged into the tight clearing with his arms raised and palms open. When the guy registered Pratt's presence, he stiffened and took a retreating step.

"How much more you need?" Pratt asked him.

The guy's eyes were bloodshot—that was plain even in the failing light—irises flicking around as if Pratt had cornered him, as if seeking out egress. Where the sleeves of his T-shirt ended, track marks were visible.

"You a cop? You gotta tell me."

"That's probably not true, but no, I'm not a cop."

"Who are you? A preacher?"

Pratt laughed.

"Well, what the hell you want with me?" the guy said.

"You're short, aren't you?"

The guy didn't say yes or no.

"I might be in a position to close the gap in your financing. A little information is all it would take."

"A little's all I got," the guy said. Safety pins hung off his shorts. His Converse sneakers were riddled with holes. "Nobody tells me nothing. Nothing worth knowing."

"All I want to know is his name. The dealer there—what do they call him?"

The guy looked amused. "His name? Everybody knows his name. Where you been?"

"Out of circulation," Pratt said.

The guy wiped his nose on his sleeve. "What do you want to know for, if you don't know already?"

"I'll ask someone else," Pratt said. "I'm not looking for a hassle." He took one step, as if he were going to walk away.

"Flave," the guy said. "His name is Flave."

"Like, as in Flavor?" Pratt said, turning back around. "The guy that wears the big clock around his neck on MTV?"

The junkie shrugged. "Don't kill the messenger."

"I guess his real name is Alton or Milton," said Pratt. He pulled out his wallet. There were two bills inside and he held one out. "So, this guy Flave doesn't mind you coming right to his house?"

"He don't got a lot of rules," the guy said. "He's got one—payment in full, no credit."

"Fair enough," Pratt said.

The junkie held the bill up to the light, and his shoulders slacked a little. "Ten?" he said. "Twenty would be a lot better. Like, *a lot* better."

"I was thinking that same thing," Pratt said, "about the ten I got left."

Pratt swung by Tony's store, hoping maybe he was working late, but no—lights off, sign flipped. He steered next toward Tony's house, wanting to check if Bethuna Pawned even had what he needed in stock. If so, he could stop by first thing tomorrow.

The Wagoneer was in the drive, the front blinds wide open so Pratt could see the girl in the *Jaws* poster on the living room wall—like a lot of people, she was in much more trouble than she knew. Pratt knocked and, like last time, Tony answered the door in an apron, this time a chef's garment that said TROPHY HUSBAND. Pratt followed him back to the kitchen, where burgers were steaming on a George Foreman grill. An array of condiments were lined up on the counter like privates called to order. A tray of baked beans.

"People will be here in twenty minutes," Tony said. "Stay and eat. Don't worry, it's nobody you know."

"I already ate," Pratt lied.

"Well, you can hang around anyway. The new *Streets of Evil* came out—we'll be up all night playing it."

"*Streets of Evil?*"

"Let me guess—you don't play video games."

"I tried it once. I kept losing instantly, like the first button I pushed."

"Homemade lemonade. Grass-fed sirloin burgers."

"What do cows normally eat?"

"You don't want to know."

Tony finished cutting a red onion and started in on a tomato. Upbeat, hippie-sounding music was playing in another room. On the kitchen wall were three small drawings of herons and nothing else—a green one, one with a yellow crown, then the Great Blue.

"I was actually looking for a camera," Pratt said. "I stopped by the shop first, didn't know if you had any. Nothing fancy. And I'm paying you this time. I'll mail the cash to your house if I have to."

Tony cocked his head contemplatively. He was leaning forward over a pickle jar, extracting a dill half. "Shit, you know what? I have one back in my room. My old one. I meant to bring it up, but I forgot about it. It's outdated—you probably don't mind. I went digital."

"No, I don't mind," said Pratt.

"It still uses film."

"Yeah," Pratt said. "What else would it use?"

"Something smaller and faster and cheaper."

"Film is good," Pratt said. He could feel, suddenly, how hungry he was, the aroma of burgers filling the room. He was very hungry, but also very much not up for meeting people. "I'll bring money by the shop tomorrow."

"Now see, that's the bad news," Tony said. "Since it was never entered into the merchandise log, I can't charge you for it. It'll have to be a personal gift. No two ways about that."

Pratt shook his head.

"For tax purposes," Tony said. "For keeping the books. Quarter two net profits. Can't dip into the till. Columns have to even out. Etcetera, etcetera."

"Sixty bucks?" Pratt said. "Is that about fair? Yeah, I'm deciding it is. Sixty even."

"You leave me any money, I'm going to throw it out on the sidewalk. I'm serious. Now help me make this lemonade, and then I'll go find the camera. It's clutter at this point. You're doing me a favor."

Pratt didn't say anything more. It flashed through his mind—and he should've thought of this sooner—that it wasn't purely goodwill and generosity that kept Tony from ever charging him for anything. Maybe the guy didn't want to accept money he thought came from Bonne. Maybe as far as the cleanliness of his business was concerned, Tony saw Pratt the same way he saw the addicts that came in with stolen radios and jewelry they'd snatched.

He sat on a stool and faced the counter, and Tony slid a cutting board in front of him. It was loaded with lemons and a bushy green bunch Tony identified as mint. He handed Pratt a knife, then pulled a pitcher from on high and started filling it with water.

Trying for a casual voice, like he was discussing a Devil Rays homestand, Pratt said, "You ever hear of a guy named Flave? Some kind of drug dealer. Probably new in town?"

Tony had a big sack of sugar in his hands. He set it down gently on the counter and looked off, his demeanor souring. Phony nonchalance was not Pratt's strong suit. "Um, yeah," Tony said. "I've heard of him. What about him?"

"It's no big deal," Pratt said. "Forget I asked. Just a lot of new people around. I'm trying to figure out who to steer clear of."

Tony dropped a heaping spoonful of sugar in the pitcher, then another. "That part's easy. Yes, you should steer clear of him." What he wanted to say—it was plain on his face—was that Pratt should steer clear of Bonne, steer clear of all these criminals. Pratt wasn't going to tell him that when it came to Flave, he was working for himself, not Bonne. Tony genuinely cared about Pratt. Why? Why did he care?

"Look, there's way more drugged-out dudes bringing stolen stuff to the store lately," Tony said. "Discmen and radar detectors. Whatever they can pull out of cars. They get pissy when I won't play ball. I hear the name. They all hate him, but they're scared of him."

Pratt finished halving the lemons. Tony went over and checked the burgers, pulled a package of buns from a cabinet and tossed them on the counter. He had something else to say.

"What?" Pratt said. "What is it?"

"Vince Flood told me about him. You remember Vince? Well, he smokes morning, noon, and night now."

Yes, Pratt remembered Vince, a feather-haired kid who always wore flip-flops. Pratt recalled having an early class with him—geography. Vince had come in late every day, and the teacher never hassled him about it. Maybe because he always seemed sad.

"Vince says everybody who sells for this guy—they're like, terrified. He gets these strung-out dudes from Jonesville—they go missing, nobody cares. People look at him wrong and he takes them out in the swamp and pops them, leaves the bodies for the alligators. He'll sell to middle schoolers. He'll sell crack to pregnant girls. That's what Vince said. I don't know, call it rumors." Tony took off his apron and folded it up sharp as an American flag. His T-shirt said STEELY DAN. "I just say no to everything that seems stolen. Guys with their teeth falling out. I keep saying no, hoping they'll get the message."

Tony pulled the lemons in front of him. He had a contraption that squeezed them flat as pancakes, every last drop draining into the pitcher.

"I wonder where he's from," Pratt said.

"Don't know, don't want to know."

Tony did lemon after lemon until the garbage can was filled with yellow disks, pulling down the pewter handle of his juicing gadget over and over. He didn't want to say any more about any drug dealers, and Pratt wasn't going to press him. Tony shut off the Foreman and arranged the burger patties on a platter.

"I know," he told Pratt, standing at one end of his spread, as if to showcase it. "You're not in the mood for company."

"I don't really understand it either." Pratt walked over to the sink and wiped down the knife he'd been using. "I appreciate you not pushing it. I'm okay—I really am. I know I'm being a shithead."

"As long as you're aware."

"It's one of the only things I know for sure."

Tony wiped his hands on a rag and headed down the hall. As soon as he was out of sight, Pratt, on an impulse, leaned over the glass pitcher and took a slurp right from the rim. It was delicious, crisp—Pratt could've chugged the whole thing. He could feel that it was unwise to keep himself isolated and stewing, and also that there was no way he could do it right now, no way he could masquerade like his troubles didn't exist, no way he could make small talk, laugh at people's jokes.

Tony strode back into the room and tossed Pratt the old camera. It looked like a new camera to Pratt, silver, about the size and weight of a bar of soap.

"Know how to use it?" Tony asked.

"Put it in salt water overnight, then throw it in the microwave, right?"

"Oh, that's a relief," Tony said. "For a minute, I was worried you didn't know much about electronics."

This time Pratt trailed Malloy only halfway to Joe-Baby's. Just past Bay Dunes he pulled into a strip mall with a gravel lot, anchored at one end by a smoke shop and at the other by a store that sold refurbished hot tubs. He parked in the shade of an immense religious billboard that prominently featured the word "lovingkindness." Pratt was confused, but strangely calm. Conquered—that's how he felt. Like someone due to work out terms of surrender. Without knowing exactly when it had happened, the notion of offing Malloy, of pulling the deadly trigger, had shifted from repugnant and impossible to the realm of an unpleasant chore. Pratt still despised the idea, but now he could imagine himself performing the task, could see that it was within his abilities. Had dragging himself through the preparation, day after day, changed him, or had he been kidding himself all along that he *wouldn't* do it? Anyone would do anything under the right circumstances. He'd been a killer the whole time, like everyone was, secretly, and since the moment Bonne gave the order he'd been accepting this, waiting for his brain to catch up with the dark parts of his soul. He looked up at the oversize billboard advertising the Lord Jesus Christ. All the words were scripted in cursive on a scroll, and the scroll was upheld at each corner by white doves. Pratt understood now why Bonne had given him till the end of the month. He hadn't been giving him time to learn about Malloy. He'd been giving him time to learn about himself.

He could see it in detail, like it had already happened and he was remembering it, like a scene in a movie that had stuck in his mind long after he'd forgotten the rest of the story. It had been written, scouted, and filmed, off in some wing of Pratt's consciousness he had no access to. While he'd been sleeping. While he'd sat in a trance in the LeBaron, the Wagoneer, the Neon. Pratt realized he was squeezing the steering wheel. He opened his hands and flexed his fingers, the knuckles drained of blood. In a corner of the parking lot where litter collected, a skinny corn-colored mutt nosed around in the trash, the skin around its snout and paws red and raw.

Here was Malloy, clear as day in Pratt's mind, pulling down the limestone backstreet behind the party supply, hair sweaty, thumb nervously drumming the dash. What the hell was this? A car stalled in the middle of the narrow lane, right where the pine tree staked one side and the palmetto thicket spilled into the street on the other. No way around, and too risky to leave his car out front. Malloy brakes tentatively now, pokes his head out the window of the Maxima to see what the trouble is, his left hand dangling outside the door with its half-smoked cigarette. Bright blue tie. Face ruddy. Pratt emerges from the disabled vehicle—a quick wave, an apologetic smile. Can Malloy sit in the driver's seat and steer while Pratt pushes, just to get it past the pine tree and off to the side? Only take a minute. They'll have the old heap out of the way before that Marlboro is finished. Stupid car, piece of shit, this was the last straw. Malloy gets out, looks around apprehensively, his face trying to be friendly. He wants this roadblock, this complication, erased from his day, wants it gone, wants to get inside Joe-Baby's and settle up so he can call in more bets tomorrow. Right, Malloy says. Yeah, sure. Cigarette still going, he walks past Pratt and toward the open door of the LeBaron—no, not the LeBaron; Pratt will rent another car, especially for this task—walks past Pratt and here's Malloy's back, undefended, slump-shouldered, soft.

Joe-Baby's guy would hear the shot—somebody in there would—but by the time anybody got outside, Pratt would be a cloud of dust. Hop in and move Malloy's car out of the way, leave it running, nose in the palmettos. Jump in his own car and reverse full speed, frontage road, Alternate 19. Joe-Baby would be Pratt's body-removal service. His guys would have no choice but to make Malloy and his car disappear. No cops. No nothing. Just a couple geezers over in the trailer park startled out of their naps—somebody shooting a snake or something, good riddance—then quickly nodding back off in their easy chairs.

Pratt could see all that, but he still hadn't actually done it. He hadn't done anything wrong at all, he reminded himself. He was a guy who liked to park in peculiar places, who kept binoculars with him at all times in case he saw a bald eagle, who drove up and down Route 19 without a destination because the car exhaust cleared his mind. Right this minute he was minding his own business on a Friday afternoon, deciding whether he wanted to price used Jacuzzis or get some cherry tobacco for the pipe he didn't own. No one but Bonne knew anything about his intentions toward Malloy, anything about the gun in his nightstand. Pratt was innocent, or as innocent as he'd been the day he walked out of prison. He'd done nothing yet, committed no terrible act—and yet, if he didn't discover some way *not* to do it...

The yellow dog was gone. Lovingkindness still loomed. Out on 19, empty cement trucks, done with the week's work. Beer trucks, restocking the corner stores in the nick of time. A lowrider packed with idiot white kids, the speakers in the trunk thudding their teeth loose. It was easy to be angry at Bonne, bitter, but there was no escaping that he was the closest thing Pratt had to a father. Pratt had come out of prison dead set on getting untied from Bonne, but in order to do what? To accomplish what? Somewhere in his gut, the knowledge was squirreled away: to do what Bonne had asked was a homecoming. Maybe all that was missing for Pratt to fully give in was the realization that he *did* owe Bonne—not for the money he and Matty lost, and not even for losing Matty himself, but because Bonne had stuck by Pratt. Bonne had summoned him. Bonne was still around. Bonne cared enough to give him an order, even if it wasn't an order Pratt liked.

Suddenly, from somewhere, the baseball mitt was in his mind. The *mitts*, plural. In Pratt's memory, the beginning of the trouble between him and his uncle. His uncle had bought him a mitt for his freshman season of high school, a perfectly fine piece of equipment like everyone else used, had presented it to his nephew proudly and clapped him on the back and made sure he knew how to break it in, to oil it and leave it with a ball tucked in the pocket. A couple days later, Bonne had casually tossed him a Wilson 3000 Ultra-skin infielder's glove, a $300 article, as if he'd tossed Pratt a pack of gum. Pratt couldn't say now what he'd been thinking—he hadn't been, he'd been a dumb kid—but he'd tucked the mitt from his uncle under his bed and never touched it again.

But no, that hadn't been the start of it. Pratt had already been sneaking out at night, smoking cigarettes, sipping stolen Boone's Farm. Pratt and Uncle Jack used to have breakfast together every morning, and Pratt could remember these meals turning silent. The elder would've been up an hour already, would've completed his run and knocked out his push-ups, and Pratt would drag himself to the table bleary-eyed. They'd eat eggs over easy and grapefruit and toast. Music maybe, but no TV. Uncle Jack never watched TV. He never spat in the street, in a public park, on a sports field. Never cursed around Pratt. Looking back, it was a wonder he'd never hit Pratt. He must've wanted to. He probably should've, to tell the truth. That was probably what Pratt needed.

Sitting in the car all day, and more sitting on tap for the evening. Pratt pulled into Josip's store, was able to get in the door and back to the cooler case without drawing the proprietor's attention away from his hot rod magazine. He found what he sought, Jolt Cola, the apple-red can with the cartoon lightning bolt. He walked to the register and clunked it down on the counter, and only then did Josip look up from a '57 Chevy with a woman in a leopard leotard sprawled across its hood.

"Prott," he said, setting aside the glossy periodical and spreading his arms in greeting. "My number one honky. How you live, son?"

"No complaints," Pratt said.

Josip picked up the Jolt and shook his head. "Something better now," he said. "The Red Bull. Right down there—grab one, OG." He pointed over the counter, cocking his wrist around to the left.

Pratt saw it. A display cooler brimming with ice, shaped like the cans that filled it, slender and metallic. He took one out and set it down, dripping. "What, do you get a kickback?"

"I care for my customer," Josip said. "For you, free. Stay away from the Jolt."

Josip reached across to the sunglasses rack before Pratt could do it himself. The pair he grabbed had green wasps on the earpieces, their stingers oversize and brandished for action.

"See," said Josip. "I know what you need. I notice everything. I see you get rid of ridiculous automobile. This make Josip happy."

"I still have the LeBaron," Pratt said. Wasps—why not? He was going to lose them soon, anyway. "Sometimes prosperous people own more than one car. That's how things work here in the first world."

"Prosperous?" Josip bellowed. "Jesus of Bethlehem, you probably don't have the health insurance. This is the sign of prosperity in this country—the health insurance."

"I don't mess with insurance."

"Well, no. Too expensive, homie."

"It's not the cost—it's that I never get sick. Not even the sniffles. I have a strong, American immune system."

Josip leaned back, grinning tolerantly. "You do not appear immune, my friend. You appear... afflicted. Beleaguered."

Pratt plucked a baggie of trail mix off its peg. "Word-of-the-Day calendar?" he guessed.

"A goal is to speak your language better than you. Is goal of many immigrants. In this country—how do you say?—a *doable* goal. Natives speak like shit."

"They speak better in other places?"

"Yes. Oh, yes. Much pride, other places."

"I'll have to take your word for it," Pratt said. "I've never been anywhere else."

"Yes," Josip said. "You take my word, P-Man. You always take Josip's word."

Pratt knew enough about Gianakos for the time being. Instead of tracking the detective, he went back to his spot one block over from Flave's place—who knew, he might wind up seeing Gianakos again without trying. Might get a picture of him this time. He didn't know what he was looking for, exactly, but he was growing fond of being somewhere no one could find him.

Here was the familiar bald shoulder of the quiet street, the view over and past the tortured-looking fence, the sky above draining of luster. Pratt opened his front windows all the way, drew in breaths of the humid air and expelled them mechanically. Ten minutes. Fifteen. He turned on the radio to find mournful, Spanish-sounding guitar music, no singing, just the strings and a drum somebody played by hand. Pratt turned it down a notch. He smelled the grease again, the smell from last night.

Three houses up the street, an old man, followed by an adolescent, came out onto their front porch and sat down, probably having finished a meal, the old man gesturing in an unhurried way with his arms, patiently explaining something to the youngster. The old man was smoking—Pratt could see the pale ribbons winding up into the porch roof. He took up his camera and powered it on. It was half the size of any other camera Pratt had ever seen. Its autofocus button made the lens telescope out from the body. Pratt raised the machine to his eye. He pressed the button and let the camera home in on its target, unblurring first the house and then the figures on the porch, their clothes, their faces. It was like Pratt was thirty feet away.

He studied the old man, his rimless glasses and wooden pipe. He was still lecturing, his face serious. Pratt shifted ever so slightly to spy the boy, and it wasn't a boy at all. It was a guy of forty-five or fifty, short and clean-shaven and wearing red running shoes. As if Pratt's realization of the subject's age gave permission, the guy now brought out a pack of cigarettes and knocked one free and dug out a lighter, nodding coolly at what the other was elucidating at such length.

Pratt rested the camera on its back and the lens retracted with an efficient, robotic whine, and for another hour nothing of interest happened. An SUV came and went, followed by an Acura sports car, both staying less than five minutes. The gloaming pulled down its gray curtain, Pratt's stomach growling and his resolve to keep the watch flickering. A few laughing kids walked past. A woman with a basket of oranges bicycled through. Nothing, nothing, and nothing happened. And then a K-car—one of those bland driver's ed cars, like an unimaginative child's drawing of a car—caught Pratt's eye. It slowed down in front of Flave's and idled for a long moment. Late, pointless blinker, and then it pulled slowly into the circle drive. This was the kind of car Pratt needed, the kind you forgot even while you were looking at it. The door swung open with a grating creak that could be heard from the next block, and out came the driver in a brightly colored ball cap and jeans, his movements jerky and restless, arms held a few inches out from his body in the classic tough-guy posture. He twisted his hat on tighter. Started up the drive. Pratt raised the binoculars, and for a dizzy moment his eyes wouldn't believe what they saw. Western shirt, half-untucked. Boots. The sauntering gait up to the front entry. Before the man stepped up to the door, he turned, making sure the street was empty—outsize fishhook on the brim of his cap, horse-choking wad of tobacco jammed in his lower lip. Beady eyes. It was Nairn. None other than fucking Nairn. He was staring at the pad now, punching in the code. He extracted his dip, dredging it from his mouth with a stiff index finger, and flung it in the yard. Wiped the finger on the seat of his pants. Wiped his stupid Johnny Cash boots on the mat.

Pratt dropped the binoculars and fumbled the camera into position. Remembered he had to hit the power button. Waited a few seconds for it to wake up—an eternity—and make its noises and ready itself for duty. He aimed the thing, saw Nairn's sullen face in profile as he looked side to side, shuffling a little. Pratt snapped, snapped—you couldn't do it as fast as with a cheap camera. He needed only one picture to come out clear, one single image of the man and his surroundings, but he wouldn't know if any were good until he developed the film. He snapped again, his fingers clumsy, the door opening now. There was a thin glow from the streetlights, and now a little light from the foyer, but already Nairn was stepping away, into the house.

Pratt lowered the camera. It was like the gun, its weight perfect. He set it down gently on the passenger seat. His heart was pulsing like a jogger's, but not with fear. With what, then? If these photos turned out, he had something, didn't he? He had an asset. If they didn't, he was still leaving with knowledge—whatever it meant. He pulled the binoculars back up and, following his own stale protocol, scribbled the K-car's plate numbers on his notepad, the date and time. In big, dark letters, he added, *SLIMY GODDAMN SNAKE HILLBILLY*. Another two minutes and Pratt would've left. Another two minutes, he would've called it a night and missed the prize.

And now Pratt *was* leaving. He'd probably sat there too long already, and didn't need to be around when Nairn came back out. He shut off the radio. He'd left it on the whole time, and it had switched from the despairing guitar to airy desert flute music without his noticing. He three-point turned and got away from Flave's quiet headquarters and out of the neighborhood. Out on the four-lane road, one red stopped him, then another. What did it mean? Probably that Gianakos and Nairn were in bed. Those two were in it together is what it meant. Gianakos had no intention of putting Nairn away is what it meant. Pratt passed a nail salon, every detail inside lit as if for a TV show. He passed a hardware store with a bunch of wheel-barrows and shovels out front, one shovel leaning on each barrel, like you should buy them as a set. Nairn wasn't going to flip on Bonne—not publicly. Anyone who flipped had to watch his back forever. In reality, but secretly, Nairn had already flipped. Once Bonne was behind bars for life, Nairn, for appearances, would do a couple months—hell, a year—at some other prison, and then he'd pretend to have no choice but to find new employment. He'd be another victim of Pratt's singing. That's what it was meant to look like. Poor loyal Nairn, whose outfit had disappeared from beneath him, who now had to work for this upstart with a foolish name. It might even have been Nairn's and Flave's idea—they may have brought it to Gianakos. It was possible. And what about Roger? What would happen to him, the guy who actually was loyal, too loyal to risk involving in the plot? They'd get rid of him, of course, collateral damage—make it look like he'd moved away, disappeared into the American ether to dedicate himself fully to his studies.

Pratt heard himself chuckling aloud. He was driving ten under the limit, passing an unpretentious Mexican joint with hot peppers chalked onto its windows. A quickie oil change hut. Gianakos—Pratt didn't know whether to be more or less afraid of him now. Maybe the detective was as desperate as anybody in this whole mess. Gianakos was playing with losing his career, Nairn with losing his life. But if they won, they ran the county. Pratt was in possession of new knowledge, but he felt more like a pawn than ever. And yet somehow, underneath all that, witnessing Nairn in the act of treason had only strengthened his feelings of allegiance toward Bonne. The feelings were there, right in the middle of his chest. Bonne, this old man who had always done it the rightest way he could. This old man whose trust had been thrown away, like a spent lighter, by a backwoods dipshit with a dozen brain cells.

The car behind Pratt honked impatiently and he let himself drift into the turn lane, then pulled into a distant corner of a Kmart lot. He came to a stop under a huge, high rack of ballpark floodlights, bugs swarming up into the buzzing corona like sinners rushing the gates of heaven.

Nairn was going to keep giving Gianakos dirt he could use to scare Pratt, until Pratt finally flipped. That was the plan. Or part of it. What it probably meant was that Gianakos was correct when he'd predicted that Bonne's days were numbered, and that there'd be a wrong side to be on, if not necessarily a right side, not for Pratt, when the chips fell. A wrong side and a less wrong side.

The next day, Pratt didn't join the living until after ten. He was groggy, could barely open his eyes. He threw on the shirt he'd worn the day before and drove the Neon back to the rental place, the hot sun through the windows almost putting him to sleep behind the wheel. He had the AC pumping, getting what he could out of it for the last few minutes he possessed the car. Ten o'clock—it was the latest he'd slept since, well, since before prison, for sure. He hadn't drunk anything last night. He was just exhausted.

The same guy with the eyebrow ring was behind the desk. He looked the car over, marking things on his clipboard, collecting trash from the floorboards with a gloved left hand. Pratt put on his wasp-adorned sunglasses. He hadn't forgotten them.

"How do you know whether someone left the state," Pratt asked, "or just drove around a bunch inside the state?"

The guy looked up from poking around in the backseat. "Why, did you leave the state?"

"That's how?" Pratt said. "You ask?"

"I guess sometimes it's the honor system. Let me ask *you* a question. How'd you get it to actually smell like the dumpster behind a fast-food joint in here?"

"That's just what I smell like," Pratt said. "Always have."

The guy's pager went off. He unfolded himself from the car and stood up, held the gadget at eye level to see the number, registering no pleasure or displeasure at what he saw. He shut the door and leaned on the car, like a senior striking a pose in a high school movie.

"I guess you think you're smart for not getting the *in*surance. You think you outfoxed lady luck."

"Insurance again? I'm tired of talking about insurance."

"Luck runs out," the guy said. "Luck don't play nice."

"The answer is no, I don't think I'm smart."

"You do. You all do. And then I get to deal with everybody crying when I charge them for a dent—they don't want to pay forty dollars, and then they have to pay four hundred. I'm the one that delivers that news."

"Every job's got something wrong with it," Pratt said. "You're not supposed to complain about it to the customers."

"World full of things trying to ding you, and they think they're above it."

"You need a vacation," Pratt said.

"See, you *are* smart," said the guy, chuckling. "That's the smartest thing I heard all week."

* * *

Pratt methodically emptied the office supplies out of the old lady's oven. Big green file folders meant to be hung. Cases of colored pencils. A commercial-size box of paper clips as heavy as a brick. Excavated from the oven, the stuff took up a lot of space, further cramping the kitchen. How long had the lady not cooked anything in the oven? No cookies? No pies? Pratt took the measure of the control panel, found the right dials to fire the thing up. He peeked back inside—yes, the coils were turning red. And yes, he smelled that charred-dust scent, hot metal, old food that had fallen down into the element years ago.

He pulled a frozen pizza from the freezer, an icy disk, craggy as a mountain range on top, smooth as a beach on the bottom. He followed the directions, and in eighteen to twenty-two minutes was sitting at the little table, just enough room on it for a paper plate and a teacup of rum and Coke, chewing the salty triangles and staring at the old lady's hundreds of magnets. Still not awake. Feeling hypnotized. The lady had bought a magnet at every place she'd ever gone except the post office, and now that Pratt surveyed them, every single place was inside Florida. St. Augustine. Miami Beach. Mount Dora. Pratt had been to Mount Dora. There was no mount there. Cape Canaveral. Sanibel Island. Pratt was in the same boat. He'd never stepped foot outside Florida either. What he knew was the state's underfunded schools. Its potholed roads. Its weedy baseball diamonds. Its penitentiaries.

He reached for the bottle of rum, but once his hand was on it, he didn't want any more. He felt sick. It could've been the pizza, the grease and fake pepperoni, the cheap booze, or the recirculated condo air. It could've been how much sitting he'd been doing, sitting in hot cars and staring vacantly for hours. Too much thinking. Too much worrying.

He abandoned the pizza and dragged himself over to the couch, and soon his head nodded back onto the cushion, his eyelids heavy as sandbags. *Thwott* out on the golf course, then someone whistling. *Thwott*, then someone cursing. He was dreaming before he'd even fallen asleep, but the fact that he knew he was dreaming was no help. Where was he? He was at a fairground somewhere—those places felt dreamy and disorienting even in real life. He was wearing a mammoth sweatshirt, like an older brother's, but that was something he didn't have. A brother. A sister. He didn't even have a cousin. It had been cool earlier, but now the sun was gold-stamped on the sky. He was sweating. Thirsty. Pushing up the sleeves of the sweatshirt over and over instead of just peeling it off. He wasn't a little kid, but he wasn't grown either. He looked up at the people who passed. He'd arrived here with money—what had he spent it on? Rides? Thrills? He could see a Ferris wheel towering up into the brightness. He walked the same circuit again and again, past the games of skill and of chance, past the kiddie rides he was too big for, past the roller coasters he was afraid of. He was searching for his mother, but each woman he approached turned unfamiliar. It was always someone else's mother. This one with his mother's hair. This one with the same way of walking, the slight jounce on the balls of her feet, head held high as if searching a watery horizon. But maybe she didn't look like that anymore, after all these years. That was the problem—he didn't know what she looked like. The place was about to close, right in the middle of the day. People were heading toward the exits in their T-shirts and flip-flops, streaming around him. There had been something in the huge, stretchy front pocket of the sweatshirt, but it was gone. What the hell had it been? Something he'd won? Something he needed?

Pratt found himself back on the road three hours later, still sedate but now rested, staring from behind his sunglasses into an early sunset the color of a citrus dessert. The good old LeBaron. Low-slung seat. Wind whipping in from outside. He'd been snoring upright on the couch like a TV uncle on Thanksgiving, awakened by the determined ringing of the old lady's phone—loud, insistent, like someone clearing their throat to draw your attention. He'd leaned and stretched his arm around the brass lamp, disjointed dreams still flicking around in his head like when a movie reel snaps—something about a fair, something else about his fingers being rendered limp and useless. It was Kallie, the voice he knew so well but with extra bravado, saying Pratt was in luck, that she had the night free, that she'd canceled her other plans because she didn't want to pretend to be excited or impressed or have to rack her brain for things to talk about. She'd told Pratt not to dress like a slob, and right then he'd let himself down from the couch and, stretching the coiled, beige phone cord, slid over the carpet and started rummaging in the mess for his pinstripe sport coat.

"I'll have to cancel my date, too," Pratt had said. "Well, dates. I had two of them—a seven o'clock and another at ten."

He parked at the curb and walked onto Kallie's porch, and when she opened the door, he had to take a step back. She wore a satiny dress, her hair pinned up off her neck with a jade clasp. Earrings. Spike heels. The dress showed off her legs, her delicate collarbones. Even freshly showered and in his least worn polo and coat, Pratt felt woefully outmatched.

"You're taking me out," she said, then stood aside so he could enter. "Somewhere nice. Somewhere we probably don't belong."

All Pratt could manage to say was, "You look great," to which Kallie smirked and said that was the general idea. She said to give her two minutes and for Pratt to keep an eye on Joaquin because the sitter hadn't arrived.

She headed down the hall to do whatever else she thought she needed to do—Pratt couldn't imagine what—and he drifted toward the kitchen where he thought he heard Joaquin scuttling around on the linoleum with his toys. Yes, here the little guy was, sitting with his back against the wall, an open, innocent look on his face. He smiled when he recognized Pratt, and Pratt felt suddenly like an asshole for being so aloof. Pratt had given him nothing but bummer vibes, and Joaquin was ready to be his pal. What was Pratt going to do, literally turn his back on him? Walk out of the room? Only because Joaquin held a soft purple baseball could Pratt understand that he was saying "back and forth." Looking right into Pratt's eyes. He sighed and went down to a knee, and Joaquin pushed the ball from his chest with two hands. The squishy thing bounced once and rolled into Pratt's reach. It was slightly smaller than a real baseball, with the stitches painted on—still, it felt strange to Pratt to grip it, old muscle memory kindling in his wrist and elbow. He bounced it back to Joaquin and it landed in the boy's lap. Again, he pushed it away from him like a plate of food he didn't want. Pratt collected the ball and crouched next to Joaquin. He couldn't stand the kid not knowing how to throw. He grasped the ball and demonstrated the proper motion over and over, until he thought he could detect understanding in his pupil's eyes. He didn't know whether he was dealing with a righty or lefty—play the percentages, righty. He pressed the sphere into Joaquin's soft palm, wrapped the tiny fingers crosswise over the stitching. He raised Joaquin's arm, putting the ball above the child's ear, and then with his own arm emphatically repeated the tossing action. The boy dropped his hand, releasing the ball too late, and it bounced across the kitchen much the same as before. Pratt fetched it, set Joaquin up for another try. This time he held him by the forearm and showed him when to let go, and Joaquin's attempt was noticeably better, flying halfway across the room before it lost steam. Pratt fetched. Joaquin seemed pleased with himself, fascinated that he could cause the orb to soar so far. He hadn't been able to, and now he could. Pratt made a little pyramid out of some plastic rings, and Joaquin comprehended instantly. He threw the ball too softly the first time, then hard enough but off target. On his third try, he beaned the edifice squarely and the rings rolled off in different directions and wobbled to a stop in this corner and that. Joaquin was laughing triumphantly when Kallie clicked out from the hallway in her heels, holding an elegant-looking purse.

"Fantastic!" she said. "A new way to make a mess."

They went to a dimly lit Spanish restaurant perched on the top floor of a historic pink hotel. The walls were glass all around, one direction offering a view of the bay and the other showcasing the ritzy area off downtown St. Petersburg. Night was falling, erasing the distinction between land and water, the lights of the boats and buildings becoming one even smattering of diamonds on dark velvet. Pratt was stiff in his coat but would've felt underdressed without it. Kallie, on the other hand, kicked her shoes off under the table and breezily ordered herself a red wine, pronouncing—rightly or wrongly, Pratt had no idea—luxuriant foreign words. The waiter was better dressed than Pratt and smelled like lavender—or so he thought—and the crusty bread he brought them would've been worth the drive on its own.

"And for you, señor?"

"A rum and Coke would be great."

"Does señor have a preference of rum?"

"Señor better take the cheapest one you got," Pratt said. "Well, what the hell—give me the second-cheapest."

When they were alone again, Kallie said it had been forever since she'd been waited on. She was always waiting on somebody, Joaquin mostly, but nobody waited on her.

"I can't imagine," said Pratt. "I only have myself to wait on."

"That can be tough, too. Waiting on somebody who doesn't know what they want. A person could get old, waiting on you."

Pratt gave Kallie a look, and she met it with her own, franker expression. He went for his water, very cold even though it had no ice, but she left hers where it was and kept looking at him.

"So, who's this guy you had to cancel with?" he asked, and just asking the question made his ears hot. He had no right, he knew, to be jealous.

"Oh, we went out a couple times. He's okay. He's kind of a ... you think he's sensitive, but he's really a jerk. He's sensitive in a bad way. It's hard to explain."

"A sensitive jerk," Pratt said. "Okay."

"His name is Ferris. Like Bueller. He went to a college up north with about seventy students in it. He owns a store for outdoor gear: What's Mine Is Yurts."

"Yurts?"

"It's in New Tampa."

The waiter approached and set down their drinks, then wordlessly, with a slight bow, backpedaled away.

"Why haven't you been waited on, if you and Ferris went on dates?"

"I don't know. He likes to get street food, or else go to places where they don't speak English and hand your dinner out the window. Slumming, I guess. Or else the opposite—go out on a yacht and do the cooking himself."

"Why'd you go out with him in the first place?"

Kallie had a piece of bread spread with soft, warm butter raised partway to her mouth, but she stopped and held it there.

"Sorry," Pratt said. "Weird question."

"Yeah, it is a weird question," Kallie said.

"It's also kind of weird not to have an answer to it, though, right?"

Kallie took a bite of her bread, sampled her wine. "He was good-looking. He seemed nice. He asked. Why does anybody go out with anybody? Am I supposed to go out with nobody, like you?"

"Yeah, well, I guess I avoided the dating scene in Zephyrhills Correctional Institution."

"Oh, you avoided it before that. You'll try to keep avoiding it now that you're out."

Pratt took another gulp of his drink. It was crisp, the spice muted. Perfect amount of Coke.

"So, what happened?" he said. "What's the trouble with the handsome, small-college, sensitive jerk?"

"No problem," Kallie said. "I like him fine. It's just... it all feels like an act. Like, this *should* work, so let's both do our best to make sure it does. Like you're trying together to not let it fail."

"This is the sales pitch for dating? This is something you want me to go out and do?"

"I see your point," Kallie said.

Pratt finished off his drink, wondering if he was already feeling it. Kallie had more wine, savoring each sip, cradling the bowl of her glass beneath her chin like a delicate orchid someone had given her. That's what Pratt should've done, if he'd known the night would feel like this—he should've gotten her flowers.

"How's the bakery?" he asked.

"Good, I guess. They're giving me as many hours as I can handle. I guess that's a good thing."

"You're a hard worker," Pratt said.

"Harder than I'd like."

"When Joaquin gets older, he'll be proud of you."

"He better be."

"I'm proud of you, too," Pratt said. "I know that can't count for much."

Kallie didn't seem to know what to say to that. The meagerest sip of wine, just enough to see the color, sat in the bottom of her glass. She was about to tip it back, but a foghorn blared out in the harbor, like a warped tuba. Everyone in the restaurant looked in its direction—an ocean liner, a colossal cruise ship, gliding smoothly toward its big concrete berth. It was lit up like a birthday cake, enormous, a city that moved effortlessly around the world.

Pratt and Kallie didn't notice the waiter until their food was in front of them. Would señora like anything? Señor? No? *Disfrutar.* Pratt had known he couldn't go wrong with *bisteca*, and he hadn't. He sliced up the tender meat and piled the pillowy rice on it. Roasted peppers. Onions diced as small as sesame seeds.

"I wouldn't have guessed a few years ago my life would be what it is." Kallie had flipped her snapper over and found the succulent underbelly, was getting at it one tiny bite at a time. "But here we both are. Together. I've got Joaquin. You've got your freedom."

"You had plans and they changed. Me, I never even had a plan, I guess."

Kallie sat up straighter. In the dim lighting, she looked vulnerable, her fingers delicate on her wineglass. "The thing in common is Matty. My wrecked plan and your no plan."

Pratt must have flinched, because she pushed a stray lock of hair behind her ear and said, "I'm not going to tiptoe around him. I'm not going to keep living with a handicap like that."

Pratt nodded. He didn't think of Matty's memory as a handicap. More like a cloud, a dark cloud the sun never quite found its way through.

"We need new plans," Kallie said. "Especially you."

"You don't know how right you are," he answered.

"What does that mean?"

"Nothing. Just… you're right. I need to stop crisscrossing. I need to pick a lane and hit the gas."

The light in the restaurant was dying. It felt like Pratt and Kallie were floating on their own raft, the other tables drifting off into a fog. Pratt's head was swimming—the alcohol, the mention of Matty, Kallie's lips against the rim of her glass.

The plates disappeared. Instead of dessert, here was another round of drinks. Pratt took a greedy pull. The second-worst stuff this place carried was the best he'd ever had.

"I'm going to tell you something," he said.

"Wow, what's the occasion?" said Kallie.

"Something I never told anybody."

Kallie had been gazing at her swirling wine, but now her face sobered, her eyes finding his.

"It was Matty's fault," Pratt said. "It was all Matty's fault we got busted at the warehouse."

Kallie set her glass down. Pulled it out of the way by its stem. "You mean, why you went to jail?"

"Prison," Pratt said. "Yes." He set his glass aside, too. "The official story was I got tailed. I wasn't paying attention. Like, it was my fault, so I take the fall. That's not what happened. It was his fault. A hundred percent."

Kallie stared at Pratt with her dark eyes. The look on her face didn't match the defeat in her voice when she said, "I guess that's not a surprise."

"His fucking side deals." Pratt looked around and lowered his voice. "He was selling a little here, a little there. You knew about that. Well, that night it wasn't a little here and there. He was getting five hundred pills, stolen straight from a pharmacy. We were moving this rare Mustang from down by Temple Terrace. Matty didn't want anybody to recognize his car or my car. He wanted to do it with the Mustang. The guy he was buying from is the one who got tailed." Pratt was sweating under his coat. He tipped his glass, emptying the rest of the silky liquor down into himself. He hoped the waiter would come with another drink, and also hoped he wouldn't. "The guy didn't have the stuff," Pratt said. "Dude was there empty-handed. He was scared—he thought we were going to lose our shit. He said he could meet later that night, he needed a couple hours. Find out later, there'd been a cop on the guy all day. Tampa cop watching the whole thing. He called the Mustang in—bam, stolen. We're driving this car around—there's like three of them in the whole Southeastern United States."

Pratt paused. He'd never let a drop of this go, and now it was gushing out of him. Kallie's eyes had gone blank. Pratt wondered if she still thought it was a good idea not to tiptoe around Matty.

"He thought he could keep doing anything," she said, half-whispering. "Anything he wanted forever and ever."

Pratt didn't see the waiter anywhere. He crunched the ice at the bottom of his glass. "The road into that warehouse is a mile long. Once you're on it, there's nowhere to go. As soon as I saw running lights behind us, I knew we were cooked. Checkmate."

Pratt's fist was clenched on the table, and Kallie reached and rested her hand on top of it. Her fingers were neither cool nor warm—she and Pratt were the same temperature.

"I didn't think about it," Pratt said. "I kicked him out of the car. I gunned it around a couple curves, then slowed down enough for him to roll out into the woods. It made sense. Why should both of us go down? I was driving. I was so used to..."

"I get it," Kallie said. "I know what you were used to."

"It didn't seem like it mattered whose fault it was. It did, though. It did matter. That might've been exactly what he needed, getting locked up. That might've been his only hope."

"Jesus, Pratt, you're the one who did the sentence. You don't need to keep what-if-ing. You don't need to feel sorry for Matty."

"I guess I feel sorry for him *and* for me," Pratt said.

Kallie pulled her hand back from his. "Does Bonne know?" she asked.

Pratt shook his head.

"He doesn't know his grandson exists, and he doesn't know the truth about the son he lost. The guy who knows everything about everything."

"Ratting on a dead guy to the dead guy's father?" Pratt said. "No, thanks."

"Risking Joaquin getting mixed up in a story like you just told— no, thanks to that, too."

The waiter gently approached their table and rested the check between them in its heavy leather booklet. The restaurant was closing. Had closed. The staff was waiting for Pratt and Kallie to leave so they could turn on the lights and break the spell and start cleaning. Pratt said thank you, but the waiter was already gone. He got out his wallet and started counting out bills, overtipping because he didn't want to wait for change, the dinner so expensive that the cost seemed meaningless, like the money Pratt was forking over was from a board game.

On the ride to the beach, they smoked cigarettes. Kallie hadn't had one since before she was pregnant. She'd come across the pack in the back of a drawer, looking for a calculator. The LeBaron's red-coil lighter, they found, worked. The Marlboros were probably stale, but neither Pratt nor Kallie could tell. After the first two puffs they were lightheaded, letting the warm air from outside wash over them. It smelled like gasoline and the sea and wilting wildflowers.

"I've got a model duplex-mate, starting about a week ago." Kallie had let her seat back a few clicks, her head lolling, her cigarette hand hanging out the open window. "I guess you don't know anything about that turn of events."

"Me?" Pratt said. "No, not a thing. Maybe he got religion."

"Maybe," said Kallie. "Doesn't seem like the type, but I guess you never can tell."

Pratt took another drag off his cigarette. His lungs felt scraped out, but he was going to smoke every bit of it. "Sometimes loud music at all hours is just a cry for help."

"His friends were getting rowdy on the porch the other day, and he scolded them like a den mother."

"Wow." Pratt shook his head, flicked his butt out onto the road-side. "It's a mystery."

He slowed the car near the low dunes at the deserted end of Blue Rocks Beach, and Kallie told him to hurry up and park already, that she wanted to get in the water. The moment they stopped, she was up and out of the LeBaron, shoes abandoned on the floorboard. In the rearview, Pratt saw her prancing on the balls of her feet past clumps of sea oats that sprang from the soft white ridges. He hopped out, too, hurrying to keep up, shucking his coat after all these hours and dropping it in the driver's seat. He jogged toward the Gulf and its hushed, unscrolling waves, his steps dissolving in the sugary sand. When he came down onto the packed flats, he saw her, already in up to her knees, staring out toward the lonely barges that may as well have been towns on a lost prairie.

Pratt threw off his shoes and socks and walked up slowly beside her, feeling almost that he shouldn't disturb her. The water was a shade cooler than a bath, the gentle breakers tugging at their legs without much conviction. Kallie didn't look at him, but she reached out for his hand.

"No stars," she said.

Pratt reached across with his free arm and brushed the hair away from her face, the thick locks escaping the jade clasp. She wasn't sad. She wasn't dreamy.

"They're there," he said. "Sometimes they stay hidden till nobody's looking."

"Well, I guess I'll look at you instead."

Pratt swallowed hard, then he leaned and kissed Kallie's smooth shoulder. Her skin smelled like the night sea, only cleaner, more alive. She shivered, squeezing a couple of his fingers together so hard it hurt. Pratt was going to get something he wanted. That hadn't happened to him in a while. Something he'd wanted for a long time. And for the moment, the reasons he *shouldn't* have it had slipped off where they couldn't be found, where they wouldn't answer if called.

Kallie turned toward him. The caress of her palm on his jaw made him dizzy. She was smiling like somebody with news they had no business knowing. She was on her toes, kissing him on the cheek and saying why don't we go use those dunes like they were intended. Then she was dragging her feet through the fans of surf, making small tracks in the looser sand, her hand up behind her, tugging on the zipper of her dress.

On the drive back to the duplex, the car was filled with an awkward tension that the wind couldn't blow away. To have anything but pure fondness, unexploited tenderness, between them—it was so foreign, neither of them knew what to do. At a stoplight, they lunged toward each other and kissed in desperation, but since it didn't help, it made things worse. They commented on the thunder they heard from some distant kingdom of the yet starless sky. They remarked on places they passed that they'd frequented back in high school. Everything was closed but a diner here and there, but they were far from hungry. Pratt could feel the sand in his shoes, gritty when he pressed the gas, the brake. He stole glances at Kallie out of the corner of his eye—her dress wasn't quite straight, and she held her high heels in her lap like someone might hold a kitten. The rotten facts that had been hiding were back out in the open. Pratt couldn't get involved with Kallie as long as he was caught up in this Malloy and Bonne business. This Gianakos and Nairn business. He couldn't drag her into all that. And then there was Matty. There would always be Matty. They'd convinced themselves he could be dealt with and left in the past, but of course that would never be true. He would always be dead, and Pratt could never replace him. Even if he wanted to. Even if Kallie wanted him to. The whole thing was snakebit with guilt and regret, the venom everlasting. Matty had been the first love, the best friend more like a brother—those truths couldn't change.

The drive took forever, and yet once they were in Kallie's neighborhood, Pratt felt rushed. Once he dropped her off, it would all feel irreversible. He stopped at the curb. Got out and walked around and opened her door. He couldn't walk her to the porch. He just couldn't. They both leaned halfway for a stiff hug—it was Pratt's fault; he was the stiff one, he could feel it. Kallie seemed to stall a minute, hoping, but whatever it was she wanted, Pratt couldn't deliver, and then she was saying she had better go in and relieve the babysitter, that they were way late getting back. He said he'd be in touch and she nodded. She slipped her shoes on and marched up the walk, gave him a little wave once she had the key in the door, a forced smile, much worse to see than if she'd been crying or pouting or spitting mad.

* * *

Pratt headed back in the direction of his condo, but on a random whim, he turned. He sat at a green light until it was yellow, then finally noticed and rolled through. The streets were empty, no one to honk at him. He didn't care where he went, and after some minutes found himself in a little enclave he recognized from his childhood called Elmer, a place where time had stopped, a place passed over by the bullying rush of the future. It was like a movie set—the big, white-steepled church and quaint corner stores. Except it wasn't a rich person's re-creation. It was ragged around the edges, showing its cracks. It needed a good weeding and a fresh coat of paint. When Pratt came upon the crumbling lane that comprised the town center, something was different than he recalled. Something wasn't right. He slowed the LeBaron to a crawl right in the middle of the road. As soon as he swiveled his head, he knew what was missing. The cane farm. There used to be a half acre of sugarcane clacking when the wind blew. And a pennant-festooned barn out front for visitors. The old couple who ran it gave tours to kids who stopped in. They'd had a big press they'd crank up upon request. Pratt remembered—his parents had brought him several times, right here, except right here wasn't here anymore. *Here* was a bunch of empty steel cages, a disused kennel of some sort, the doors of the tiny jail cells wagging open. Pratt remembered the heavy, fresh wands the old man would hand out, big as your arm, to be carried around and gnawed the rest of the day. He remembered the clay-colored cat that would rub its head against your leg until you petted it. All gone, wiped out for junk. The old couple had passed, and who wanted a tiny canebrake you could barely make a living from? A floodlight hung on a diseased live oak, casting a sick yellow pall over all of it. The wheel of a bicycle leaned against the fence, the rest of the bike nowhere to be seen.

Pratt lifted his foot and the car rolled toward the flashing light ahead, bugs swarming in the beams of his headlights. Some of the good things in the world went away while you weren't around, slipped off into the fog because no one cared to defend them. And some good things, Pratt thought, you reached right in and destroyed with your own stupid hands. You couldn't help yourself and you busted them into a million pieces. Pratt raised both arms and pounded down on the steering wheel. What a goddamn idiot he was. He could never have been Kallie's big love, and now he wouldn't be her friend either. Not like he had been. It wouldn't be the same. The two of them had screwed up. They'd ruined something great. They'd screwed up and now Pratt, who hadn't had much, had a lot closer to nothing at all.

He beat his record, staying in bed until 10:30, not really sleeping, his dreams just briny clouds passing through his mind. He wanted out of the condo but did not want back in the LeBaron, didn't want to be anywhere he had any business being. He put his shoes on and went outside into the blinding chorus of sun and heat, and instantly sweat dripped off his forehead. Instead of toward the road, he wandered deeper into the complex. He passed the clubhouse where people sold Tupperware and makeup. Passed the big square pool, the whole thing four feet deep. The windblown bocce and shuffleboard courts. When he reached the back row of condos, he kept on going, tromping through high weeds and down into a shallow gully. He hopped a ditch of stagnant runoff and emerged up onto an anonymous residential street where oak branches rested on the low roofs and one stamp of yard blended in with the next, no hedges or fences. He hadn't been hungry, but now he smelled the barbecue grills. Cookouts, three to a block, fleets of minivans and rodent-colored sedans, gangs of kids chasing each other in circles. More on the next block. More on the next. White. Black. Caribbean. Filipino. The hamburger smoke hung thick on the air, pulled around in swirls by the breeze. He kept on, the neighborhoods growing better tended, the houses newer and broad-windowed, the lawns sprinkled and the children in bright, unwrinkled clothes. Some of the porches were festooned with banners—when Pratt got close enough, he understood: *Home of the World's Best Dad*; *Free Beer for Great Dads*; *Parking for Dad of the Year Only.*

Pratt crossed the street as he approached each new get-together, giving the celebrants their space. Pool-party cookouts. Church-clothes cookouts. Smiling men, young and old, slapping each other on the shoulders. At one house, a canvas pavilion had been pitched in the grass, a TV set up inside—it was a World Cup game, the United States versus, it looked like, Iran. Pratt imagined everyone in Iran gathering with their families around television sets, too, whatever time it was over there.

When he passed out of the residential zone into a series of business parks dominated by credit unions and insurance offices, everything went silent. He was on a walkabout, like Gianakos had said that day. He thought about his parents, their attitude about holidays. They hadn't cared about decorating, about eating specific foods on Christmas or even Thanksgiving, but his father had always made a production out of Mother's Day, and his mother did the same on Father's Day. It wasn't for them, Pratt understood. All the fuss—the trip to the beach with an expensive brunch, the list each parent would read of all the caring deeds the other had done in the past year—the fuss was for Pratt, to make sure he was properly grateful, to keep him from getting spoiled. They'd polish off their baby back ribs and Greek potatoes, and then Pratt's father would lead him into the shallows and teach him the different types of crabs and search for stingrays and watch out past the sandbar for the cresting roll of dolphins. They always saw one. At least one. Tony was with his dad right now, of course, and probably his mom, too, since their divorce was going so well. No beer, but Tony would've whipped up some top-of-the-line lemonade with mango or whatever in it. Kallie was with her dad, over at his double-wide, both of them tired, both of them fondly watching Joaquin and not talking much, both a little distracted, Kallie's distraction caused perhaps by heartsick thoughts of Pratt—he hoped so and he hoped not.

Walking up onto his porch, parched after his excursion, Pratt stopped short at the sight of an envelope taped to his door. Unlabeled white business envelope, one strip of fat, clear tape. He pulled it free without ripping it, looked at both blank sides—weightless, sharp-cornered. Somehow, he knew it wasn't from the Cypress Plantation management. It also wasn't an ad. He ran his finger under the flap and tore it open and pulled out a single sheet of yellow legal paper. When he unfolded it, he saw a lone name in blue ballpoint, the penmanship unharried but not too careful either.

Kalliope Pappas

Nothing else, just the name. No cursive in the writing, no loop or style.

Pratt turned around and leaned his back against the door, the envelope and legal sheet pinched lightly between two fingers, both arms hanging limp. His head was not spinning. Not this time. Pratt understood. Gianakos had tried to be reasonable, and now he was taking a different tack. He'd decided maybe Pratt didn't care enough about his *own* well-being. He was giving the carrot a break and bringing out a bigger stick. Pratt should've expected this, and maybe deep down he had. Desperate, the cop? It seemed so. And therefore dangerous? Had to assume yes. He was going all in on his hand, and probably Gianakos himself didn't know if he was bluffing. Gianakos didn't know exactly how much he could pressure Pratt, exactly how hard he could push him. He did need Pratt—Nairn would never agree to the starring role. Nairn was an asshole, but he wasn't a sucker.

Pratt peeled off his sopping shirt and dropped it at his feet on the doormat. He looked at the writing on the paper again. Kallie. Her full first name. Her last name. Just two words. He lowered the sheet, then let it slip from his fingers and float soundlessly to the beaten green carpet of the porch.

Monday morning. The rest of the world getting on with their normal jobs. Pratt foraged in the kitchen for a miniature cherry pie and brought it to the living room and sat on the couch's open spot. Through the window, he saw the first elderly golfers of the day. He sat there for twenty minutes, watching one foursome after another struggle through. He witnessed one guy look around slyly and kick his ball out of the rough. Saw another guy injure himself, grunting a swing through the high weeds and then walking back to the fairway with one arm hanging limp. Malloy was arriving at his office about now, but nothing would be gained watching the accountant proceed through the same Monday as always. Or maybe Pratt was lazy, too unprofessional to cross his *t*'s even when his life depended on it.

The phone rang and Pratt's leg flinched, his foot kicking one of the old lady's boxes hard enough to make a tinkling sound. Pratt listened to ring after ring, perfectly still, like if he moved the person calling would know he was home, and then he heard Tony's voice on the machine. He hadn't heard from Pratt all weekend, he said. Hoped he was doing okay. He reminded Pratt it wasn't too late to get on the baseball team, then said, "All right, man," left a moment of dead air, and hung up. Pratt didn't know why he hadn't picked up, unless he was tired of disappointing Tony, tired of being reminded by Tony that he was disappointing. He hadn't answered when Tony called just now and he hadn't called Kallie yesterday, even though, for more than one reason, he damn well should've.

Pratt made a fist—it felt light, weightless. The thought of rum ran through his mind. He needed to take the edge off. It wasn't close to noon no matter how you looked at it, but really, what did that rule have to do with Pratt? He hoisted himself up, wiped his pie-sticky hands clean on his shorts. He started making his way toward the kitchen, toward his one-bottle minibar, but then the doorbell sounded, like the strangled call of some ungainly bird, and Pratt froze where he was. The bell sounded again and he stalked over on the balls of his feet, realizing, as he did so, that if the person knew his car, then they knew he was here. He brought his eye slowly to the peephole. Okay, whoever this distorted form in the blue-tinted haze was, it was nobody Pratt knew. It was a woman, maybe fifty—at least a decade too young to be a neighbor. She didn't look like a Jehovah's Witness, in her green jeans and polka-dot blouse. She wasn't holding pamphlets or a petition. He flipped the lock and cracked the door enough to stick his head out, asked the woman what he could help her with.

"I'm Lulu," she said.

"Lulu?" It sounded vaguely familiar.

"You're Pratt Zimmer, right?"

"I suppose," he said.

"I'm your landlady. From Delaware."

"Oh," said Pratt. "Oh, okay."

"Sorry I didn't call first." The woman, Lulu, had plum-streaked hair and wore hiking boots. Her eyes went big and round when she spoke and then slitted when she listened, back and forth, like a child's eyes.

"No, that's fine. It's your house." Pratt was shirtless, wearing shorts and, he noticed now, one sock. "Let me just... did you want to come in or... well, yeah, I guess you'd want to come in."

"I think you'll be happy if I do," she said.

Pratt looked at her.

"Oh, no, jeez—not like that. I'm here to clear out my mom's stuff. If this is a good time. Sorry, didn't mean to..."

"It's a good time," Pratt told her. "Give me two minutes, okay?"

Pratt left the door not quite closed and went back and yanked on a shirt and brushed his teeth fast and hard, pressed his slept-on hair into shape with his palms. He stepped over to the nightstand and opened the drawer, took the gun and ammo out and slid them deep under the mattress. He wasn't going to bother making the bed. Wasn't going to straighten up. There was so much shit everywhere, in every room of the condo, what difference would a little straightening make—and anyway, only a fraction of the shit was his.

He went back out through the kitchen and pulled the door open and stepped aside, arm held out like an usher, and Lulu tentatively placed one foot inside the condo and then the other, her boots making no sound at all against the linoleum. Her lips were already a hard line of apprehension, but when she saw the state of the kitchen, the rest of her face hardened to match. With an air of stoicism, she told Pratt she was sorry about all this, her eyes creeping over the rise-and-fall topography of the clutter. She said it again, this time with even less feeling, that she was sorry, and Pratt told her he didn't like to cook anyway, and that he didn't entertain much. Lulu proceeded to the main room, her bearing grave and resigned, and Pratt quickly pulled Gianakos' card from beneath the napkin holder and pocketed it. When he joined Lulu in the living room, their elbows touching for lack of space, she seemed paralyzed.

"I didn't know it was this bad," she said.

"I'm used to it," said Pratt. "Kinda."

"It's been four years since I stepped foot in here. Well, five. There was no funeral, really. Just a little service up north with her ashes. I couldn't come down then. The place wasn't like this last time I saw it. It wasn't great, but it wasn't like *this*."

Pratt didn't know what to say. She was apparently feeling guilty, and guilt wasn't something other people could really help alleviate, Pratt had learned.

"I was at a wedding in Sanibel," Lulu said. "I figured I might as well take care of this. Take it all to the Salvation Army or whatever. There's no one else to do it."

"Right," said Pratt.

"I rented a van. I should've rented a U-Haul."

Lulu drifted deeper into the room like someone under a spell, wiping dust off statuettes with her finger, lifting the lids of bins and letting them fall shut again. "We were close when I was young," she said. "We used to get along. It wasn't only her fault how it all changed. It was my fault, too. Sorry, geesh, you don't need to hear this."

She edged over to a hulking wooden hutch Pratt had left untouched, parted its glass doors and picked up one of the safari figurines inside. She put it back down and picked up a decorative spoon, then a frosted wineglass. She opened the drawers one at a time, each giving a little squeak of protest. Souvenir smashed pennies. A magnifying glass in its own special case.

"When she was my age, she was perfectly normal. It makes you scared to think what's in your *own* future."

"Everybody's got their thing," Pratt told her equably. "Their silly thing they do to get by." He never had occasion to speak to women this age, probably just a bit younger than his mother would've been. Pratt could only guess by looking at Lulu that she was more lost now than at any other time in her life.

"Why don't you sit a minute?" he said, and she nodded and followed the advice, stepping over to the couch and lowering herself into the single spot. She sat there, knees together, hands in her lap, head bowed slightly forward.

"I know what I need to do—I just can't do it," she said. "I don't mean to be wasting your morning."

"Wasting mornings is one of my specialties," said Pratt.

Lulu picked something off her jeans, closed her eyes a moment. "It feels mean, like I'm getting the last word or something. To haul all her treasures off. To her they were treasures."

"That's always the way," Pratt said. "One man's... you know."

"It's not like I hate the woman. I love her. I don't want to insult her memory. She was a good mother when it counted. She worked hard. She got crazy after the divorce and crazier after I left for college, and then she was here for thirty years." She waved her hand toward the whole of the condo. "Thirty years. They didn't slip by, but they didn't take three decades either."

Pratt was looming over Lulu, no place to back up to. He knew he'd never find the right thing to say, and also knew there was no way this woman was getting all this shit out of this condo today. He looked out the window—a high school kid was tinkering with a stalled golf cart, had the thing tipped over on its side.

"This is out of the blue," Pratt said, only realizing what he was saying as he was saying it, "but could I offer you a rum and Coke? I find them helpful when nothing else seems to be working."

Now Lulu looked up. She chuckled with patronizing amusement, like a dance club bouncer at the sight of a five-dollar bill. Pratt could do it when he wasn't trying, make people laugh. Lulu looked at her watch, then threw up her open palms, a gesture that meant she'd try anything at this point.

Pratt maneuvered to the kitchen and got two cups down, plinked ice into them, pulled over the liquor and unscrewed the cap on the Coke. As he poured the drinks, it struck him that he and his guest had the same problem. He didn't want *his* parents' stuff either. The sight of it, every time his eyes fell that way, depleted him. It didn't remind Pratt of his mother and father in any good way; it only reminded him they were dead. What's more, his parents wouldn't have wanted their old possessions sitting around forever, in the way, a burden. They wouldn't want Pratt to cart around these objects that could never stand for their lives anyway. That was most of the reason they'd put instructions in their will to be cremated, he knew. They didn't want there to be some sad plot of land Pratt would be forced to visit, that he'd feel guilty not visiting, always dragging himself back to some flower-scattered couple acres that in time would have a freeway rushing past it.

Pratt brought the drinks carefully over to the couch, the little lavender-hued cups already sweating. He handed one off to Lulu and she immediately took a sip, holding the cup by its finger loop daintily but making no face, not at the teacup or the taste of its stiff contents. She said thank you and smiled half-heartedly and drew her free hand underneath the cup like a saucer.

"I think maybe we can help each other out," Pratt said.

Lulu looked at him steadily. She didn't wear glasses or a single piece of jewelry or anything in her hair. She didn't even have a purse. She was the opposite of her mother, the opposite of a hoarder.

JOHN BRANDON

"Here's the trade," Pratt said. "Even up. You get rid of these boxes right here..." He pointed up and down the stack of boxes that had come from the storage unit, battered from when he'd kicked them, the top one an inch from the ceiling. "You take those with you in the van—except the top one, it's got most of my clothes in it—and I'll take care of all this stuff your mom left. Simple as that. You scratch my back, I'll scratch yours."

Lulu cocked her head to the side, making a face like Pratt was a simpleton.

"I'm serious," Pratt said. "I'll even find a good home for some of it."

"It's too much," Lulu said, scoffing. "It's not fair. And it's crazy, anyway." She was shaking her head, but she stopped in order to take a bigger sip of her drink. "It's not right," she said. "It's not your responsibility."

"Look," Pratt said. "It's not your fault your mom left so much, and it's not my fault mine left so little, but neither of them wants us carrying this crap around the rest of our lives."

"Your mom is..."

"Yeah, she's dead, too."

"Shit," Lulu said. "I'm sorry."

Pratt drained the rest of his rum in one pull, then set the cup somewhere without looking. "It happened a long time ago."

"That's her things?"

"And my dad's. And some of it's mine, but I don't want it anymore."

"Your dad, too? Jesus."

"They died in an accident when I was young."

Lulu raised her teacup and finished it all at once, like Pratt had. Now she made a face. Determination showed in it more than anything else. "I'm supposed to leave with a stranger's family heirlooms? Leave all my mother's stuff behind?"

204

"You can call it heirlooms, but it's crap," Pratt said. When Lulu didn't respond, he said, "And yes, we're supposed to do each other a favor here. That's what we're supposed to do."

Lulu slowly scanned the room, looked down at her lap and then up at the ceiling, as if searching for another argument to make. She wasn't going to find one. All she had was her empty cup.

"Another rum and Coke?" Pratt said. "They're really small."

When his landlady's rented van disappeared from sight, a wave of panic washed over Pratt. The boxes were gone. Out of his hands. Deleted from his life. A woman he'd met an hour ago was going to do God-knew-what with them. But then the worry subsided as fast as it hit, a quickly receding tide that withdrew and left Pratt slightly unnerved but mostly just hot and hungry. He'd solved a problem. He'd hatched a good idea and put it into action, and now he had to live with it. And anyway, he had another problem to deal with. Even if he dreaded calling Kallie because of what had happened over the weekend, he had no choice but to warn her about what he'd found on his door. The envelope. Her name. He should've called yesterday. Should've called Saturday night. She was probably sleeping now, but that was just another excuse not to pick up the phone. There would always be an excuse. He didn't think Gianakos would do anything to seriously hurt Kallie, but he didn't want that psycho harassing her in any way, talking to her, watching her.

He sat down on the available sofa cushion, where he could still smell Lulu Stamper's perfume, a scent like gentle rain, and got hold of the phone and punched in Kallie's number. Listened to it ring and ring—yes, he was waking her up—until on the seventh appeal he heard her pick up and heard, "Yeah, Kallie here," her voice drowsy and impatient.

"Who is this?" she said, when he didn't say anything.

"Me," said Pratt.

He heard her exhale into the receiver.

"It's Pratt."

"I know who 'me' is," she said.

He could hear her sitting down at her kitchen table, could hear the creaking.

"Sorry to wake you up."

"Yeah, well..."

Pratt had only her tone to go by. There was something in it besides annoyance. Something more supple.

"I'm not only sorry for that," he said. "I'm sorry about the other night. I mean, I'm not *sorry*, but—"

"I'm glad you called," Kallie said. "I could've called, too, but I didn't. I'm glad you did. Look, Pratt, we made a mistake, but I think it's the two of us that get to decide the punishment. I don't think there's anyone else to judge us. That's what I've been thinking. I'm thinking we could take it easy on ourselves."

"A slap on the wrist?" Pratt said. He was untangling and untangling the phone cord. It was so twisted, and he never talked on it.

"I know we can't be together that way, the way we wanted, but... I'm glad you called."

It felt like Pratt's turn to say something, but a lump was in his throat. He was thinking of Kallie trotting off ahead of him into the dunes, her hand groping her back for the zipper of her dress. He was thinking of her playing soccer in high school, chopping the tall girls down with shrewd slide tackles. He was thinking of the way Joaquin looked at her. Her stupid little bed in the living room.

"Kallie," he said.

"Yes?"

"There's something else I need to tell you."

Now it was her turn to be quiet.

"I'm just gonna say this."

"Please do."

"You need to go somewhere for a couple days. Till the end of the week, maybe. You need to be somewhere. You need to be where nobody knows you're there. You and Joaquin."

"Go somewhere? Jesus, Pratt." Now she was standing. Pratt could hear it. "Go somewhere?"

"I know there's nothing I can say, but I'll fix this. I promise I'll fix it."

Kallie clicked her tongue. "Bonne?" she said.

"Sort of," Pratt answered.

"Fucking Bonne?"

"It has to do with Bonne, but he's not the reason you have to go. Bonne has no idea about you. I'm trying to get clear of the guy, but it's not that simple. I'm—it's just, it's a mess. I mean, a lot of it's not even Bonne's fault. It is, but it's not. He's... I'm all he has left. I'm the closest thing he has to family."

"I'm sure it's a mess," Kallie said. "No debate there."

"I can't believe I let you get involved in this. I'm so sorry."

"I have to work, Pratt." Now he could hear her making tea. The idea of Kallie going back to sleep was blown out of the water. "I can't go hide somewhere and not go to work."

"I really don't think you should. Just this week. You and Joaquin and your dad, go to a hotel out on the beach. Use your vacation days. I'll pay for the hotel. I'll pay the whole thing. Tell me which hotel you pick, and I'll take care of it."

"Vacation days," Kallie said. "You're cute."

Right. Kallie wouldn't have vacation days. Wouldn't have sick days. And paying for a hotel for the better part of a week would more or less wipe Pratt out. What did it matter? He'd be broke soon enough anyway. He'd been right to think he should steer clear of Kallie, to not allow his life and hers to overlap, right to think his presence was poison.

"All right," Kallie said, sounding more defeated than he'd ever heard her. "We'll go to the beach."

"Go right away," Pratt said. "Go right now. I'll fix this. I'll fix everything."

"Let's get off the phone then, I guess."

"Yeah, we better." Pratt glanced out the window. A low-flying prop plane was dragging a sign through the sky that read AUTO ACCIDENT? CALL 1-800-JUSTISS. "It sounds corny," he told Kallie, "but check in under a fake name. Leave a message on my machine with the name of the hotel, so I can get in touch."

Kallie didn't answer that. He couldn't hear any sounds from her end. "Don't get yourself hurt, Pratt Zimmer. I don't ask much, but I'm requesting that you don't get hurt. That one request. If you think you have amends to make, that's how you can make them."

Pratt wanted something real to eat, and he needed out of the condo. He couldn't think in the clutter. The bar up the street would open soon. If he walked there, the door would be unlocked when he arrived. And so he walked. And the door was indeed open. The place was empty. Not even the bartender was in sight. Pratt stood there a minute—when no one came out, he stepped around and poked his head in the back room. He saw the tank-topped proprietor wrestling cases of tallboys from a cooler. "Morning," Pratt called. He ordered his cheeseburger and the man gave a thumbs-up and kept at his work.

Pratt went back out and found a booth in the back corner, sat down and pushed the plastic ashtray against the wall. A song by the Doors was playing, one where the singing was somber. Pratt's father had loved the Doors. His uncle had liked Creedence Clearwater Revival. Pratt didn't know what music he himself liked. Maybe that was something you figured out when you were older, when the world had changed and the new music didn't make sense to you.

Pratt took a survey of the barroom and saw, on a nearby table, a big leather book, closed, its place held by a yellow pencil sharpened with a pocketknife. The author's name on the spine was Russian. Just as Pratt was deciding it must be the bookish bartender's, he heard boot landings from near the restrooms and turned his head to see Roger emerge, tugging his rolled sleeves into place. At the same time Roger appeared, the bartender saw fit to show himself. Roger paused briefly and asked for a Scotch and black coffee, then strode over to the jukebox and dropped in some quarters. The first Doors song ended and another started. On the way back to his table, Roger noticed Pratt—without any acknowledgment or hitch in his step, he altered his course and came and sat himself down on the other side of the booth. His posture was ramrod straight, and Pratt felt himself sitting up straighter to match. Roger didn't speak right away. He put a meaty fist on the tabletop and rested the other atop it, like he was gripping an invisible bat.

"Mixed together?" Pratt said. "Or a Scotch and then a coffee?"

Roger didn't need to answer. Here came the bartender, who set down one steaming mug and one tumbler with a generous pour of whisky. He asked if Pratt wanted a rum and Coke, remembering his customer's order from a single previous visit, and Pratt nodded.

When the guy was gone, Roger took a sip of each of his beverages. He placed the coffee in front of him and the Scotch to the side. "I come here when I don't want to feel like the universe is getting bigger," he said. "They say it's always expanding, but I don't follow that. I don't know what that means. It's the universe. It's already everything. What's the point of zoning off the new and old parts of an abyss?"

Pratt was looking at Roger's scarred fists. "Maybe the universe is, like, something," he tried, "and the void the universe is inside of is nothing."

"If one's nothing," Roger said, "the other's nothing. How does airless space fill up airless space? I guess maybe I don't have a mind for science. With science, the more you learn, the more you doubt yourself."

"As opposed to?" said Pratt.

Roger grinned, like Pratt had made a witty remark, and then the bartender was back already, thank goodness, with Pratt's drink. He set it down and retreated to his customary spot, staring into a book at the end of the bar. Pratt wondered if there was someone else in the back to make his burger. It was more like a library at the moment, this place, than a drinking establishment.

"People want a border," Roger said. "The entropy. The wandering. They want it contained."

Pratt took a swig of his cocktail and felt it trickle inside him. The singer from the Doors was in an exalted mood now, letting out joyous yawps.

"How come you do it?" Pratt asked, figuring he might as well try. He gave a nod that vaguely indicated the world outside the bar.

"What, philosophize? Navel-gaze?"

"The business," said Pratt.

"Oh, that. Well, that's easy." Roger did his routine again—a sip of coffee, a sip of whiskey. "I was meant to," he said. "People always wind up doing what they're meant to. Some people think you choose your fate, but you don't. Personally, I have a talent for never getting scared—that's rare, and that's how I make my living. I'm also pretty good at reading—that's not rare, and that's my hobby."

"How'd you get started, though, with Bonne? I've never known that."

"Get started?" Roger said.

"Something happened. It's not like jury duty."

"Yeah, something happened. That something was my brother. He owed money. I thought I'd be in and out. But you're not listening—something always gets you in if you belong there. It doesn't matter what."

Pratt felt like guzzling his whole drink, but he was overmatched in this conversation as it was. He wanted to say that what had gotten *him* into all this was his parents' accident, but it was also ignoring his uncle. It was also his bond with Matty. He wanted to say he wasn't good at this shit, but that remained to be seen.

"You planned to do something else," Pratt said. "Like in high school, you must've had some career goal."

"Whoa," Roger said. "Hard to remember. I was kind of a loner. I didn't sign up for a bunch of clubs. They wanted me to play football. They weren't too worried about me after that, so I wasn't either. Now look at me. I got two English degrees, working on a third. Do them through the mail." Roger sipped. "They say you can't do anything with an English degree but teach. I guess I teach somebody a lesson sometimes." He smiled a moment. His teeth were straight, and two of them were capped in gold. It reminded Pratt of Bonne's bird dogs. "That's a play on words," Roger said, "but it is *not* a double entendre."

Pratt remembered a story he'd heard about Roger. Somebody had snuck up on him from behind in a parking lot and he'd stabbed them in the neck with his #2 Ticonderoga.

"I hate reading," Pratt said.

"Then I guess you don't know much about the world and your place in it."

"I think that's right," said Pratt.

"You might not even know about Florida."

"I know it's hot," Pratt said. "I know nobody's happy but the snakes."

"People been fighting for Florida for hundreds of years. The Spanish—Narváez and Cortés and them. Like a pretty girl, they fought for her and fought for her, then decided she was too much trouble. A haven for the unruly. Gave her to the US for a utility infielder and a box of balls."

"I guess we're unruly, you and me," Pratt said.

"Ranchers and orange growers had it, now their grandkids can't wait to sell off, build houses for Long Island retirees. The common thread is folks not *from* here thinking it's paradise."

"I guess it should've been left to the Indians," said Pratt.

Roger let out a quick, sharp laugh. He dlopped his finger in his whiskey and put it to his lips. "That's not how history works, young fellow. History's just a big list of things that never should've happened. How else could it be? Everybody stays put and shares what they have?"

Pratt went ahead and finished his drink. The bartender had slipped away. Roger, across from him, stirred his coffee with a tarnished spoon, working the lumpy muscle of his forearm.

"Here comes the expressway," Roger said. "More strip malls, and you can get those heroin pills faster. That's what the Europeans have accomplished here. Stores full of plastic and pharmaceutical misery."

"I'm white," Pratt asserted. "I don't go shopping or pop pills."

"You're approximately white," Roger said. "You're off-white."

The music ended. Roger looked over at the jukebox but didn't get up. Now cars could be heard sweeping past outside.

"How's Nairn doing?" Pratt asked, trying to make the question sound casual but, to his ear, blurting it.

"Nairn," Roger said, smirking. "He's doing all right. Same as ever. You concerned about Nairn's well-being?"

"I wouldn't say that. It's to my benefit to track his moods and pastimes, as much as I'm able."

"That's right," Roger said. "Moods and pastimes."

"He hasn't been, you know... acting strange or anything lately?"

Roger smoothed down one of his eyebrows with his pinkie. "You mean aside from getting in bare knuckle fights over by the tracks and tearing up the AARP ladies? You mean strange other than that?"

"Good point," Pratt said. He'd been picking at his nails. When he looked down, he saw that one of them was bleeding. "I don't trust him, that's all. I don't recommend anybody trusting that snake. I'll go on the record with that. I don't know what Bonne sees in him—I really don't."

To this, Roger gave a nod. He tapped his spoon twice on his coffee cup. "Sometimes the crazier side wins. Or the side that *seems* crazier. There's a certain kind of task where Nairn excels. I imagine Bonne was looking for a complement to *my* skill set. I think differently from most guys, and Nairn doesn't think at all. It's better that we're not friends, he and I. You don't want to be best buddies with your work partner."

Pratt let his posture fall slack. He'd been buddies with his work partner and it hadn't worked out, but he didn't see how things would work out for Roger and Nairn either.

"Why you think I read so much?" Roger said. He looked off to the side, and then Pratt looked over with him. The bartender was walking up with Pratt's burger and a bottle of ketchup. Another rum and Coke.

"I never know," Roger continued, this time not waiting for the bartender to move out of earshot, "when the book I'm holding will be the last one I'll ever open."

* * *

Next morning, Pratt again stayed away from Malloy. He ate a bagel without toasting it, fetched the gun from the nightstand where he'd restashed it after Lulu had left, and packed the blue-black weapon into a vinyl lunch box he'd found in a kitchen cabinet. He drove through the sticky silver-glare morning, the clouds stretched in strips across the sky like silken scarves, all the way to Winter Garden, thirty-five minutes away, to a gun range he knew of called Town & Country.

Pratt had never been inside the place, and from the parking area it looked impossibly low-ceilinged, the front windows pasted busily with signs that said BAN IDIOTS, NOT GUNS and IF GUNS KILL PEOPLE, FORKS MAKE PEOPLE FAT and, hand-painted on cardboard, LADIES WELCOME! At one end of the building was a shop. Pratt walked across the gravel lot and went inside to buy earplugs and more ammo. While he waited for the clerk to ring him up, he looked around at the hundreds of posters and bumper stickers for sale, stamped with the same puns that had been around for decades, as many bumper stickers as the old lady had magnets in her kitchen. They may have liked guns, these people, but they loved, absolutely loved, *saying* they liked guns.

Pratt went down to the last lane and loaded and unloaded the pistol a few times, moving his fingers around on the grip to get the feel. He pushed the button until the target was twenty-five yards away, set his feet and aimed and missed his first two shots high because of the kick—before long he was hitting shoulders, an arm, and soon enough was peppering the chest of the crude paper figure. He could feel the recoil reverberate in his elbow, could smell the scorched powder. This was the goal, to make all this feel normal, to hear the flat percussion and the echo, to kill the mystery of how the weapon would jump in his hand. He was comfortable from twenty-five yards, and in real life people rarely pistol-shot anyone from such a distance, rarely shot anyone, or at least hit anyone, outside point-blank range.

This was the next step for Pratt if he was following Bonne's order, which he wanted to appear to be, even to himself. This was due diligence, getting weapon-competent. This was his punishment, he thought—coming to this awful place was punishment for not yet devising a way out of all this.

Pratt reloaded again. Chest, chest, shoulder, stomach, chest. He lowered the gun. This was easy. It was too easy, killing someone. The hard part was *deciding* to do it. He relaxed his stance and took a step back. When he looked down the lane at the other shooters, his stomach soured. Wannabes. Posers. Little boys who'd grown up and gotten ahold of bigger, louder popguns. Posers, but posing as what? Guys Pratt's age, with backwards hats and goatees, who lived with their parents and spent all their minimum wage earnings blasting hunks of metal into inanimate objects. Big slobs in overalls who got rejected by the KKK. Pratt hoped he didn't blend in with this crowd, but why wouldn't he? His uncle, it occurred to him, would never come to a place like this. His uncle had two handguns, one rifle, one shotgun, but he went into the wilderness to shoot them. He never talked about them. He wasn't proud of them. The man knew how to kill a game animal and use every part of it. He was capable of blowing a rattlesnake in half with one shot and tucking the gun away before anyone even saw it—Pratt had seen this once at a campsite when he was young. The only wild animals these gun range guys ever saw were lazy alligators sunning themselves in man-made ponds. These guys were shooting hundreds of holes in blank silhouettes, but none of them had ever killed a real person. Pratt's uncle had, in the Marines. Bonne had—if he was telling the truth, which he had no reason not to. Roger had. Even Nairn—even he was superior to these jerkoffs. He'd actually done the thing. He carried it around inside him, a limp, dead soul tacked to the wall of his heart.

* * *

Pratt got Tony on the phone and told him he could have whatever he wanted out of the old lady's condo, that anything he didn't take was bound for the dump. He told him he'd need more than the Wagoneer. Told him he'd promised the old lady's daughter a favor, but it was Tony who had to perform the favor.

An hour later, Tony was gingerly backing a canary yellow panel truck up to the front steps. He rolled up the door in the back and pulled down a stack of hard plastic crates and tossed Pratt several rolls of bubble wrap. Inside, he allowed himself one brief tour of the place, then set to work in the spare bedroom, his practiced hands releasing dust plumes into the air as he wrapped item after item with the efficient panache of a cowboy tying up a steer. He explained to Pratt that many of these objects were so profoundly hokey as to be sought after by young people who liked to celebrate old-fashioned sensibilities and simpler times. Celebrate or make fun of—it was hard to tell.

"Hipsters," Pratt contributed.

"Exactly," said Tony.

"You're saying I'm the hippest guy in Hernando County."

"You're one of them. You need a French press and a record player."

Tony said somebody would buy all the kitchen magnets in one lot and make art out of them, that smart-ass kids going off to college would covet the embroidered pillows. He said he could take probably 40 percent of the stuff, but that Goodwill was in for a bonanza, too. He filled a crate and Pratt hauled it out and loaded it in the truck. Filled another, and Pratt loaded it.

They didn't take a break until sun slanted sideways through the rear windows. The place looked larger, a significant portion of its clutter stacked in the panel truck. It was too dusty to stay inside, so they took teacups of water and a bag of chips out to the porch and sat down. Tony asked about the outdoor treasures, the large and small dolphin statues, the family of brass gnomes huddled in the corner, the wind chimes, and Pratt told him it was all up for grabs but the cactus. It looked better than ever, the spiny little loner, deep green and plump.

"I have a proposition," Tony said. He was sitting with an ankle crossed over a thigh, dangling his cup almost to the ground in his pitching hand. "It's not a small one."

"Okay," said Pratt.

"I want you to really consider it."

"If it's a proposition it's got to be big, right? Otherwise, you'd just call it an idea."

Tony had some chips cupped in his palm. His teacup had a graphic of a sunset on it. "I won't accept an answer today. Not even the one I want."

Pratt waited. He looked at Tony, who was looking out at the parking lot.

"I'm too busy at the store." Tony let out a laugh, gesturing toward the truck. "Even busier after today. I've been needing help for a while, but I want someone I can trust. Someone invested in the shop. Somebody who won't need me to negotiate every price. Who can be a little tough with the problem sellers, not a pushover." Tony took a drink, then set his cup down on the shabby turf. A cardinal in a nearby tree was chewing another bird out, reading it the riot act. "It's you, man. I know you won't stay forever, but until you figure things out. I mean, I'd be happy if you stayed forever, but I don't expect it. What I can give you is twelve dollars an hour plus ten percent of the profits. I can concentrate on advertising, putting time in at the flea markets, answering the phone instead of messages piling up, maybe even looking for a better location. Or *another* location."

Tony had said he didn't want an answer today, but the way he was looking at Pratt, Pratt had to say *something*. What he wanted to do was scoff at Tony's absurd generosity. A percentage of the profits? It was nuts. It was totally unfounded. Pratt felt flustered at the kindness aimed his way. He drank what was left in his teacup, trying to get his feelings in order. Why did he have this friend? Why was Tony so good to him?

"I'll think about it," he said, keeping his voice steady. "No shit, I will. But there's no way I'd take a percentage. That's idiotic. That's not how life works."

"The way life works is the boss makes the rules." Tony's smile had snuck back, his lightheartedness.

"You're a good dude," Pratt said.

"I'm okay," Tony assented. "I'm okay until people start hogging the chips." He put his hand out, and Pratt reached down and held out the bag. "If I don't get my share of chips, a whole different side of me comes out."

"A side no one wants to see," said Pratt.

Tony chewed and swallowed. Found his cup down on the turf. "Really," he said. "It's a win-win. So think about it."

Pratt nodded. He had himself in check, but not completely. A job offer. A job that wasn't dangerous and that he could turn down. That he could turn down even though he wished he could shake on it and start tomorrow.

"China cabinet next?" Tony said.

"China cabinet," Pratt said. "Might as well face the music."

"Well, china cabinet first," Tony said, "then the music boxes."

* * *

The next day, Pratt got back on Malloy. He'd felt a creeping anxiety about leaving him unattended the past two days—plus the weekend, so four days—but everything was exactly the same. Everything except the secretary's getup, today a one-piece number, a jumper, Pratt thought they were called, platform shoes, hair like Princess Leia.

In the afternoon, Pratt tailed Malloy most of the way to Joe-Baby's, but pulled off before the Alternate 19 split, into the high-weeded lot of a defunct drive-in theater. Pratt could hear the wiry undergrowth scraping hard against the bottom of the LeBaron. There was one open patch of pale, packed sand, occupied by three crows who were engaged in tormenting some small creature, a scorpion or newborn turtle or something. Pratt brought the car to a stop in the sun. He could see, hiding out in the brush, the waist-high stands that held the speakers. The screen was gone, no sign of it. Pratt turned off the air and opened the windows. He got out and loped over to where the crows were, and instead of flying away, they just backed up a step. It was a young snake they had, all but dead. They weren't eating it. Not yet. Just picking at it, harassing it. Pratt gritted his teeth and stepped down with his heel on the snake's shiny black head. When he looked at the crows they stared right back at him, not seeming surprised at all that he'd ruined their fun. "If you're going to eat the thing, then eat the fucking thing," Pratt told them. He picked back through the way he'd come and sat down in the LeBaron and watched the crows flap off to a distant power line. They hadn't been hungry. Just bored.

Friday would be the day. Friday would be showtime for this movie Pratt was starring in. He was out of time. He wasn't in control and hadn't worked out how to get control, and now he had to play this part. Bonne would have something on him, sure. But he'd also have something on Bonne, something big. Neither of them would ever cross the other. It was fair, when you thought about it. Pratt had done time for Bonne, and that time would never go away, would never get shorter. But Pratt had eaten a thousand meals Bonne provided. He'd driven around on hundreds of Bonne-funded tanks of gas in a Bonne-financed Jeep. Whatever Matty had, Pratt was always free to share in. His clothes. His barbell and dumbbell set. His beer. Even his tutor, who'd driven all the way up from USF so both of them could get their geometry grades in order and be allowed to play baseball. There was an open door in front of Pratt, and all he had to do was turn off his lightweight brain and walk through it. If he did what was expected of him, at least the decision would be made. He could tell Gianakos to fuck off and take on whatever consequence Gianakos wanted to dole out. At least Kallie would be out of it. Back to her normal life. At least the game would be over, even if Pratt wound up losing. He had no choice. He had to go ahead and become the thing he was supposed to be, for better or worse, to surrender to his fate, as Roger might put it, because fate was fate—you couldn't fight it.

Inside the corner store, Pratt grabbed a package called Lunchables from the cooler. When he set it on the counter, Josip shook his head, an expression of pity weighting his face.

"Answer is no, my friend. None of this today. Come on, eat like a man."

"How's that?" Pratt said. He was in his own world, as if wads of cotton were shoved in his ears.

"Lucky day for you, Mr. Prott. Fortune smile. My *baka* is visiting from Zagreb." Josip gently took hold of the Lunchables package and set it below the register, out of sight. "If customer come, say Josip is back soon. I go upstairs very quick."

Pratt nodded, but Josip was already headed down where the counter ended, past the least popular cigarettes and the products meant to help you quit them. He disappeared up a staircase, only the first two steps visible from where Pratt stood. He heard a door creak open quickly, then slowly groan closed, and a moment later, light, quick footfalls right above, like a cat walking on Styrofoam. Across the ceiling and back. Across again.

Pratt's attention shifted back to the store when a pair of middle school girls shuffled in, both wearing jeans that were too long for them, the cuffs walked to tatters under the soles of their Vans. They took a sharp right and parked in front of the magazine rack and looked unlikely to move.

"Just don't bend them," Pratt called to the girls, surprising himself. "You can look, but don't dog-ear them." The girls regarded Pratt with mild curiosity, their faces like empty rooms, and then turned back to their reading. Dog-ear? Was that something his parents used to say?

The creak of the door, and here was Josip again, down the stairs and turning toward the register. He was carrying a few stacked glass containers, balanced heavy against his chest. He had to bend his knees to ease the dishes onto the counter, then he took a step back, admiring his offerings. Pratt could already smell the stuff right through the glass, rich and foreign-scented, sharp with herbs and unfamiliar oils.

"Do not heat in microwave," Josip instructed Pratt. "Oven only, but not too hot. Warm. You know oven? It's like microwave, but big, and food doesn't spin around."

Pratt stared at him, feeling suddenly famished.

"This one is dessert. *Rozata*. This one *pašticada* with gnocchi. This one *brudet*. No chemicals, so Mr. Prott's stomach may not like it. May go into shock—too healthy, too many vitamins."

By the time Pratt stepped into the condo with all the glass kitchenware, his mouth was watering. Space in the living room—what a luxury. Pratt spread a duck-print tablecloth right on the carpet, too hungry to bother heating the food in Edith Warner's relic of an oven, and sat down with nothing but a fork and dug in. Three or four bites from the first container, three or four from the next, no memory of what any of them were called. He'd sat on the floor like this once when his mother had taken him to a Japanese restaurant in Orlando. This food was better. This food was better than his mother's food, for that matter. She was from New Jersey but had learned to cook Southern because his father liked it. Pratt's mother had spent time learning those recipes because Pratt's father missed *his* mother, who Pratt had never met. Is that what *baka* meant? Grandmother?

Pratt leaned back from his meal, reclining on his elbow, and caught sight of a red light blinking on the end table. The answering machine. He did a half roll on the carpet, no clutter to negotiate, and hit the button and waited as the mechanism rewound with a thick hiss. He expected it might be Lulu, calling to say it had been a mistake getting rid of their parents' possessions, angry at Pratt for talking her into it. It might be Tony imploring him to play baseball, inviting him to a party, sweetening the terms of his job offer. It could be Kallie, letting him know where she was. It turned out to be none of them. The first thing Pratt heard was laughter, brittle cackling, cocky and a bit crazed. He knew the voice. Just from the laugh, he knew it right away.

"Pratty, Pratty, Pratty. Peppermint Pratty. All-beef Pratty." It was Gianakos. He was into the old ouzo, by the sound of it. "We gotta quit flirtin' and get some clothes off here, Prattrick Henry. You gotta choose liberty, my friend. I like a little teasing. A little teasing is nice. But nobody likes blue balls. And hey, you go back to the clink, I'll make sure nobody in your cellblock has blue balls. I'll get you a two-hundred-fifty-pound boyfriend who's in love with love."

Pratt could hear Gianakos' radio in the background, predicting bummer weather for an Aerosmith concert. The good detective was in his car, it sounded like. He must've been on a cell phone, either paid for by the police department or by his buddy Flave. He rambled on, explaining to Pratt that when a useless cracker assistant goon was offered a fucking future, the smart move for said cracker was not to sit around with his opposable thumb up his rectum. He knew some people were beyond help, beyond bettering, and he hoped Pratt wasn't one of those people.

Pratt scooted himself into a sitting position, rear end on the carpet and back against the couch, his eyes drawn to the orderly lines of identical ducklings on the tablecloth, marching forward with full trust in their leader. He wondered how long the machine would let Gianakos blather on.

"Friday is the deadline, genius. There's been new discoveries. Guy who used to deliver for Bonne when his fishing charters got slow—we busted his poker game, and he's looking to trade his way out of the stewpot. Nine miles, shit—could've *swam* in from where this dude anchored. I can do this without you, Pratt Benatar."

Pratt heard Gianakos belch, heard a bottle skitter across concrete, heard the honorable officer of the law yell at someone to get their punk ass the fuck out of his way. "I don't hear from you in the next forty-eight, I'll consider you a bad guy and any friend of yours the associate of a bad guy. Your sweetie, Kalliope. I found out something real interesting about her. I already knew she was interesting to look at, but I found out that cute kid of hers has a pretty fascinating bloodline."

Gianakos performed a subdued version of his opening chuckle, almost choking on his own smugness. Pratt's hands were clenched in wooden fists. He was glaring at a blank wall that had once been obscured completely by pastel flowers and rowboats and little girls grasping watering cans. This motherfucker. Seriously, how long was this stupid tape going to let him blab?

"But don't worry," Gianakos said. "Just keep reclining on that thumb. You'll be better off in prison. No decisions to make. No hard choices." He sighed histrionically. "Two days, Pratty Cake. Two short days." The last thing on the message was Gianakos coughing, and then a loud clank that was probably the cop hurling the phone onto the floorboard.

The answering machine sounded its optimistic beep and went dormant, the blinking red light gone. Pratt pressed his knuckles into the carpet and raised himself to standing, then stepped over and found the cord that connected the phone to the wall and pushed the little plastic tab down and slid it free. From the electrical socket, inches away, he unplugged the answering machine. He stood up straight and paced over and closed the window blinds, darkening the already dim condo. Paced to the front door and locked the dead bolt. He got his dinner dishes from the living room, each container more than half full, and covered them with foil and slid them into the refrigerator.

Gianakos had said Kallie's formal name, pronouncing it with that slight accent Greek people never lose when they say Greek words. Pratt had been forced to hear that dickhead say her name. Joaquin—Gianakos knew about him. Of course he did. He was a cop; he could find out anything. This was a line. This was a clear line Gianakos was crossing. Pratt wouldn't have guessed there were any lines in this particular mess, but Gianakos had found one and he'd danced across it with both feet. He'd brought a child into it. It was a tactic. A good one if it was supposed to scare Pratt. A really good one if it was supposed to piss him off. A very clear line. A line everyone was supposed to understand. Gianakos either thought he was untouchable—the same fault he accused Bonne of—or he felt he had no choice but to cross that line. Either way, there were supposed to be repercussions for this sort of thing. Everyone was dirty, but there were supposed to be consequences for playing *this* dirty.

* * *

When Joaquin wasn't splashing around, Kallie could hear the Gulf breakers rolling in. The pool was open another hour, and this was already the latest Joaquin had ever stayed up. Kallie and her father had watched him go down the slide fifty times until he got bored of it. Now he was jumping in and dog-paddling back to the edge over and over, splashing an old woman in a tropical muumuu every couple leaps. Kallie called out to him to move down so he wouldn't splash the nice lady, but she wasn't a nice lady. She was shooting Kallie dirty looks instead of simply relocating to a chair at one end of the pool or the other. The air in Clearwater stank of fryer grease and sunblock and car exhaust. Calypso music from a few hotels down wafted on gusts of wind.

"*He's* having fun," Kallie's father said, "but looking at you, nobody'd guess this was supposed to be a party."

Kallie had told him they were taking a few days at the beach to celebrate her raise. As if the math on that added up.

"I'm fine," she told him. "A lot on my mind."

"I get that," he said, "but how about taking a worry break. Punch out. Start worrying again early tomorrow. Whatever it is, it'll be there in the morning."

Kallie looked at him but didn't answer. He was gripping his cane even though he was sitting, tapping along to a faint Caribbean beat. His hair was a nest. Full as a thirty-year-old's. He combed it tame every morning, and as the day wore on it grew more unruly. She didn't think he'd *ever* worried. Not really. Not like a parent is supposed to. He was thinking that if Kallie was going to pay for this place—which she'd probably wind up doing—she ought to enjoy it, and of course he was right, but she was getting only more irritated the more she thought about the situation. She had been born and raised in Hernando County and now she lived in the next county south in order to avoid Matty's father. She worked hard and honestly and still she had to look over her shoulder, had to endure a secret that quietly gnawed at her, whether she ignored it or whether, like now, she couldn't get it off her mind. She was hiding now, and she'd been hiding for three years. Here she was, passive, in the dark, waiting for Pratt to fix whatever was wrong.

"Joaquin!" Kallie yelled. "Come this way. Not too far. Stay away from the steps."

He'd gotten a drop of water on the dowager again. She was theatrically toweling off her shin.

"Your mother's birthday is next week." Kallie's father leaned forward—it required an effort in the lounge chair. He'd been nursing the beer on the table next to him for an hour. Kallie had had an iced tea for just as long. "I'm guessing we won't make the Mucky Duck. We should do something else, though, right?"

"Yeah," Kallie said. "We'll do something. Joaquin has to feel like she's still part of the family. I'll nab a tres leches cake from work first day I'm back." Joaquin's grandmother, Joaquin's father—the kid had more family he'd never meet than family he would.

"As long as we're together," said her father. He raked his hair to the side with his stiff fingers. "That's it, buddy," he called toward Joaquin. The boy had found a little rubber basketball and was shooting it toward a kiddie hoop that sat in the corner of the pool.

"I really appreciate how good you are with him," Kallie said.

Her father grinned wryly. "Because you wouldn't have guessed I would be, judging by how I was as a father."

"I didn't say that," Kallie said. "But yeah, it's been a very nice surprise."

Kallie's father rested his cane across his lap. "Part of it was my fault. Part of it was, she just did everything. She loved it. I couldn't... I don't know, find my way in. She *liked* when you woke her up at night. She sang little songs when she changed your diaper. Then you were older. Then you were even older. My drinking didn't help."

Kallie's mother had died eleven years ago, of a urinary tract infection that had turned septic and killed her in days. She was there and then she wasn't. Kallie had been fourteen, old enough to take care of herself, and so that's what she'd done. She'd neglected her grades, sure. She'd partied more than she should've, but all in all, she'd been a good parent to herself. It was only since Joaquin was born that her father seemed so different, not muted with sadness, not distant—he didn't get mad when his sports teams lost, didn't get drunk anymore. Kallie's parents hadn't been a love match, and he'd been much older than she, but he never said a less-than-glowing word about her. He'd been in a hundred fistfights when he was young, and no few knife fights, and here he was now, this serene fellow who smelled like Dial soap and cut up bananas for a child several days a week, who read Dr. Seuss, who rode a bicycle up to the chess park on his days alone and happily lost match after match.

Pratt's voice popped into Kallie's head, telling her that Bonne wasn't really a bad guy. Saying he was only doing whatever he was doing because Pratt was all he had left. The closest thing to family Bonne could grasp at. She didn't know how much she bought that, and how much it was just Pratt being loyal to a fault.

"It was him," Kallie's father said, startling her. He nodded toward Joaquin, who was throwing the ball the way Pratt had taught him, overhand like a baseball, pounding it against the dinky plastic backboard. "You trusting me with him. That made it a whole new life. Another chance. Us old guys, we can't do what we always used to, or if we can we don't want to, but we don't have anything else in place of it."

Kallie reached over and tapped his knee with her fist. "I was looking for the cheapest babysitter I could find, and nobody could touch you on price."

"That's true," he said. "Nobody undersells me."

Just then, the ball slipped out of Joaquin's little paw and of course flew right over toward where the old lady still sat with her paperback romance. That's why she wouldn't move—she had the best-lit spot. She made a yelp when the ball bounced off the chair next to her. She held her book aloft, like a tidal wave was about to wash through.

"I better go lay the charm on this old biddy," Kallie's father said, getting his cane into position and leaning his weight on it as he stood. He tapped it three times on the concrete and winked at Kallie. "I'm gonna make her book come to life," he said. "She won't know what year it is."

Somehow, the idea of keeping tabs on Malloy that Thursday was comforting—something predictable, at least. No gun ranges overrun with phony tough guys, no stewing at the condo where he was a sitting duck for Gianakos' threats, no more of Tony Castillo's bighearted help. Keeping eyes on the target—this was something he could do, this was his routine, his cozy rut. He'd do the whole day, watching intently like it was the first time, and see Malloy all the way to the gates of his thoughtfully detailed development. Pratt would be a realist. A professional. He'd get in the groove and ride out the final revolutions of this record.

He parked in his original spot at the edge of the stereo shop's lot. Like before, a months-old newspaper sat on the passenger seat beside him. Like the opening of a sitcom rerun, Malloy arrived right when he was supposed to. Briefcase. Cigarette. Pratt looked at the notes he'd jotted—*Maxima, green, dirty, sunroof*. The handwriting didn't seem like it could be his. It was the handwriting of a cool, collected person, a person who only had to wait for their patience to pay off. Malloy had gotten a car wash. An optimistic thing to do. An ignorant thing to do, in Malloy's case. Pratt put down his Cracker Jack and raised the binoculars. The slyly waving cat. The poster of the Grand Canyon. Malloy disappearing behind his closing office door. An hour later, the secretary appeared. She had a bit part. Jeans and shiny boots and red-checked button-down—Hollywood's idea of a cowgirl. An hour after that, lunch for Malloy. Sushi and a glazed doughnut, exactly like the first day. Back at the stakeout lot, the woman with the stroller, crocheted blanket hanging out and dragging on the sidewalk. Old men, half a dozen of them, tottering past in light coats in the ninety-degree heat.

The slow afternoon wound down, Pratt exhausted but not drowsy, his brain feeling poached but resilient. A stray cat—the one he'd seen before? A troop of tiny birds hectoring a blue jay until it flew up gracelessly, against a gust of wind, and alighted at the top of a tree like a damaged kite.

Quitting time for Malloy, like clockwork. Pratt started the LeBaron and followed the accountant onto Moon Road. On a dumb impulse, he turned the stereo on—yes, W.A.S.P. were still doing their loud, peacockish work—and just as quickly snapped it back off. A stand that sold boiled peanuts. One that hawked fireworks, erected in haste ahead of the Fourth of July. Flycatcher Road, which featured the expected trailer parks and then a vast, sandy field punctuated by a lone cow standing stoic in the sun. But well before Masaryk Road, his usual turn, Malloy put on his left blinker, the conscientious citizen, and slowed and pulled onto a nondescript weed-flanked lane that cut unassumingly into a sparse woodland. Well, okay. Not part of the scheduled route. This didn't seem like a shortcut. More like a road to nowhere.

Pratt waited until Malloy was out of sight to hang the same left, and shortly he came upon and passed an unmanned fee booth, finding it hard to imagine someone paying to delve farther into the pale, flamingo-leg pines and burned-out swale grass. Past the booth was a tipped garbage drum, rolling slowly back and forth in the wind, and beyond that, barely visible in the roadside weeds, a loose company of barbecue grills were staked into the ground near an engulfed picnic table. The road took two sharp curves around swampy patches and then went straight again, open land ahead, fences, Malloy's car in view and more cars in the distance. This narrow pike was going to deliver him, Pratt saw, into a spacious parking lot. He slowed, no one behind him, cruising for a stretch on the car's momentum—nearing the lot, he veered into the loneliest quadrant, side-eyes on the Maxima but also taking in the clumps of people gathering out on the mown, yellow-green grass, smiling and waving at each other. It was ball fields. Pratt saw the metal bleachers and the stucco concession stand. Actually, he remembered the place. He'd played baseball here as a kid—T-ball and then coach pitch and then the real thing. He'd played here for years, his parents in the six-row stands cheering for him, until Bonne's company had thrown in for the new diamonds over near County Line. Real dugouts at Bonne's place. Floodlights. Batting cages. But here it was all unchanged. The parts of the complex Pratt couldn't see, he could picture. The cracked, uneven clay of the infields. The crooked, rain-hardened bases. The chain-link backstops, curled up at the bottom, that always let pass balls roll away. And now he could see Malloy parking next to a clot of other cars near some soccer fields, pulling up to a throng of adults that was trailed by meandering kids, those kids trailed by smaller kids who scuffed their sneakers through the grass and picked dandelions. Malloy moved with the crowd toward distant, netted goals, balls rolling away from the motley parade and getting fetched, water bottles being passed about. Pratt's foot was on the brake, his unthinking eyes trained on Malloy, when he finally registered his mistake. Children running up to Malloy—a knee-high boy who hugged his leg, and then a boy a bit older, wearing a blue jersey, accepting a pat on the back and saying something that made Malloy laugh. A girl with a pale red ponytail, the oldest child, kissing the accountant on the cheek. And here came the children's mother, Malloy's wife, carrying a Starbucks cup like so many mothers did and wearing a bleach-white visor, squeezing her husband's arm affectionately. The whole brood conferred a moment, maybe hammering out plans for after the game, maybe asking one another how their days had gone, and then they proceeded toward the field in the wake of the greater party, the girl already back in her book as she walked, the older boy jogging to catch up with his teammates, Malloy's wife with her hand on her husband's back. They got smaller as they progressed into the humid, shabby, everyday landscape, but no matter how long they walked, Pratt could still see them clearly. Smaller, smaller, but they wouldn't disappear.

Pratt had no memory of driving home. He dragged himself up the shallow steps and into the kitchen, poured some straight rum, and breathlessly tipped the liquor into him, chest burning. He caught his breath, staring from ten inches away at a lonely magnet Tony had neglected to take. Destin, Florida. A smug seagull wearing a fishing hat. He glugged out another drink, and this time carried it back out front and lowered himself into one of the plastic chairs. He sipped without tasting anything, the sun dropping into hiding behind the scrappy oaks that picketed the far edge of the complex. He felt no need for dinner, and somehow none for sleep. He hoisted himself a couple inches off the chair to pull out his wallet, folded it open, leafed through the small bills and crinkly receipts. He stared at the picture on his driver's license, the face so familiar it was inscrutable, a face trying its best to smile. The eyes half-squinting. Two days of scruff. In a flap meant to hold a credit card, Pratt had the slip of paper that read "Suncoast Accounting Professionals" in Bonne's cramped hand.

In another compartment was the green jai alai envelope with "Chama" written on it. Pratt ran his fingers over his license, over Bonne's scrawl. There was nothing else in the wallet. Eleven dollars. He scratched the hard, pebbled arm of the chair with his fingernail and the sound grated in his ears, too loud, like an acoustic trick in a nature show where you could hear ants like you were one of them, like you were an impossibly small creature going about its percussive daily labor.

When a tee shot out on the course woke Pratt, he didn't know where he was. He felt pain in his back and hips and smelled honeysuckle. He was in the cheap patio chair still, his shoulder propped against the condo wall. He was on the damn porch. He'd slept there all night. The armrests of the chair were slick with dew, and mosquito bites speckled his forearms and the backs of his hands like chicken pox. He tried to blink himself out of grogginess. His wallet in his lap. Empty teacup down on the decaying turf.

Exhausted, Pratt washed up and changed clothes, limping around the condo with legs stiff as boards. He'd grudgingly hooked the phone and answering machine back up, in case Kallie called, and the red light was on again. He bent and hit the button, and it was indeed Kallie, thank God. He fetched a pen, not trusting himself to remember the hotel since all of them were named with the same six or seven words. Shore's Edge Resort. Kallie didn't sound upset. One sentence to judge by, but she sounded okay. Like she actually believed Pratt might get everything worked out, or at least wanted Pratt to think she did. Pratt had listened hard, but hadn't heard Joaquin in the background, hadn't heard anything but Kallie's voice. She didn't say anything else, only where she was. What else was there to say? Pratt wouldn't have wanted to speak to her, wouldn't have wanted to try and make the best out of anything. Make any more promises. Any more apologies.

*　*　*

The teenage clerk at the Eckerd's photo desk was so tall—until he started shuffling around back there, it seemed he was standing on a box. Had to be six foot seven and probably weighed less than Pratt, with his bird-bone wrists and sunken cheeks. Pratt had been worried about whoever developed the pictures looking at them, but besides this kid's obvious lack of interest in his work, what would the pictures look like to a stranger? Just a guy standing outside a door. A shifty hick waiting to be let inside some random house and then fifteen shots of anonymous roadside trees, taken to fill the film, Pratt thinking it might look strange to drop off a partially used roll.

The kid had loud violin music playing on a boombox, and Pratt raised his voice to ask what it was.

"Oh, that's me," the kid said matter-of-factly. "That's my audition to Juilliard. I'm listening for flat passages. Juilliard is a music conservatory in New York City."

"I've heard of it," Pratt said.

The kid turned the music off and slid Pratt's pictures into a paper sleeve. When he stepped over, he was looking steeply down at Pratt.

"It sounds good to me, even if Juilliard didn't go for it," Pratt told the kid, handing over a ten dollar bill.

"Juilliard liked it fine." The kid pushed back a lock of his hair that was dyed turquoise and started making change. "I got in. I'm just listening for places I could've done better."

Pratt nodded. He accepted a couple bills and some coins and shoved it all straight in his pocket. "Let me ask you," he said, "because I'm from around here, too. How does a Bethuna Pond kid wind up going to New York City for violin school?"

The kid shrugged, but seemed to consider the question seriously. "The first thing I would recommend," he said, "is not having any friends."

"Oh," Pratt said. He was looking up at the kid's face, hoping to see a crack of smile.

"If you have zero friends and no aptitude for sports, but *do* possess a natural ability to elicit human emotion with organized noise, then I'd say you're off to a promising start."

Pratt gave a nod. "I thought maybe it had something to do with being tall."

Still no amusement from the kid. He pulled a rubber band off his wrist and tied his hair back with it. His Adam's apple was the size of a lime. "I'll make some friends in New York," he said. "Friends, or maybe enemies—either way, more than I got here."

Pratt didn't arrive at Suncoast Accounting Professionals until after ten. This time he parked right on the street about a block down from the office, eyes on the Maxima, behind a high-sitting 4x4 with a homemade topper. He wore an old T-shirt, but a button-down and tie hung in the back seat. Pratt had picked them up at Sears so he could look like he was driving home from his cubicle shift when he ran into Malloy later in Dunedin. Shit—he realized he'd never rented a car. He'd meant to sideline the LeBaron and get something different for today. Well, it was too damn late now. Nothing to do now but tell himself he'd been careful, that Malloy wouldn't recognize his Chrysler convertible. Having to use his regular car—that wasn't really the disturbing part. It was that he'd forgotten part of his plan. It was that his brain wasn't working like it needed to be. Once you got tired enough, he knew, your mind started taking shortcuts, started shirking its duties without telling you anything about it. You had to watch your mind like a hawk. Had to double-check everything.

When Pratt finally glimpsed Malloy at lunchtime, the accountant was buoyant, a spring in his step, no suit jacket, his tie loosened in a way that seemed carefree rather than weary. He seemed younger, to tell the truth. Pratt waited until he was several blocks down to fire up the LeBaron and head toward Publix. He found a good spot, waited—when Malloy emerged from the store, he was still beaming idiotically, dropping change in the charity bucket and surprising an old man with a salute. Pratt watched him through the binoculars as he talked on the yellow phone, his grin never waning. Watched him greedily devour his chicken tenders and deviled eggs. Pratt finally comprehended: Malloy had won. That's what it was. His wagers had hit last night and so now he could enjoy his Friday—his job, his lunch. This was the problem for gamblers. Sometimes they won. They guessed right, and they thought it was for some other reason than dumb luck. They thought they'd cracked the code. But somewhere deep down, in some dark nook of themselves they had to ignore, they must've known their luck had run dry the first day they started betting. They had to, right? Deep down? Pratt watched Malloy finish his meal and contentedly stretch, reaching his arms above his head so that his shirt came untucked. Watched him wipe his mouth with his napkin and then tilt his face toward the sun like it was some benevolent, life-nourishing god rather than a mean eye of torment.

On the way back to the office, three cars behind Malloy, Pratt could feel his face heating up with anger. He wanted to ask Malloy who the fuck he thought he was. The guy had an addiction, Pratt acknowledged that, but Jesus—people never thought of who *else* their actions affected. Because this doughy shithead couldn't quit putting money down on the Montreal Expos or the Seattle SuperSonics or whoever, his kids were going to lose their father and his wife her husband, and Pratt had to be the one to take him away. Grown men were playing with a ball somewhere and Malloy, this numbskull, thought it had something to do with him, thought lucky bounces and bad refereeing and twisted ankles should be the basis of his financial destiny. And because of that, Pratt was supposed to become a killer. Pratt was supposed to end this guy's life, this guy he'd never spoken to.

Pratt watched his quarry hop onto the curb with the aplomb of a teenager, watched him perform a deep, gentlemanly bow to a woman in a halter top walking a bulldog. How dare he be so cheerful? So light? How dare he act like he had things figured out when Pratt would lay five to one, a wager of his own, that Malloy hadn't started with Joe-Baby's book. He'd begun his patronage at Joe's, odds were, to try and cover debts he'd run up somewhere else, maybe betting there to cover the place before.

Pratt pulled around the block and stopped the car near an abandoned building that had once been an Arby's. He looked left and right and saw no one. He shut the air off and rolled down the windows and took a minute to breathe, then leaned over and opened the glove box and took out the gun. It looked the same. Felt the same. The gun didn't care if it ever got used, or for what. It was all patience, no plans—see where that had gotten Pratt. Black grip, black barrel. When you held a gun, it really held you—he couldn't remember where he'd heard this. His uncle? Roger? Inside? He slid his finger under the trigger guard and slid it back out. It was loaded. It was ready to go, but it was indifferent to Pratt, to Malloy, to whoever had bought it or stolen it or traded for it in the first place. It made Pratt feel desolate to hold it, and also nostalgic for something he couldn't name—just choice, maybe. Options.

A mockingbird called nearby and Pratt dropped the pistol back in the glove box with the LeBaron's three-inch-thick owner's manual and the rest of the hair metal tapes, the ones he'd listened to only once. He pressed the plastic door closed until it clicked. Turned the key in the ignition halfway and rolled up the windows. Got out of the car, locked the doors, and walked over to the crumbling sidewalk, his sneakers trudging through clumps of weeds, tiny thorns nipping at his shoelaces like kitten claws. He proceeded to the next block, to a pay phone out in front of a mom-and-pop video store Blockbuster had put out of business, and pulled Gianakos' card from his back pocket. He lifted the receiver off its cradle and thumped the side of his head with it, feeling no pain, told himself "fuck it," then dropped in his coins and pressed the numbers he needed to press.

The phone pealed in Pratt's ear distantly, like a sound coming from the other end of a pipe—once, twice. The pay phone was beneath a myrtle tree that hadn't been pruned in ages. It didn't offer much shade, but dropped tiny, fluttering flowers of white each time the slightest breeze blew. Three grainy rings, four, then here was the click and, sure enough, the cocky, forbearing exhalation.

"Gianakos—what do you need?"

"A hundred thousand," Pratt said, feeling like a nervous actor, the moment unreal because something real was finally happening. "I don't say a word without all the money up front."

"Prattrick Swayze. At the eleventh hour. So, you do have a survival instinct."

"Apparently."

"Pretty useful, if survival is indeed your goal."

"Be at the skinny section of the canal by the power plant in one hour. After it bends into the swamp—nobody's ever back there."

"An hour?" Gianakos chuckled. "Five zeroes in sixty minutes? Um, okay, what the hell—for you, I can make it happen. You're a preferred snitch. VIP. That comes with privileges."

"I'll be waiting. I'll come out when I see you."

Through the phone, Pratt heard nuts cracking. When Gianakos spoke again, it was to tell Pratt in his soberest voice that he'd better be sure. "The po-lice get a bad rap for brutality," he said, "but compared to the fellas you're getting in business with, we're the Little Sisters of the Poor."

"You're just the messenger boy, huh?" said Pratt.

"I assumed you'd deduced that by now. I did the poor-cop-with-integrity thing for a few years. Romance wore off."

"You're gonna ruin the town. You're gonna make the whole thing like Jonesville." Pratt had no idea, once he'd said this, why he'd said it. Why he felt the need to stick up for Bethuna.

"This runoff ditch?" Gianakos crooned. "Ruin is part of the fabric. Jesus, you should take these jokes on the road. Except don't, because you're not allowed to leave town. You accept this money, you better not go anywhere until your obligation is fulfilled."

"You didn't grow up here," Pratt said, "so of course you're not worried about it."

Gianakos clicked his tongue. "Neither of us need to worry about anything but doing what we're getting paid to do. I guess you got an hour to think on it. Once currency changes hands, you're talking and you're saying whatever I tell you. And Pratt, for what it's worth, saying someone's not from here is a way to pay that person a compliment. You don't need to stroke my ego. I get stroked enough."

"Whatever I need to do to get clear of the whole mess of you," Pratt said. "Before I go crazy."

"There's nothing more dangerous than a cracker gone bonkers."

"That's the truth," Pratt said.

"Pratt the Rat. It's got a ring to it."

"I'm hanging up now."

"I'll miss you," Gianakos said.

Fifty-six minutes later, Pratt was standing in a tangle of palmetto and turkey oak, getting harassed by horseflies, when he saw Giana-kos' form stalk coolly around the bend of the canal—more a marshy spillway than a canal at this point—the detective stepping high in the waterside reeds, comically out of place in his aqua-colored silk shirt and ivory suit coat and Italian loafers. One of his hands was empty and from the other dangled a flimsy plastic grocery bag. Pratt stepped out into a clearing where the sun was intense, and the flies did not follow. Gianakos strode near with a half-hearted smirk on his face. He took off his silver-framed sunglasses and hung them from his collar.

"Been shopping?" Pratt said. "Get some BOGOs?" The Publix bag was doubled or tripled because Pratt couldn't see what was in it.

"What'd you expect, a leather briefcase with a combination lock?" Gianakos held the bag open a moment, and Pratt could see rolls of hundreds. Pratt could smell Gianakos' cologne, and his teeth were blinding in the glare. "Unless you have religious obligations, we're gonna get started Sunday morning. That's a day off for a lot of folks, but not for us at the station. Most people who work up there lost faith a long time ago."

Gianakos had made no move to hand the bag over, and Pratt wasn't going to reach for it. "Just let me know what time," he said.

"You can't put this in the bank or anything," Gianakos said.

"No shit."

"Don't go buy a Porsche."

"Why would I buy a car? I got an awesome one already."

Gianakos nodded his subdued appreciation. He raised an eyebrow and slowly held the bag out toward Pratt, and Pratt made him wait a moment before he put up an arm as well. When he took the bounty, it was heavy on his two fingers. It was enough legal tender to actually be heavy.

"Don't come back to the world for a half hour or so," Gianakos said. "Go for a nature walk. Commune with the biting insects."

Pratt shrugged affably, feeling lightheaded. The sky above was too close, an attic ceiling, something about it unfamiliar. It could've been a sky from anywhere—some other country, some other time. There were factions of clouds everywhere, but it didn't feel like rain.

Gianakos sighed, looking down with tolerant humor at his hand-made shoes covered in burrs and sandspurs. "What a way to make a living," he reflected.

When the detective turned his back to begin his canal-side return trek, Pratt rested the bag on the dirt and slipped the gun from the back of his waistband and hoisted it slowly. Though he was looking the other way, Gianakos halted in his tracks. His head ticked upward and to the side, looking in the direction of the endless, green Gulf of Mexico that couldn't be seen from where he and Pratt stood.

"Fuck are you doing, Prattrick Dempsey?" Gianakos' voice was annoyed now, like he'd had enough of Pratt's amateur hour.

"Don't turn around," Pratt told him, but Gianakos scoffed and rotated to face Pratt as blithely as an old Cuban man pulling a dance move. Of course, he had a gun holstered under his jacket, but he didn't make for it, his arms hanging limp and posture casual.

"Jesus, man, something good is trying to happen to you. I know you're inexperienced with favorable luck, but do you have to be *this* dumb? The SS Bonne is taking on water, and there's not a reason in the natural world—"

Pratt interrupted Gianakos' lecture by means of pulling the trigger, introducing a calamity of noise to the scrappy, half-tropical landscape. Birds flew in every direction, gone from the world in one long blink. The slight current in the canal gave out, the breeze stilled. It had taken Pratt weeks to get his mind around the idea of shooting someone dead, and now he was standing in the freeze-shock of the act, no way to reverse it, vibration ringing in his elbow. He hadn't imagined this part, this moment of bright equilibrium, all held in place by the after-roar—it would evaporate in the next breath, he knew, and then he would be dizzy, overmatched, out of step with standard time and normal rules. It wasn't that mysterious, was it? How else would you feel except like you were on the ocean floor with a thousand feet of water pushing down on you? If you'd just shot a cop, how else would you feel? If you'd murdered an officer of the law?

Gianakos was crumpled down in front of Pratt, on the ground, still moving, wheezing, trying to talk. Pratt couldn't hear what he was saying or else didn't want to. The sweat running down his spine was like melting ice. He stepped over and bent down and tugged Gianakos' gun free of its shoulder holster, the writhing Greek making no effort to stop him, and tossed the piece out of reach. Pratt swore he still heard the blast reverberating, but that couldn't be right. He wanted Gianakos dead already. He wanted to be alone. A dark stain had formed underneath the detective. The clouds above were closing ranks—maybe it would rain after all. Pratt could smell blood and Drakkar and dank, rotten water. He wasn't going to shoot Gianakos again. He didn't have that in him.

Pratt, either too cowardly to look the man in the face or wanting to give him solitude, shuffled around behind the detective. If he was hiding, he didn't feel guilty about it. He knew guilt—this wasn't it. Time was passing—minutes, it was hard to say how many—the buzzing and chirping of the mongrel floodplain returning in full throat. The sky dimmed—maybe just the clouds in front of the sun. Pratt's mouth was bone-dry. His fingertips were numb. Finally, inevitably, Gianakos breathed no more. Without seeing the man's face, Pratt could tell. A stillness only dead things possessed, bodies that would never move on their own again. He stepped over and put his hand on Gianakos' arm and he was touching a carcass, no doubt about it. He rolled his victim onto his back and the man felt full of gravity, twice as heavy as he should have been. His face retained a trace of that smirk... you couldn't really disappoint a cop, not deep down. Pratt got hold of Gianakos' wrists and leaned his own living strength against the dead heft and dragged the well-dressed payload into the loose morass of turkey oak and let it slump there out of sight. Gianakos' watch had been yanked half off—Pratt had a rogue impulse to take it. A trophy? A last insult? Was this the watch Pratt thought belonged on his own wrist, instead of the farcical Rolex? No, he didn't deserve anything. He arose and dragged his sneakers over the track Gianakos' body had raked in the dirt. The man had lost an Italian loafer and Pratt tossed it near him. He found Gianakos' service pistol and wiped it clean on his shirt and tucked it back in its holster, which was yanked askew on the corpse's torso, the gun under the wrong arm now. Pratt's mind felt strangely clear, but like it might be someone else's—it was the only mind he had right now, he had to trust it. He went back over to the money. A few rolls had fallen on the ground, and he dusted the sand off them one by one and dropped them in the bag. A beetle was crawling on one and Pratt blew the creature off and peeled the outside bill free. Good old Ben. He'd brought a Bic pen along in his front pocket, and he slid it out and bit off the cap. Flattened the hundred on his thigh. Right over the founding father's stately portrait, he scrawled *Property of Flave*, then traced it again to make sure it was legible. He took the bill to Gianakos and folded it once and tucked it neatly in the front pocket of the dead man's garish dress shirt, well clear of the blood stains, then pulled the lapel of his coat closed and gave his bested opponent a single game, sporting slap on the meat of his shoulder.

Pratt backed away and gathered the handles of his triple-bagged bribe and pulled them tight in his grip. He would need to cut back through the woods to reach his car, staying clear of the power plant. And so he began trudging in that direction, resisting any urge to glance one last time at Gianakos, his eyes trained groundward for snakes, his ears full with a mean aria of all the raucous insects of the sumped peninsula. There was, he realized, another noise ringing in his head: the remote after-racket of the bullet he'd fired into the flesh of one Dimitri Gianakos.

Pratt's hands were shaking—to still them, he wrapped his fingers tight around the steering wheel at ten and two o'clock. The gun and the money should've been hidden somewhere, away from Pratt, but there they sat in plain sight on the passenger seat. The oyster-colored sky had released a throw of tentative drops, not enough for the windshield wipers, but Pratt pulled the lever anyway, staring through the glass into the darkening afternoon.

At the condo, he loped here and there and tried to keep his cool as he packed his duffel bag, tried to keep his hands moving while silencing his mind. Luckily, he could just pack everything he had—the same stuff he'd reentered the world with a few weeks ago. Same old clothes. Some snacks. A thermos of water. He finished the last of a Gatorade and filled that bottle with water, too. Standing at the kitchen table, he culled a single roll of bills for traveling money and tucked it in his back pocket, then took two more rolls and flattened them out and clipped them to a note for Lulu—a shade over three months' rent, fair recompense for Pratt's early disappearance. The rest of the cash he tucked tube by tube into an oversize red Folger's coffee can, packing them in like sardines and pressing the lid down all the way around the rim to make sure it sealed. He tore off another sheet of stationary and sat at the table with it. Grabbed the pen. The top of the page was stamped *The bad news is time flies, The good news is you're the pilot.* Pratt had no idea what he wanted to write, or maybe he had a hundred ideas and none of them felt correct. He gazed out the little window. He didn't have all kinds of time; the gray afternoon would soon become a gray evening. Five cars in view—a Grand Marquis, two Lincoln Continentals, an Oldsmobile 98, and Pratt's LeBaron, looking like a compact in comparison with the others. He tapped the ballpoint on the Formica. He couldn't say he would see her again—maybe he would, but probably he wouldn't. I love you? What a gutless way to say that for the first time. And what a pointless claim. What was love? It was a thing that hung around just out of sight and laughed at you. Say hello to Joaquin for me? Best of luck with everything? Jesus. He cocked his arm as if to whip the pen across the room, but kept himself from following through. He looked over at the rum bottle but didn't go for it. He was hungry. He was tired. He could smell Kallie's skin, somehow. The smooth skin of her bare shoulder—coconut and heat and clean white powder. Her neat fingertips holding her wine glass, her mug of tea, a stray toy of Joaquin's. The acutely neutral face she put on, not fooling anyone, when she was intrigued with something. *I'll never forget you*, he wrote. He pressed his eyes shut until he saw colors, then opened them back up to the thin light. *And I'll never want to*. Pratt stared at the words. He knew he wasn't going to come up with anything better. He signed *Your friend for all time*, then peeled the lid back off the Folger's can and tucked the note in the bottom, squeezing it between the stiff off-green cylinders.

He arose and dumped what was left of the rum down the drain. There were a couple dirty dishes in the sink, Pratt didn't even know from when—he washed and dried them and placed them up in the cabinet. The counter was nearly bare, and Pratt straightened the few items that sat on it. He walked in and out of each room, making sure the windows were closed and lights were off. There was nothing for him to forget—everything was in the bag. He backed the AC off a few degrees. Pulled the broom out of its narrow closet and swept the short hallway that connected the kitchen to the bedrooms. What was he stalling for? He'd never even liked this place. Duffel bag. Coffee can. Keys. He stepped out onto the front patio and locked the door behind him. Slipped the condo key under the dolphin statue. The one with the green waves on it. About to hit the steps, he noticed the cactus. He backed up and set the duffel down and knelt to get a better look. It was alive, of course, doing just dandy. The spiny paddles were miniature like a baby's fingers. Pratt pushed the chair out of his way and plucked the plant up, and it weighed nothing—truly nothing, like a Wiffle ball. "You won't slow me down much," he said. He wouldn't water it. He'd bestow on it no special treatment. Special treatment from me, he thought, the thing won't stand a chance.

Pratt wasn't sure what time it was. The car was off and his watch was in the glove box with the damn gun. Through the windshield, a couple scraggly lawns up the street, was Kallie's place. He needed to sneak around to her kitchen window and stash the can on the ledge where she couldn't miss it—again, like at the condo, he didn't know what he was waiting for. He *wanted* to do this part. This was the only righteous detail in the whole jumbled shit heap. He'd place the can and then call from a pay phone and leave a message at the hotel that she could go home. He didn't know what name Kallie would be under, but he'd describe her and Joaquin and say the message was urgent. He'd tell her to enjoy her little view. He peered up the block again. He could see the bench on Kallie's porch, Joaquin's toys underneath. The spoonbill statue. The neighbor's side of the duplex was immaculate. Not a single piece of litter on the property, the porch as ordered and tasteful as a model home. The car on blocks was still there, but with no stray tools lying around or beer cans resting on its roof. Pratt rummaged on the floorboard and found the binoculars and brought them to his eyes. Here it was. Here's what he was looking for. On a low branch, the sturdy wooden bird feeder he'd requested. Steep green roof. Little perches on each side. No customers at the moment, but when Pratt looked closely, he could see that the thing was overflowing with seed.

He was sitting at a backed-up stoplight on Nunn Pass, trying to ignore both the Christian metal blaring from the car in front of him and the techno bumping and ticking from the car behind, when he took notice, off to his right, of a low yellow glow in the sky. Above the roof of a sports memorabilia shop, a row of floodlights on a high rack. Sumner Road was the cross street. It was Friday night, ten minutes to eight. This was it. A tidy little serving of luck. The game would still be going, and Pratt owed Tony this much. He owed him more, but this was what he was able to do. He pulled into the turn lane when the traffic moved again, driving past the cluster of stands that sold fruit weekend mornings, past the decrepit dentist office, and into the cramped lot of the city fields where Tony and his guys played ball. Pratt saw the Wagoneer. He exited the LeBaron carefully, trying not to ding the door of the car next to him, and shoved his keys down in his sock. The gun was still in the car. The whole situation was ridiculous. The whole month of June was a confusing dream, and now he was going to step out onto a baseball diamond. He'd stolen a white trash fortune from a drug dealer and killed a cop, and now he was stopping off on the way to telling off a crime boss in order to play this cheerful child's game.

He heard the ping of an aluminum bat, saw a shallow fly float down into someone's glove. It was the third out for Tony's squad, and as they jogged out to their positions, Pratt blended in among them, stopping in front of Tony as he took the mound. When his friend saw him, his eyes got round as saucers.

"Holy shit," Tony said.

"I told you I'd come out once I got some other things straight."

"Well, still—holy shit."

Tony turned to a guy with a gut like a medicine ball and asked if he could guard the cooler for an inning or two, and the guy said he'd guard it with his life. He started walking toward the dugout and Pratt asked if he could borrow the guy's glove.

"Hell," the guy said, "if you can get anybody out with it, you may as well keep it."

"That's Carl," Tony said. "Best plumber in town, but also the worst shortstop."

Pratt held the mitt in both hands a moment before sliding his fingers into it. Too snug, but it was genuine leather and opened and closed as easily as a bird's wing. Tony threw him the ball—when it found the pocket, Pratt didn't even feel it. It was the sixth inning, Tony told him. They were down 5–1. He told the third baseman to play the line so Pratt could patrol most of the left side. When the batter stepped in, Tony went into his stretch, looking exactly like he used to—skinny legs and dopey haircut and then the ball exploding out of his hand like magic.

The contact rang out, a glancing sound, and Pratt instantly charged, barehanding the dribbler. He sensed the batter tearing toward first, a fast little dude for a Friday league. Pratt's patented sidearm fling—it looked too high at first, like always, then dipped right when it needed to, popping into the first baseman's glove, the runner out by two full strides.

When the next batter stepped in, Tony came toward Pratt with his glove obscuring the lower half of his face. Pratt knew what he was going to say. The batter was a lefty, so Tony would pitch him low on the outside edge and he'd hit a grounder to Pratt's territory.

But that wasn't what Tony said. He lowered his glove and put a hand on Pratt's shoulder. "I appreciate this," he said. "It feels like real baseball. It feels like before."

"Yeah," Pratt said. "It does."

"I know you're not a regular guy that someone can be regular friends with. That's fine with me. If you don't want the job, that's fine, too. Just know I always liked you and I always will. Sorry to have to talk to you this way. Every once in a while, it's necessary."

Pratt nodded. "Same here, Tony," was what he could muster.

From the other dugout, someone yelled, "You gonna gab or pitch the ball?"

Tony turned away from Pratt and strode back toward the mound. "Both," Tony yelled back. "I like to chitchat, and I like to paint the corners. You know that."

Pratt hurried to wipe his eyes on his sleeve. He didn't plan to bobble the ball because tears were blurring his vision. He saw it now, not that it was ever complicated: Tony wanted to feel like a kid again, and wanted that for Pratt, too. He wanted to do the thing that couldn't be ruined by your parents fighting or your parents not being around anymore. Baseball was a perfect thing adults couldn't screw up. When you played baseball, baseball was all that mattered—nothing in the world could drag you down while you were between those foul lines.

Tony uncorked a sinker, outside half of the zone, and next thing Pratt knew he was diving to his right and stabbing a worm-burner. He was up. The sidearm fling.

"You can't bring in Ozzie Smith in the middle of the game." This from the other dugout.

"Ozzie Smith is a bum compared to this guy," Tony yelled back.

Pratt batted once and laced a double to opposite field. They lost 5–3. Another thing that happens when you play ball: it went from dusk to full night without Pratt's noticing. Immediately after the final out, the two teams intermingling and beer cans cracking open, Pratt tossed the glove back to the plumber and shook Tony's hand.

"I know," Tony said. "You need to run."

"I don't know what you see in me," Pratt said.

"One-two-three innings. That's what I see. Go do what you gotta do."

"We would've won states," Pratt said.

"Yeah," Tony replied. "Or at least it would've taken a truckload of luck to beat us."

Out past the incongruous lonely-road billboards. Past the burned-out ranchland. Past the rotting trailers half hidden in clumps of cypress. The taco huts, closing up. Here were the mulch elevators, looming up in the night. Beyond them, the reddish foothills of chipped bark. Pratt pulled off and taxied back to the ten-car lot, and here was Bonne's plain four-door Ford, looking like a salesman's rental. The guy probably *never* went home anymore. His wife didn't recognize him, no more than she recognized the nurses Bonne hired to attend to her. At home, there'd be pictures of Matty on the wall—Mrs. Bonne probably didn't even remember he was dead. And hell, maybe Pratt was in some of the pictures, smiling, he and Matty wearing matching ball caps.

Pratt shut the LeBaron door hard. He walked up to the warehouse and knocked, but didn't wait long before he tried the knob and felt it turn in his hand. Bonne was watching him on the closed-circuit camera, had likely unlocked the door from his office by pressing a button. The place looked like an overgrown metal barn, but Pratt knew it was wired like a savings and loan. He wasted no time crossing the cavernous space, shrink-wrapped pallets parked at odd angles here and there, weak fluorescent lights hanging high above, the smell of topsoil and rust.

When Pratt pushed Bonne's door open, the man was sitting at his desk and looking right at Pratt, calm but alert. Laid out before him were three or four county survey maps, geometric plots outlined in grainy blue, the whole thing zoned, gridded with latitude and longitude lines. A sandwich sat on a file cabinet in its deli paper, abandoned with two bites missing. Bonne held a pencil aloft by its eraser like a conductor. He didn't move or speak.

Pratt stepped all the way inside. He wasn't going to sit down in the yellow kitchen chair. "I didn't take care of your Malloy problem," he said, "but I took care of a bigger one. I cut down a more immediate threat."

Bonne pursed his lips. One of his eyes was slightly rounder than the other. "You gotta be more specific. I got a lot of problems."

"You'll hear about it soon enough," Pratt said. "You really had nothing to do with it, for once. You'll see it on the news like everyone else."

Bonne's face slowly hardened, like mud drying—either at the thought of unknown messes or at the revelation that Pratt hadn't carried out his assignment.

"We're even now," Pratt said. "And you *are* losing me. If that was your goal, to keep me, you didn't accomplish it. I'm about to disappear."

Bonne tapped the sharpened tip of his pencil against one of the maps, then opened a drawer and dropped the pencil in. He left the drawer standing open. "We're not even," he said. "Nobody's even until he dies. Till that day, the scales are tipped some sorta way."

Pratt didn't let his eyes wander to the drawer. He imagined a pistol resting inside, maybe the same make as the one out in his car. "Is that religion?" he asked Bonne. "You have to die before anything good can happen? I didn't think you were into that."

"Religion depends on faith," Bonne said. "I'm talking about time and debt. The time always runs out first, that's all." Bonne shifted in his chair. His eyes were the color of a hard, rotten lime and betrayed nothing more than a businessman's jadedness. "I know a lot more dead people than alive people, so maybe I got some authority on the topic."

Pratt didn't tell the old man he might not know so many dead people if he stopped having them killed. Malloy wasn't dead yet, but he would be soon enough.

Bonne held out his hand as casually as if asking for a lighter Pratt had borrowed. "Gun?" he asked.

"I decided to keep it. Going-away gift. Memento. Call it what you want."

Bonne let out a humorless laugh. "You balked on your given mission and now you want to leave town with a stray gun, a gun that by the sounds of it has been used for business recently, a gun that might conceivably be tracked back in the general direction of me? That's what you hope to do?"

"Look," Pratt said, louder than he'd ever spoken to Bonne, "I'm about to turn my back and walk that way. You can shoot me between the shoulder blades with that gun in your desk drawer or let me drive off and try to pull the sun up somewhere no one knows me, somewhere most of the people I know aren't dead. We got that in common, you know—we *both* know mostly dead people."

"Sun comes up no matter what happens to you and me," Bonne said, an alien strain of sorrow infecting his voice.

Pratt slowly raised his left hand and showed his palm. With his right, he reached into his pants pocket, slipped out three pictures he'd taken of Nairn at Flave's place, and dropped them on Bonne's desk, right on one of the blue-inked maps, blotting out a lonely orange grove that hadn't yet been bulldozed for mini-mansions.

Bonne eyed the photos without leaning forward, and if his face changed, if it hardened a measure more, Pratt missed it. The old man reached and slid one photo off another, so all three were visible, then calmly flicked a pencil shaving off the desk.

"You know whose house that is?" Pratt asked him.

Bonne sighed. He twisted the big ring around on his middle finger—Matty's grandfather's ring. "It's the house of a dead man," he replied. "I give this one a job," he said, nodding toward Pratt, "and he doesn't do it. I give this other one a job, and he goes Judas on me. Fucking idiot."

"Nairn was supposed to kill Flave?"

Bonne stacked the photos neatly, then flipped them face down. Tapped the stack with his fingertip like a man asking for another playing card. "They're both going down now. Roger's the only one I can trust. I guess I knew that. You think you're the only one who wouldn't mind getting out of this life? There's no brakes—you just have to keep steering. At least in the old days, your own crew wasn't against you."

Pratt backed up a step. Nothing could be seen out the office window but the dead tree, the glowing marble-white relic. Bonne was looking off now, his eyes aimed a tick to the left of Pratt, at a blank wall. He'd drifted into his own world, and so there was nothing left for Pratt to do except about-face, with false coolness, and make his exit, breath held and shoulders tense. He heard nothing as he stepped toward the door, nothing as he took leave of this office he'd stood in so many times, not the slightest creak from Bonne's chair, and though he felt the exhilaration of escape, he also felt like exactly what he was: a young person deserting an elder to the confused closing scenes of their once-grand life. Not a parent, but close enough. The world was

going to pass this guy by, no matter how long he'd been an institution. Flave wouldn't do it, but it would happen next month, the
month after. Pratt heard nothing but his own footfalls as he crossed
the shadowy expanse of the warehouse, nothing but a muffled click
as the heavy door eased itself shut behind him.

Outside, it was hard to see. He let out the breath he'd been holding, then lowered himself into the car and started the engine with its
flinty, determined little roar, tried not to hurry as he rolled past the
sheds and the towering chutes, the elevators and the dark ridge of
planter fill. He went through the open gate—Bonne still in a trance
or letting him go—and bumped up onto the two-lane county road,
nothing moving in the mirror behind him, the looming forms that
made up Bonne's landscape supply blending in readily with the rest
of the eerie night. Pratt flicked on his headlights. Pulled on his seat
belt. At the next empty rural intersection, he cut west, trying to get
to Route 19, where there would be other cars, the highway taking
you south through half a dozen scorched, stucco, grumpy-retir-
ee-and-juvenile-delinquent-infested counties to the very low point
of the United States, or north and west to places with clean air and
more stars in the night sky than lost people to look to them.

Finally, 19, straight as a high wire this far up, no more traffic lights.
There wasn't much on the roadsides but wetland, creepy cypress and
leaning pines, the bottoms of their trunks rotting out from beneath
them. Wasn't much *on* the road but occasional pickups—mud flaps
and eight-foot radio antennas and loaded gun racks. The gun. That
was the next problem on the list. Pratt wasn't about to leave it with
Bonne, but he didn't want it, either. Every half mile, a rough dirt
lane spoked off the highway, lightless tracks that led to nothing,
to swamps full of malicious snakes and spiders big as silver dollars.
Alligators. If there were people down these potholed strips, they were
people who minded their own business and answered questions from

strangers with an over/under shotgun. The only reason to turn off 19 on this stretch was to get rid of something you wanted to stay rid of, to make irreversible dedications to the steaming, eternal, stinking dump of the world, and there was no way Pratt was bringing that damn gun with him into the tomorrow he was driving toward. He wasn't bringing anything there but himself.

Bonne remained in his office chair, the uneaten sandwich still in its nest on the file cabinet, the desk drawer open, nothing in it but rubber bands and paper clips and cash and an old address book for numbers that weren't listed, most of them no longer current. Inside, a man past his prime. Outside, the skeletal white fingers of the dead tree, crowded at its base with flower bushes.

After no one other than Bonne had been in the office in days, two visits in an hour—moments ago, Pratt, and just before him, the Greek girl with the mop of silky black hair and a backbone like a telephone pole. She'd been nervous, all but drawing blood with her nails against her knuckles, but she'd pushed through, saying everything she meant to say. Bonne, no idea who she was, had closed the front gate behind her car, locked the warehouse door after she'd walked inside. A messenger from Joe-Baby? In that case, why so pretty? A messenger from one of the new dealers in town? Nothing more dangerous than a lone lovely woman where she wasn't supposed to be. But this one was already talking when she crossed Bonne's threshold, finding him easily in the big empty place, not sitting down, not letting him interrupt. Once he knew what was going on, he feigned resignation. Received her monologue with the air of a man suffering a single bad hand in the midst of a hot streak. She wanted Pratt free without knowing exactly what he needed to be free of. In truth, Bonne didn't *want* to keep Pratt any longer. Pratt had a long road ahead of him. Not so for Bonne. Bonne had no more fire—what he had was spite, bitterness. Things always got messier. Always got worse. When the girl visited him, he didn't even know about Nairn and Flave. And whatever bullshit Pratt was talking about, whatever "threat" he'd addressed—Bonne would probably wake up to that news in the morning. This was for the young, all this shit—an old man couldn't be expected to put up with it forever.

Kallie had made it clear she wanted nothing *but* an old man, a nice old grandpa. She said Bonne could see the child, but no money, no favors, nothing at all to do with the business. A simple deal—lose Pratt, gain a grandson. Bonne put on his show, pressing his lips grim and squeezing a fist atop the desk, but he didn't want the boy near the business and didn't want to spoil the kid. Didn't want to spoil him like he'd spoiled Matty. Kallie wanted Bonne to know that Joaquin wouldn't be another Pratt, that Joaquin—this was his grandson's name—had a mother. Joaquin had a family already. The girl went on, her voice growing lower and calmer, not more frantic. She didn't want Joaquin to be angry at her later, when he found out how close his other grandfather had been all the while. She knew it wasn't Bonne's fault that she and Matty weren't careful and made a baby. Bonne, by that point, could hardly hear her. He'd been glad he was sitting down, because his knees would've been jelly. He was picturing the boy. Picturing a kid who looked like Matty as a toddler, but with black hair and a philosopher's eyes.

Now, in the fluorescent-lit office with darkest night out the window, Bonne smelled wildflowers, burgers grilling, sun on skin. He heard the sound of a ball in a glove. He was playing catch with Matty, the boy eight or nine. Bonne's shoulder ached, but he kept throwing and throwing. He'd bought Matty half a dozen gloves, but didn't have one of his own, so his fingers were jammed inside a child's mitt. Bonne remembered the yellow sun in his eyes, the beams lancing through live oak branches. He remembered Matty's blinding smile after he dove for one of Bonne's errant tosses and came up with it, rolling in the soft grass then holding his glove aloft to show he'd made the improbable catch. Five more throws. Five more throws, Pop. Just five more.

EPILOGUE

THROUGH THE WINDOW OVER his kitchen sink, Jack Prescott saw a barely moving sparkle far down the ridge road that he knew was a car. Four miles away. A bit more. He made no haste washing his dinner dishes—one plate, one drinking glass, knife and fork. He'd grilled an elk steak over mesquite and sided it with a pan of oil-fried peppers, and the aromas were heavy in his clothes, his skin, his hair. The car had to deal with the incline and the handful of shallow switchbacks, the late afternoon sun slanting into the driver's eyes—it was white or beige, not a large vehicle, not a farm truck or livestock transport. White or beige or *champagne*—that was a color for cars now, Jack knew. He dried the dishes. Rested them gently in the mostly bare cabinet. Dried his hands on the scrap of towel.

He shut off the radio, the third time in the past forty-five minutes he'd heard tomorrow's weather report, calling for hot and dry and then cooling fast after sundown, just like it would today, like it had yesterday. He stepped out onto the shaded front porch, hand against the wooden screen door so it wouldn't slap closed. If he was seeing right, the car was a convertible. It took the bend near the raft of juniper trees, pulling up an almost transparent sheen of pink dust behind it. The smart money was on someone lost, someone who'd missed the turnoff for the bird park at the bottom of the rise where people went at dusk to watch the pinyon jays and listen to the thrashers. It wasn't impossible that it was that twice-divorced woman with the movie-star eyelashes who rented a fancied-up hiker's cabin a couple ranches down, off early from her job at the diner and coming to see him like she'd threatened over a week ago. But no, Jack could make out that it was a man—the height, the haircut, some other indefinable quality in the form's bearing. A man in a white convertible—not beige or champagne, just dirty.

He was about to descend the five plank steps to solid high-desert rock, but a quick wave of dizziness washed over him and he reached for the rough-hewn post. Somehow he knew who drove the strange topless sedan. Through the late-day haze and the horizontal sunlight, somehow he knew, so that when he willed the automobile even closer, drawing it near with his attention, tentatively off the ridge road and onto the long, narrow drive that cut an easy curve over his acreage, he was only confirming the fact. Instead of treading the stairs, he sat down on the uppermost one, taking the half minute the car would need to reach him to regain whatever dignity he hoped he carried around with him in the world. So much space, and usually it felt as empty as a mayor's promise.

The convertible rocked to a stop. One brief swell of the breeze and the disturbed dust was gone. It was time to stand. Time to right-left-right the oversize steps. Jack Prescott's heart was making an effort to tilt sideways in his chest. Down off the porch, he could hear noisy guitar music, electric instruments buzz-sawing toward a melody and three or voices chanting something unintelligible. Music—well, some might call it that. But then it was gone, along with the clanging whine of the car's engine, a whole program of noise evaporated, and instantly the crisp, wolfish silence of northern New Mexico was everywhere, close, far, part of the air.

His nephew didn't raise his eyes until he was out of the car and standing full straight. His clothes looked weather-beaten, like they'd been machine washed and then thrown into a wet heap. He could see in the boy's face, the *man's* face now, the sown seeds of regret, or maybe it was his own regret he was seeing reflected there. He'd learned not to treat regret with too much patience. The thing right now was he was going to get another shot at this. They both were. Pratt had aged, but Jack had aged more. People who spent their time in the sun, in the elements—at a certain point, every year that passed did the work of five.

"I been around a long time and fought in wars," Jack said, "and I don't think I've ever heard so hideous a sound."

Pratt smirked, relief brightening his expression. "I don't even hear it anymore," he said, his voice half an octave deeper than Jack remembered. "I was using it to drown out the noises from under the hood."

"I know that trick," Jack told him. "Got a guy down the road'll sell me American car parts at cost. We'll get you fixed up."

"What does 'down the road' mean out here?"

"It means pack a snack."

"I probably met him already," Pratt said. "I stopped three times for directions."

The breeze mustered again, and Jack's visitor brushed the hair from his eyes. A big duffel bag, looking like it had been beaten with a stick, was crammed in the passenger seat of the car. Atop it sat a tiny plant in a terra cotta pot.

"Been thinking about you," Jack heard himself say.

At this, he could see determination settle on Pratt's face. The person before him was thicker-muscled than before, but also seasoned in a way that was only coincidental to age. Some guys couldn't build themselves up right until they were burned to the ground. Jack hated to think of Pratt behind bars, but maybe it had done him good.

"If we've got any sorries, either of us," Jack said, "let's chuck those in a canyon somewhere. I'm not feeling real interested in sorries right now."

Pratt nodded. He still hadn't taken a step toward Jack. Getting here had taken everything he had. Jack went ahead and moved his boots, closing the space, and once in reach he shook Pratt's hand.

"I was about to sit on the porch and enjoy a golden beverage, and you're welcome to join me. It's my evening ritual, and I'm not going to change it just because of company."

"I'll accept a beverage," Pratt said. "Except for a catnap at a rest stop, I been driving since last night. Straight through. Fifteen over with the manual cruise control."

"I know that drive. Ugly, then uglier, then you hit the Ozarks and things start to look up."

"But when you come into the Ozarks it starts to rain," Pratt said. "And your roof is stuck, so you have to drive right through it."

Jack laughed and it felt like a surge of tonic water gushing up out of him. He guessed he hadn't laughed in weeks, but it could've been longer than that. "How long's the roof been stuck?" he asked.

"Since I was sitting in a traffic jam in Mobile and wanted some air. First time I ever opened it. Pretty stupid, because then I was in direct sun."

"Well," Jack said, placing his hand on Pratt's hard shoulder, "speaking of the sun, let's not miss the big finale. The sky turns orange and the hills go purple and the boulders glow, and then the half million stars wink on. If that's anything that interests you."

Pratt did not look out toward the western horizon. He was looking at Jack, and maybe at the gust-scoured, flat-roofed two-bedroom behind Jack, this place out in the middle of the desert that might be his new home. That *would* be his new home.

"You did good," Jack told him. "You did real good coming here."

He loped around the other side of the car—a LeBaron it was—and took the little cactus in hand and hoisted the duffel bag onto his shoulder, then he led Pratt up onto the porch and pointed at a chair, waited a moment to watch his nephew sit and release a sigh of sighs. He went inside and deposited Pratt's stuff in the kitchen, opened the fridge and reached in the back for two cold Lone Stars. He'd need to clean out that spare room, currently used for drying wet gear, polishing boots, cleaning guns. He was looking very much forward to this beer, to having someone to drink it with—this someone, in particular.

Back on the porch, he handed Pratt a can and sat next to him, and for a moment he saw the property with new eyes, as his young relative must have seen it. The vastness. The mesas falling off into soft shadow, where anything might lurk. The majestic craggy ranges so far west they were two counties away. Closer, the hoard of firewood under a leaning old rectangle of tin roofing. The plain white beehives Jack had restored to working order. The archery targets stored against the little smokehouse.

"How is it," Pratt said, "that something made of wood is more comfortable to sit on than something made of cushion?"

Jack took his first big pull of the beer, pleasantly bitter at the back of his throat. "Are you making metaphors at me, kid? Once I got a golden beverage open, it's too late for metaphors."

"I'm doing no such thing," Pratt said. "I'm just saying the Chrysler LeBaron is not a comfortable choice for a six-state cruise."

"And the chairs get some credit, too," Jack said. "I made them. They're an inch and a half higher than a normal chair."

"Could you teach me how to do that?" The seriousness returned to Pratt's eyes. "I want to learn how to do some things. Learn how to *make* something."

Jack nodded. He couldn't do more than nod, couldn't do anything with his voice for the moment. For three years, he'd been passing on everything he knew to tourists from Chicago and California. He watched Pratt take a couple quick sips of his Lone Star, then hold the can in both hands like something he was afraid of losing.

"There *is* one problem," the kid said.

For a moment Jack thought Pratt might be teeing up a joke, but he could tell by his face that wasn't the case.

"Try me," Jack told him.

"Well, I'm not really supposed to be here. There's a part I haven't figured out yet. I just started driving. I had a bunch of other things to think about, so I didn't…"

"You're supposed to be here," said Jack. "What is it? What's going on?" Jack was making sure to sound matter-of-fact, but part of him expected to hear Bonne's name in the next ten seconds. That small-town thug who hadn't done his own dirty work in thirty years. If it was Bonne, Jack decided, then so be it. If Bonne wanted to be a problem of Pratt's, then Jack would be a problem of Bonne's. He'd be happy to.

Pratt exhaled. Jack could smell the kid. He needed a scalding shower and twelve hours of sleep. He needed to burn the clothes he was wearing. "I'm on parole for another eleven months," he told Jack. "The guy will be expecting me in a week or two for my check-in. I'm not supposed to leave the state. If they knew I was here right now, I'd be back in lockup."

Jack thumped his finger on the armrest. He'd spent a whole day on these armrests—the trammel, the spindle sander, the drum sander, gluing and vicing the maple veneers. He didn't want to show any relief that it wasn't Bonne. Whatever it was, Jack would've handled it, but he was glad it wasn't Bonne.

"I can't live back there," Pratt said. "I can't go back there." He took another gulp of his beer, like medicine he had to get down. The sunset was beginning to unfold, corn-yellow beams underlighting lavender cloud banks, the mountain faces to the west taking on the detail of an etching, but Pratt paid no attention to it.

"Parole," Jack said dismissively. "Jesus, man, I thought there was a *real* problem."

Pratt looked confused. He looked right in Jack's face.

"When I was younger, I did missions with a lot of guys, Pratt. I don't want to brag—well, what the hell, what's so bad about bragging once you get old? I saved a lot of dudes. Saved their lives. You know what I'm saying? These religious people always talk about saving people. I literally kept the blood inside these folks. Blood on the inside and fingers wiggling. I talked a lot of United States military personnel back into their heads so they didn't *need* saving. I stayed awake so a lot of guys could sleep. I need background music for this, don't I? I saw men sob. These are tougher men than they know how to make now—the factory where they made these fellows, it's been converted to artists' lofts with a smoothie shop in the lobby." Jack took a pause. His nephew had a poker face, but relief was there. He wanted to believe Jack could help him. The older man tipped back his beer can and the younger followed suit.

"Point is, Pratt, I got dozens of if-you-ever-need-anythings from persons who, at this point, don't got no higher to rise in the corporation. When they say 'anything,' they mean it. Guys I served with and those guys' sons, too. You know how many of those favors I've cashed in?"

"I can guess," Pratt said.

"We'll get your probation moved to New Mexico. No problem. Done deal. Anybody back in Florida who doesn't like it, I'll be talking to that person's boss's boss. We'll switch it like a baked potato instead of fries."

Pratt frowned, keeping his composure. "Jeez, thank you," he said. "Thank you so much."

"Thank *you*," Jack said. "Nobody wants to go to their grave with a bunch of uncashed favors. It's a great fear among the aged."

Pratt tipped his head back and breathed the air like it was a delicacy. He finally cocked his eyes off toward the horizon. The colors were in full psychedelic swing, vivid and dreamy.

"We gotta go down to Santa Fe once a month anyhow," Jack said. "Have a meal that ends with sopaipilla and see some ladies in dresses."

Pratt sniffed hard, recovering himself. "What's sopaipilla?"

"Sopaipilla is only one reason this place is better than other places. Feel that cool strain in the air?"

Pratt nodded.

"You work hard all day, you get a break at night. I swear to God, sometimes in Bethuna midnight was hotter than noon."

Pratt chuckled, though nothing was funny. It was a chuckle Jack was familiar with. It was the cautious laugh of a man who was trying to figure out whether he was the same person now that everything around him had changed, now that he'd done things he never imagined he would.

Something caught Jack's eye out in the darkening landscape and he leaned forward and pointed so Pratt would look, too. You could just make them out, their jaunty, long-legged trot—two coyotes, one sure and eager, one trailing behind, sniffing everything twice. Colorless silhouettes. They were nothing but their fears and desires and that didn't trouble them a bit. They were as real as anything, as real as human memories, as real as the churches and city halls people raised out of timber and dust, as real as the mountains that cast late-day shadows miles long. But they were also ghosts, apparitions that could disappear in a watery blink—ghosts, or as close to ghosts as the fortunate men spying them from afar would ever see with their own eyes.

JOHN BRANDON has been awarded the Grisham Fellowship at Ole Miss, the Tickner Fellowship at Gilman School in Baltimore, and has received a Sustainable Arts Foundation Fellowship. He was a finalist for the New York Public Library Young Lions Award. His short fiction has appeared in *ESPN The Magazine*, *Oxford American*, *McSweeney's Quarterly Concern*, *Mississippi Review*, *Subtropics*, *Chattahoochee Review*, *Hotel Amerika*, and many other publications, and he has written about college football for *GQ* online and *Grantland*. He was born in Florida and now resides in Minnesota, where he teaches at Hamline University in St. Paul.